Crab Bait

A Sylvia Avery Mystery

BOOK THREE

Jan Bono

Sandridge Publications
Long Beach, Washington

Who's guilty?

Jan Bono

This is a work of fiction. Names, characters, places, and incidents are either the product of the author's imagination or are used fictitiously, and any resemblance to actual persons, living or dead, business establishments, events, or locales is entirely coincidental.

First Printing, Summer, 2018

Printed in the United States of America
Gorham Printing, Centralia, WA 98531

Cover Photo: Allan Fritz, Ilwaco, WA

Sandridge Publications
P.O. Box 278
Long Beach, WA   98631

http://www.JanBonoBooks.com

ISBN: 978-0-9906148-6-9

DEDICATED

to the steadfast and amazing women
who encouraged, supported, and gently pushed me
(despite many personal challenges and set backs)
to complete this third book.
I am forever grateful for your faith in me.
I love you, too.

OTHER BOOKS BY JAN BONO

Sylvia Avery Mystery Series:
> *Bottom Feeders,* Book 1
> *Starfish,* Book 2

Health and Fitness:
> *Back from Obesity:*
>> My 252-pound Weight-loss Journey

Collections of humorous personal experience:
> *Through My Looking Glass:* View from the Beach
> *Through My Looking Glass:* Volume II
> *It's Christmas!*
>> Forty-three stories and three one-act plays
> *Just Joshin'*
>> A Year in the Life of a Not-so-ordinary
>> 4th Grade Kid

Fiction:
> *Romance 101:*
>> Forty-two Sweet, Light, Delicious,
>> G-Rated Short Stories

Poetry Chapbooks:
> *Bar Talk* and *Chasing Rainbows*

A number of Jan's books are now available as eBooks at Smashwords.com. Find them at:

http://www.smashwords.com/profile/view/JanBonoBooks

NORTH BEACH PENINSULA

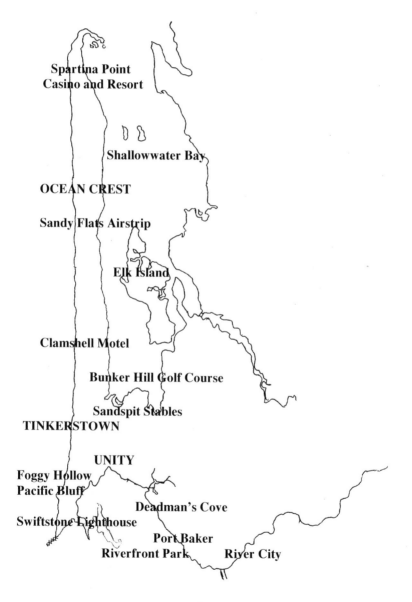

Spartina Point
Casino and Resort

Shallowwater Bay

OCEAN CREST

Sandy Flats Airstrip

Elk Island

Clamshell Motel

Bunker Hill Golf Course

Sandspit Stables

TINKERSTOWN

UNITY

Foggy Hollow
Pacific Bluff

Deadman's Cove

Swiftstone Lighthouse

Port Baker

Riverfront Park   River City

CRAB BAIT

CHAPTER 1

"Deputy Frederick Morgan! What in heaven's name are you doing here standing on my front porch at—" I grabbed his left hand, brought it up close to my face, and peered at his wristwatch. "—at 5:30 in the freakin' morning?"

Freddy grinned, his dimples immediately softening my imitation morning mad. It was hard for me to keep a stern face around him, especially when he looked so darn handsome in his police uniform.

"Good morning to you, too, Sylvia," he said, making no attempt to disguise his elevator eyes running up and down my body. I had come to the door clothed only in a well-worn navy and gold high school football jersey—his jersey, at that.

I dropped his hand and made a half-hearted attempt at modesty, moving to step behind the partially-opened front door. "I repeat, Deputy Morgan, what in the world are you doing here at this ungodly hour?"

Freddy's smile evaporated, and his eyes narrowed. Suddenly he was almost all business. "As much as I hate saying this, Syl—" he said, interrupting himself to shake his head and run his tongue across his lips, still giving me the once, or maybe the twice-over, "—but this isn't a social call. You're going to need to pull on some publicly-acceptable clothes, and come with me."

"Come with you—where?" Was it my imagination, or had his words suddenly increased my heart rate—and not in a good way?

"Down to the docks in Unity."

"Unity? The docks? Oh my gosh, Freddy, is your dad okay?"

Freddy's father, Rich Morgan, was sole owner and operator of a charter fishing vessel. He'd gotten into a bit of unintentional legal trouble a few months ago, and was making it right by occasionally taking special needs students out on the Columbia River in his boat. I sure hoped that whatever was putting such a pained expression on Freddy's face had nothing to do with Rich—or any of the school kids.

"No, it's not Dad." Freddy cleared his throat. "Sheriff Donaldson called me out early today to come pick you up. I'm not at liberty right now to tell you much more than that."

I resisted the urge to punch him in the upper arm, remembering just in time that you can usually catch more flies with honey than with vinegar.

Instead of popping him in the shoulder to get his attention, I calmly asked in the softest, sweetest voice I could muster, "So exactly how much more *can* you tell me, Deputy Frederick Harold Morgan, hhmmm?"

I turned before I could resort to batting my eyelashes, and quickly headed to my bedroom to dress.

Freddy stepped inside the house and closed the front door, following me, without invitation, back down the hall.

He knew the way; it wasn't as if we'd never spent time in there together, despite the fact that Deputy Morgan was nearly 15 years my junior.

"I guess I can tell you that the Coast Guard is currently escorting a crab boat in from the ocean, and your presence at the dock has been requested by someone on board."

I had already pulled on a pair of jeans and was struggling to get a hot pink hoodie over my head when his words slammed into me like a bug on a motorcycle helmet's visor at 70 miles per hour. It was a crazy, mixed-up metaphor, or maybe it was a simile, but frequently being the one on the inside of the helmet, I knew from experience that his words left me feeling utterly gobsmacked.

I began to hyperventilate, unable to find the neck hole in the hoodie for my head. Panic threatened to engulf me when two strong, yet tender hands, aided me in getting my flailing arms into the sleeves, and I gasped for air as my head emerged.

"Freddy!" Even I could hear the uncharacteristically high pitch of my voice. "Who asked for me by name? Who do I know who's in trouble, Freddy? Tell me, Freddy! *WHO?!*"

Freddy looked down at his shiny, but non-regulation, cowboy boots and sighed. Then he lifted his dark eyes to mine and said softly, "Meredith."

"Meredith?!" I echoed. *"Meredith, my mother?!"* Without waiting for confirmation, I crammed my feet into a pair of slip-on tennis shoes, grabbed my purse from the bureau, and began running for the squad car in the driveway. "Lock the door on your way out!" I hollered over my shoulder. So much for me playing it cool.

As we wheeled out of the driveway, Freddy turned on the flashing blue lights, but not the siren. He stepped heavily on the accelerator, and shot me a quick look of compassion.

"The fact that your mother was able to ask for you by name should be some kind of reassurance," he said. "If Meredith were totally unable to communicate, then you'd have something to worry about."

The very suggestion of my mother not being capable of talking nonstop evoked a wan smile, but there were too many unsettling variables for me to take more than the smallest comfort from Freddy's words.

"What else do you know, Freddy?"

"I've probably told you too much already," he said. "Sheriff D's going to have my scalp."

Under normal circumstances, I would have laughed. Freddy Morgan is one-eighth Native American, and only because of this heritage can he get away with such politically incorrect comments. But these were not normal circumstances, and I thought I might chew my way through my lower lip before we finished the 10-mile trip from my house straight down Sandspit Road to the Unity marina.

A few minutes passed in silence, then Freddy asked, "Do you have any idea what your mother might have been doing out on a crab boat last night?"

As a matter of fact I did, but it rather miffed me that Freddy was plying me for information when I couldn't get any back in return. Nevertheless, I took a deep breath and honestly answered his question.

"Her friend Nova Johanssen asked Mom to come along with her when she headed out to pull up crab pots yesterday."

"Whoa!" said Freddy, shooting just a quick glance my way. "Since when does your mother moonlight as a crab fisherman?"

I knew he was trying to make light of the situation, but his attempt at humor wasn't helping. I blew out a deep breath. "Meredith was asked to come along in case any medical issues arose with Nova's husband back on board."

"You better start at the beginning," said Freddy, this time without taking his eyes off the road. "Why might her husband need the services of a retired registered nurse?"

"Nova's husband Matthew has Parkinson's. He was diagnosed a couple years ago, about the time he turned 62. That's when he started training Nova to run the boat, and do the crab fishing by herself. She's been doing the lion's share of the work for the past year or so, but at the start of this season, Matthew was no longer able to come along.

"His disease had progressed enough that although he could stand with a cane and take a step or two by himself, he needed a wheelchair almost full time.

"Nova just finished having the boat modified to accommodate him. He's not able to be much help with the crab pots, but he can still pilot the boat, and he was eager to get back out there on the water. He's worked on the ocean his whole life."

Freddy's face brightened. "Oh! I think I've met Nova. Does she wear a lot of plaid flannel and have short, spiky gray hair?"

"Uh-huh." I smiled at the thought of her hair. "Her hair looks tousled and windblown whether the wind is blowing or not. She calls it her patented 'beach do.'"

"She must have been the gal down at the dock a couple months ago, asking Dad all kinds of questions about how he modified his boat for the Special Needs Students."

I nodded thoughtfully. "Now that you mention it, I'm sure I remember Nova mentioning Rich's helpfulness."

Freddy slowed, but did not stop, at the first

intersection of three between my house and the port, then picked up speed again. He shot me yet another quick look.

"To tell you the truth, I kind of hoped Nova was single. Dad sure seemed interested, and it would be good for him to have a woman in his life again."

I couldn't tell for sure if Freddy were sincere, or being snide. Rich and I had been friends for years—just friends—but lately Freddy had gotten the idea he was in competition with his dad for my affection. I'm not quite sure just how I really feel about Freddy, but dating Rich was not, and had never been, on my radar.

I decided to dodge the comment about his dad's love life and changed the subject. "Yesterday was the maiden voyage of the Estrella Nueva with Matthew on board."

"Estrella Nueva?" asked Freddy.

"It means 'New Star' in Spanish," I explained. "Matthew named his boat after Nova. A lot of fishermen name their boats after their wives. A New Star is a Nova. Get it?"

"Uh-huh," said Freddy, nodding. "But my dad named his boat 'Geraldine,' after his mother, and I'm sure it was a contributing factor in her decision to leave us. My mother considered the Geraldine my dad's true mistress."

"Oooooo.... Sounds incestuous." I tried to make it sound like a joke, but my words fell flat. I knew Freddy still felt deep emotional pain over the fact that his mother abandoned both his father and him when he was just a child. Not everyone is cut out to be a fisherman's wife—or, for that matter, a mother.

Freddy said nothing, maybe because there was nothing he could say that would make the situation any better, and I felt bad about trying to make a joke about the boat name. An apology might only make it worse, so I quickly turned the conversation back to the matter at hand.

"Nova was hoping that being back on the water would help Matthew's depression. She said he'd been really despondent since he became almost totally reliant on the wheelchair. Mom was invited along in case it was all just too much for him." I sighed. "Gee, I hope everyone's okay."

Freddy had already navigated the second and third intersections, and adeptly wheeled into the port parking lot. He pulled in and parked as close as he could get to the docks. Sheriff Donaldson's Inceptor SUV was there, along with an ambulance, but neither vehicle had its lights flashing. I wondered if that were a good sign or a bad sign.

Sheriff Carter Donaldson, at 6'4" even without his Stetson, towered above the cannery workers gathered to see what was going on. He took a few steps in our direction, nodded politely to acknowledge me, but then narrowed his eyes and scowled at Freddy.

"I thought I asked you to retrieve Sylvia without sharing any information with her about why she was being summoned here."

Freddy looked uncomfortable, but said nothing.

The sheriff continued, "No need to deny it. Sylvia's wringing her hands, and anyone with half a brain could see the stress written all over her pale face."

Again, it struck me that under other circumstances, I might have made some kind of politically incorrect joke about him not being the Native American in the group, and therefore not the one to talk about me being a pale face, but this was obviously not the time for any superficial attempt at levity.

"My pale face?" I tilted my head and glared at him. I was used to going toe-to-toe with the sheriff. "Well then, since you're going to criticize my appearance, maybe you would have wanted me to waste time getting here by stopping to put on make-up?"

Sheriff D shook his head. "That's not what I meant, Sylvia, and you know it. You look just fine. More than fine."

I didn't want to consider what he meant by that, so I put my hands into the pouch of my hoodie and once again returned the conversation back to its original theme. "Don't be so hard on Freddy, Carter. I forced the information out of him—what little I got."

Sheriff D almost smiled. "Just trying to help my deputy learn to keep his personal and professional lives separate, Syl. No need to rush in to defend your boyfriend."

My boyfriend! Normally, I would have jumped all over Carter for saying something like that, but at that moment, the Estrella Nueva, closely followed by a Coast Guard cutter, rounded the breakwater and entered the marina. A hush fell over the three of us, each lost in our own thoughts, for our own reasons.

Then, as if by magic, Captain Richard Morgan, Freddy's father, appeared at my elbow. I looked up at Rich, my eyebrows arching in an unspoken question.

"I heard it on my fishing radio." He shrugged and took a sip from his ever-present stainless steel coffee mug. "We're all connected on the same frequencies down here."

Then to the sheriff, Rich asked, "Is it true there's been a fatality on board?"

Sheriff Donaldson's normally ruddy face became a shade or two darker red. "That's exactly the kind of rumor we want to avoid, Captain Morgan. If you're going to speculate on what has or hasn't taken place on the Estrella, you'll have to continue that kind of talk a little farther from the dock ramps."

Two thoughts collided in my head. The first was that

the sheriff had spoken unduly harshly to Rich, and the second little voice was screaming that when Rich used the word fatality, the sheriff had not immediately denied it.

"Carter?" my voice squeaked out. "Is it true? Has someone on board died?"

Not unkindly, Sheriff D placed his hand on my shoulder. "Now Syl, you know I can't confirm or deny anything at this point."

"That's what you always say when you're in the midst of an ongoing investigation. Are you— Is this—" I fought for just the right words. "Will there be an investigation into something that did or didn't happen on the Estrella Nueva?"

Blast him and his adherence to protocol! Didn't he understand? My mother was on that boat, damn it! I took a deep breath. Of course he understood. He's the one who had sent Freddy to come get me when someone on board had requested my presence on the dock. But was that someone who asked for me to come really my mother, or had someone else asked for me because my mother had been hurt—or worse?

For my money, the Coast Guard was taking far too long to maneuver the Estrella into her usual slip, and the only people I could see onboard were one Coastie at the helm, and another on the back deck, waiting with rope in hand to be close enough to tie up.

Sheriff Donaldson turned to Freddy. "Son, you stay here on the port walkway with Sylvia. Under no circumstances do I want her on any part of the docks. Under no circumstances—do you think you can manage that?"

It was a rhetorical question, clearly a dig at Freddy's earlier inability not to tell me anything about my summons to the dock, but Freddy officiously replied, "Yes sir," to Carter's fleeting back. I was surprised he didn't salute.

The sheriff worked his way down the ramp and along the dock toward the mooring vessel. He climbed aboard, entered the cabin, and was gone almost longer than I could bear. I doubt he was inside for more than a few minutes, but my world had suddenly come to a complete halt, and everything around me seemed to move in slow motion.

I felt a wave of nausea, and my knees started to buckle. Freddy quickly reached out and grasped my upper arm to steady me at the same time his father took my other arm. I gave them each a small smile, looking first to Rich, and then to Freddy. Then I took a deep breath, and hoped they weren't going to get into some crazy game of tug-of-war.

Sheriff Donaldson re-emerged from the boat and started up the ramp. His expression was unreadable, and I had a totally inappropriate-for-the-occasion thought flit through my head—don't ever play poker with this man.

Then, when he cleared the top of the ramp, instead of joining our group standing off to the left, he walked straight ahead, back to the edge of the parking lot. He bent down to speak briefly to the driver of the waiting ambulance, and the wagon started up, backed around, and pulled away, headed, I presumed, up the hill to the hospital—empty.

Again I wondered if that were a good sign or a bad sign, as the sheriff took his sweet time coming to fill us in about what was happening on the Estrella.

"Don't worry, Syl," said Sheriff D as soon as he was close enough so that he didn't have to shout. "Meredith is fine. She's inside the cabin, finishing up her official statement for the Coast Guard. She'll be up here in a few more minutes."

I let go of the breath I'd been holding, and my ability to

stand seemed to leave with it, and for the second time that morning, I was grateful the Morgan boys were both there to keep me from collapsing.

"And Nova?" Rich asked, his brow deeply furrowed.

"What about Nova, Sheriff? Is she okay?"

"Nova's also fine," said Sheriff D, nodding in affirmation. "She's understandably exhausted from being up all night, but otherwise, she's fine."

That left only one person unaccounted for, and none of us seemed eager to ask the obvious question. As it turned out, we didn't have to.

A middle-aged Hispanic man left his cannery co-workers and quietly approached us. He took off his worn ball cap and held it in both hands in front of his chest, clearly uncomfortable at being the designated spokesperson for the group.

"Señor— Sheriff Donaldson," he began. "Mi amigo, Mateo... Qué..." He shook his head as if to clear it and began again in English. "What— What about Mateo Rodriguez? Is my friend Mateo okay?"

"Who is Mateo Rodriguez?" asked Freddy, of no one in particular. "How many people fit on that little boat?"

"Mateo is Spanish for Matthew," I replied. "Matthew, or Mateo, Rodriguez is Nova Johanssen's husband. She chose to keep her birth name when they got married."

"Most of us on the docks just call him Matt," explained Rich. "Matt is a shorter form of both Mateo and Matthew."

Freddy shot Rich a look that said he was either thankful for the information, or annoyed that it was his father who had to explain it to me. I couldn't tell which.

The sheriff, not sure if any of the men and women from the cannery gathered nearby were members of Mateo's immediate family, and wanting to follow precise protocol, hesitated in giving the man an answer to his question.

Finally, Sheriff D carefully replied, "I'm sorry." He spoke more softly than I could ever have imagined he could speak. He made eye contact with the man and gently shook his head. "Mateo is not with them."

"Mateo is not with them?" I echoed the sheriff in disbelief. "But—" Then the full force of his words hit me. I gasped, my right hand flew to my chest, and I turned to face the sheriff for clarification. "Carter?!"

Sheriff Donaldson held up his hand to keep me from saying more. "Now don't go jumping to any conclusions, Sylvia."

He turned back to Mateo's friend, still standing there, scowling with the effort of trying to process what the sheriff was saying, or not saying. His eyes were wide with disbelief. "No Mateo?" he asked in disbelief. "No Mateo?"

Movement in the marina suddenly turned all our attention in that direction. Nova and Meredith were being escorted up the ramp by the Coast Guard. They walked in single file, one uniformed man walking ahead and one walking behind them. The man bringing up the rear was pushing an empty wheelchair, wrapped in yellow crime scene tape. The expression on everyone's face was grim.

Sheriff D turned back to the cannery worker and placed a hand gently on the man's shoulder. "What is your name?" He scowled, then managed, word by word, "¿Cuál—es—tu—nombre?"

The man's expression was one of fear and confusion. "Me llamo Miguel."

"I'm sorry, Miguel," said Sheriff Donaldson. "Lo siento. Your amigo—your friend Mateo—has been lost at sea."

CHAPTER 2

Once at the top of the ramp, Meredith turned left to come join our group, but the Coast Guardsman at the front of the procession put his arm out to hold her back. She looked at him in surprise, then looked plaintively at Sheriff Donaldson.

Sheriff Donaldson silently signaled to the Coastie to let her approach us. Merri took a couple steps, and her knees visibly wobbled. In a flash, I moved to her side and put my arm around her waist.

"You okay, Mom?"

"No problem, Syl. I'm fine. I just got to take a minute to get my land legs back," she said, but her voice was uncharacteristically weak. "Thanks for coming, Honey. It was good to see a friendly face on the dock when we tied up this morning."

"What happened?" I asked. "Was there an accident out there?"

"Hold on." Sheriff Donaldson cut me off with two words, then turned to Meredith to finish his thought. "We'll need to go down to the station to take your statement before you say anything else, Mrs. Avery."

"It's *Ms.* Avery," replied Meredith, "and I already gave my statement to the Coast Guard. Can't they just send you a copy of it?"

Sheriff Donaldson cleared his throat. "The Coast Guard and the Sheriff's Office work independently of each

19

other, although we do cooperate in any investigation where jurisdiction might be in question. Nevertheless, you'll need to repeat your statement for our official records, *Ms. Avery.*"

Merri had recovered just enough of her emotional balance and spunk to snap back at the sheriff. "Is this the part where you tell me not to leave town?"

The sheriff didn't flinch, but he sighed and pushed the front brim of his Stetson up about an inch with his right forefinger before giving Meredith a meaningful look.

"No, this is the part where I tell you it's your lucky day. Today you'll be getting a free ride in the county sheriff's big, shiny police car, straight to the station in Tinkerstown, to answer a few questions."

"More questions?" said Merri. The wind suddenly left her sails, and she leaned heavily against me. Like mother like daughter, I thought, surprised at both her apparent vulnerability and the sudden tenderness I felt toward her.

"Nova and I have been interrogated by the Coast Guard for the past three hours, and now you want to ask me a few more questions?" Meredith looked like she were about to cry, and I had never in my life seen my mother cry. "Can't I at least go home and get a shower and change my clothes first?"

"Afraid not," said Sheriff D. He sounded almost sympathetic, but I knew underneath he was all business. "And the sooner we get this over with, Ms. Avery, the better. Believe it or not, questioning witnesses and potential people of interest who are still obviously in shock is not my favorite thing to do."

Meanwhile, Freddy had Nova by the elbow and was guiding her toward the squad cars parked side by side. "Sheriff?" he called out. "You want them taken in separately?"

Sheriff D nodded. He placed his left index finger and thumb on the middle of his salt and pepper mustache and drew his fingers apart along his upper lip. "Yes, thank you, Deputy Morgan. Sylvia will ride with Ms. Avery and me. You can go on ahead."

My mind was still fixated on one particular word. "Mom? Why would the Coast Guard be interrogating you? What do they think happened out there?"

Sheriff D held up his hand to stop Meredith from answering. "Not another word until we get you to the station," he warned her. "Not another word. Whatever you say—even to your daughter—needs to be on the record and officially documented."

A sick knot was building in my stomach, and if I'd had any breakfast in there, I knew it would be thinking about leaving me. "Are you going to read her her rights?" I asked. "Are either of these women under arrest?"

"Arrest?!" Meredith exclaimed. "I should say not!"

Sheriff Donaldson glowered at Meredith. "I told you, not another word!" He pulled himself up to his full 6'4" plus his Stetson height and gave her a glower that could have seared flesh.

I looked over at Mateo's friends, gathered in a tight group, all talking rapidly in Spanish. I couldn't pick out a single word, but the somber expressions on their faces, as they flicked their eyes over to watch what was going on, spoke volumes.

Rich had distanced himself from either camp, standing back under the eaves of a charter office, taking everything in, but staying out of the way. He'd already had his fair share of trouble when his high school fish delivery system had been found transporting drugs inside live sturgeon bellies, and he wanted no part of any investigation now. He was on probation, and so far, he had followed the rules to a "T."

Freddy and Nova pulled away from the dock in Freddy's Inceptor, Nova's drawn and pale face looking out anxiously from the back of the cruiser.

I turned to Sheriff D. "What are we waiting for?"

"For that—" He motioned to the Coast Guardsman climbing up the ramp carrying three large heavy-duty plastic bags—two in one hand, one in the other. They looked like the kind of plastic bags the charter fishermen use for the tourists to bring the salmon up the dock. They use clear plastic bags to show off their catch. But there were no fish inside any of these bags today, and what I could see gave my stomach another cause to lurch.

The first plastic bag contained a well-worn medical go-bag. The second held the GPS from the crab boat, and the third held what I assumed to be the Estrella Nueva's lap top, which would contain a record of their crab pot drop points, their catch log, delivery prices, and other information pertinent to Nova and Mateo's crabbing business.

The Coastie handed all three plastic bags over to the sheriff, then pulled latex gloves off both his hands.

"There you go, Sheriff. Chain of evidence followed. You can take this to your crime lab for processing. Please remember to send us a copy of the finished report."

Chain of evidence? What was he talking about?

"Ms. Meredith Avery," asked the sheriff in his most officious voice, "does this nursing kit belong to you?" He held up the bag with the medical go-bag in it.

Merri's face turned even whiter than it was when she'd gotten off the boat, if that were possible. She said nothing, but looked back and forth from the sheriff to me several times in nothing short of terror.

I knew without a doubt that the medical duffle was hers, but I still couldn't figure out what it had to do with anything. Nova had asked her to come along on Mateo's first trip over the Columbia River Bar since his wheelchair confinement, and having her med kit with her should have been no big deal.

"I asked you a question, Ms. Avery."

Meredith recovered just enough to reply, "You told me not to say another word, and by gosh and by golly, that's exactly what I'm going to do." She exaggeratedly clamped her mouth shut, and I almost expected her to pantomime zipping her lip.

I couldn't take it any longer. "Carter! What exactly do you think happened out there last night?"

All business, despite our long-term friendship, Sheriff D only said, "Would you like to ride with us to the station, or not?"

"Of course I would! You know good and well I don't have my car here!"

"Then we best get going," said the sheriff. He carried the bags to the Inceptor SUV and placed them in the far back. Then he assisted Meredith into the back seat, same as Freddy had done with Nova. I guess I should have counted my blessings that I got to ride up front.

The show was over, for the time being, and the cannery workers sadly dispersed. Rich started back down the ramp to his boat, and on the far end of the dock, I could see the Coast Guard was stringing the familiar yellow "Do Not Cross" tape around the slip of the Estrella Nueva.

The ride to the station seemed to take forever, and my head reeled with several different, and all unsavory, scenarios. Obviously, Mateo had gone overboard during the night, but under what circumstances?

Sheriff D only broke the silence to radio in for the crime lab guys to meet us at the station to take immediate possession of the three plastic bags in the back of the car. That business settled, we lapsed back into our own thoughts for the rest of the trip.

Our small town police station has only one interrogation room, and Freddy had already seated Nova inside, so the sheriff could either put Meredith in his office to wait her turn, or the holding cell. When he chose the holding cell, my stomach lurched again.

"Carter! Is this absolutely necessary?"

"Afraid so, Sylvia." He looked genuinely sorry. "Your mother can't get any special treatment. In my office there's a phone, a computer, and too many items that could be used as a weapon if she wanted to escape."

"*Now* who's been watching too much crime TV?" I shook my head. "You know Merri's not going anywhere, and she's not about to hurt herself, or any of us, either. There's no reason to put her in lock up."

"Non-negotiable," Sheriff D replied.

Surprisingly, Merri did not put up a fuss, and we left her there, sitting on a wall bench, staring down at her hands, looking as sad and forlorn as any person I'd ever seen.

"Would you like to observe the interrogations?" asked the sheriff, when he'd closed the holding cell door behind us. He stood facing me in the hallway between the interrogation room and the observation room. "You know these women pretty well. Maybe you'll see something we might miss."

"So now you're asking for my help?" I frowned at him, then sighed. "Of course I want to observe, but just what is it you want me to watch for?"

"I'll be frank, Sylvia. We don't know for sure what happened out there, but at this time I have three working theories. It could be as simple as that Mateo tried to get up from his wheelchair, lost his balance, and fell overboard.

"But it could be that he intentionally went out there for the sole purpose of hurrying the end of his own life."

"Suicide?" I started to say no way, that he'd never do that, then changed my mind. "I know Mateo was pretty depressed about spending the rest of his life in a wheelchair, and the progressive nature of Parkinson's, but I can't honestly say if he was suicidal."

"Fair enough," said Sheriff D. He adjusted his service vest and put his hand on the interrogation room doorknob. "I know it will be hard for you to be objective, but I'm asking you to do your best."

"But Sheriff— You said you were working on three theories, and that's only two. What, besides accident or suicide, are you considering?"

As soon as I heard the words coming out of my mouth, I was sure I knew exactly what else he was thinking, but this was one time I didn't want to be right.

Sheriff D sighed, and nodded. "You already know, Sylvia: It was either accident, suicide, or murder, and if it turns out to be murder, then it's my sworn duty to make sure justice is served, and the woman, or women, responsible, are punished for their crime."

I didn't like it one bit, but I was glad he wasn't pulling any punches with me. "You really think Nova and my mother would conspire to murder Mateo? For what possible reason would they do that?"

"I make it my business not to jump to conclusions, Syl. We're after the facts, no matter where that might lead us.

Possible motives will be considered as we gather the facts, and no speculations before we have enough information. Understand?"

"Got it. Thank you." Then I went without another word into the Observation Room, a recent and pretty high-tech addition to our small rural community police station. It wasn't the first time I'd watched an interrogation from behind the two-way mirror, and I flipped on the speaker as soon as I entered the room.

Freddy was making small talk with Nova, asking general questions about crab fishing, and Nova was explaining how each fisherperson out there had his or her own colored buoy markings on the pot lines so that they each pulled in their own catch and didn't accidentally haul in the wrong pots.

I felt a surge of something like pride, knowing Freddy was in there doing his best to help Nova relax. An interrogation room, even without the stereotypical single light bulb hanging from a wire overhead, can be darn intimidating.

Nova looked pretty rough. Her hair, though cut and spiked exactly as I had described it earlier to Freddy, looked matted and oily, like it had been plastered down from being underneath a ball cap or something. Then I remembered that was most likely exactly how it got that way.

She wore jeans and a red sweatshirt with "Got Crabs?" written in big white lettering across the front. And she still had on the rubber boots she'd been wearing on the boat, heavy-soled and non-skid.

"Sorry for the delay," said Sheriff D, entering the room. "I needed to sign for the evidence transfer," he explained. "Deputy Morgan, you'll be overseeing the crime lab's findings, and I want to know what they know as soon as they know it."

It was a confusing statement, and I almost laughed. Freddy just nodded, and left the room. Sheriff D took the vacated seat across from Nova, with his back to me. He had brought in his digital recorder, and now asked Nova's permission to use it. She nodded, and he had her repeat her consent aloud, then state her full name.

I watched from behind the two-way mirror, and listened as the sheriff went through some pretty routine questions. Nothing seemed out of the ordinary until Sheriff D asked her about the GPS on her boat.

"Educate me," began the sheriff. "Your GPS shows that your boat ran in circles for most of the night."

"Yes," said Nova. "We set the boat's controls so that we stay in about the same location while we sleep. That way we can both get some rest without fear of running aground."

Sheriff Donaldson nodded his understanding, then stroked his mustache while he considered his next question. "So how do you explain that when the Coast Guard arrived, you were many miles north of your original night's resting spot?" He leaned forward and studied her face.

Nova, bless her heart, looked like she considered this some kind of trick question, and began to babble. "About 10 p.m., I set the boat to slow circles and we all went to bed. Something woke me up about 2 a.m. and I got up to check on Mateo. Mateo was not in his bunk, but Merri was still asleep on the cushions that fold down when we put the table away. I discovered Mateo's wheelchair out on the deck, lying on its side, and empty."

At this point, several sobs escaped Nova, and she had difficulty drawing a deep breath. Sheriff Donaldson handed her a box of tissues, but said nothing. Nova wiped her eyes and blew her nose, and struggled to compose herself.

It took a few minutes for her to continue, but when she did, it all came out in a rush. "I turned on all the deck lights. I thought maybe the chair had slipped out from under him and he had crawled to some sheltered spot. When I couldn't find him, I woke Merri, and we searched everywhere on the boat again. I put the floodlights out on the water, and we both called and listened, called and listened and—"

I thought she was going to break down again, but she did not.

"And then I radioed the Coast Guard, reported the emergency, requested assistance, then opened up the frequency most of the other crabbers out there have on stand-by and sent out a general SOS. Then I took the Estrella off autopilot and turned north, slowly weaving back and forth, but staying parallel to the shoreline."

That seemed to be the end of her monologue, or maybe she had simply run out of steam, and it took the sheriff's prompting to get any more out of her.

"I'm sorry, I still do not understand. Please explain to me why, exactly, you moved the boat from the spot you suspect Mateo went overboard."

Nova looked at him like he had straw sticking out of his head. "I was following the pattern of the currents along the coast. I didn't know how long Mateo had been gone, but I knew the current would be taking him north."

The light finally dawned for Sheriff D. "Oh, of course."

Nova's explanation of the events, along with her emotional and physical responses, had led me to conclude that Mateo had either committed suicide or had been the subject of a terrible accident, and from the way the sheriff was wrapping things up in the interrogation room, I could tell he felt the same way. That is, until Freddy came into the room and pulled the sheriff outside for a quick conversation.

When Sheriff D returned, he sat down and tapped his pencil on the tabletop for a few seconds before he said to Nova, "I understand you're the beneficiary for Mateo's life insurance policy?"

His question caught Nova off guard. "Yeah. So? I'm his wife. Of course I'm the beneficiary. Who else would it be?"

Freddy entered the observation room and stood next to me. Together we silently watched the drama unfold inside the interrogation room.

The sheriff continued, "And I understand you took out this policy fairly recently?"

I sucked in a breath of air.

Nova's shoulders slumped, and she sighed deeply. "Yes. Yes, I did. After Mateo's Parkinson's diagnosis, he insisted I get good insurance on him. We didn't know how fast the disease would progress, but he didn't want me to have any financial worries after he passed." She scowled. "His exact words were, 'at least the boat will be paid off.'"

I involuntarily took another huge gasp of air.

"It gets worse," said Freddy, breaking the silence between us. "The insurance policy is for a cool one million dollars."

"Is Nova going to need a lawyer?" I asked.

"They both will," said Freddy, without thinking. "Not only is Meredith the secondary beneficiary on the policy, but there's the little matter of—"

Suddenly realizing to whom he was talking, Freddy clamped his mouth shut and abruptly left the room.

I started to go after him, and demand he explain just exactly what he meant by that, but Sheriff Donaldson was now holding the interrogation room door open for Nova, and Freddy was already there, handing over my mother in exchange.

It was hard for me to think of Meredith as my mother. She hadn't displayed a lot of maternal instinct during my youth, but as I've aged, we've grown a lot closer—rather like equals rather than parent and child.

A hard lump formed in my throat as I saw her take the seat facing the mirror, look up into the mirror and fluff her hair a little. Then she smiled a soft smile and wiggled a couple of her fingers at me. Of course, she couldn't really know I was back there, but it must have suddenly dawned on her that it was certainly possible that someone was watching, and I was currently the only one not accounted for.

She asked the sheriff if it was okay to remove her pea coat, and he consented. I watched as she unbuttoned the double-breasted wool jacket, pulled her arms out of the sleeves, and folded it neatly before setting it on the table in front of her. She seemed to want some control over her environment, and I couldn't blame her for that.

Sheriff Donaldson took her through the same recording instructions and verbal permission as he had with Nova, then tipped back in his chair, looked at the ceiling and laced his fingers behind his head.

Uh-oh. I knew that posture all too well. Dollars to donuts Sheriff D was about to drop one heck of a bombshell.

CHAPTER 3

"Ms. Meredith Avery," Sheriff Donaldson began.

"Please call me Merri," interrupted my mother.

"Ms. Meredith Avery," repeated Sheriff D, "please explain how it came to be that you refilled a prescription for 30 Triazolam just two days ago, and today there are only 8 sleeping pills left in the bottle."

The room was suddenly much too warm, and I wondered if I were having another of those seemingly never-ending hot flashes. When my knees started to buckle, I braced them against the wall beneath the mirror.

Freddy re-entered the room, I assumed after securing Nova in the holding cell. I didn't dare look at him, but continued staring at the drama unfolding in front of me.

"Ms. Avery?" said Sheriff Donaldson a second time. "I need you to answer the question. What happened to the 22 missing pills?"

"I'm invoking the 5th Amendment," my mother said immediately.

I could feel my eyes trying to pop right out of my head. "The 5th Amendment?" I asked incredulously.

"She refuses to answer on the basis that it may incriminate her," said Freddy.

"I *know* what it means!" I jabbed him with my elbow. "I just don't know why she'd say such a thing."

Sheriff Donaldson shifted his weight forward, and the front legs of the chair slammed against the floor. He grabbed his digital recorder from the table, and I assumed he switched it off. I was doing a lot of assuming lately.

"Meredith!" exclaimed Sheriff D. "For crying out loud! You are not on trial here, and I'm hoping you won't need to be on trial any time soon. Now work with me."

Meredith took a deep breath. "But what if something I tell you could get me into trouble in a way totally unrelated to Mateo being missing?"

Sheriff D blew out a big breath. "Ok, fine. We're off the record here. Just tell me what happened to those 22 pills."

"At a certain age, sheriff, insomnia becomes the norm, rather than the rule."

"But what about the pills, Meredith?"

Merri looked down at her hands. "Two of my close friends aren't able to afford prescription sleeping aids. I gave 10 pills to each one, and last night on the boat, I took two myself because I wasn't used to the constant movement of the boat, and I didn't think I would be able to get to sleep without assistance."

Freddy gave my hand a squeeze. "It sounds reasonable, but we'll have to get statements from both of the women she gave them to."

I jerked my hand away. "And just what had you *thought* she had done with them?"

"We weren't jumping to any conclusions," stammered Freddy. "But if you gave a guy a handful of those pills, it would sure be a lot easier to hoist him overboard."

"Frederick Harold Morgan! How dare you think my mother was a co-conspirator in a homicide! For all we know, Mateo committed suicide."

"Unlikely," said Freddy. "His life insurance policy doesn't pay off on suicides, and Mateo probably knew that."

"So... You think you have it narrowed down to either

an accident or a murder?"

Freddy sighed and cleared his throat. "Well— At this time, those are the two most likely options."

I couldn't argue with him on that point, but I sure hoped it could be proven to be an accident—for everyone's sake.

Sheriff D and Meredith had left the interrogation room, and Freddy and I joined them in the hallway. "What now?" I asked.

"Now," said the sheriff, turning to Meredith, "this is where I really do say 'don't leave town.' But since you and Ms. Johanssen both have solid roots here, I'm not really worried about that."

"You're not going to charge us?" asked Meredith.

"At this time, there's no evidence to indicate that either one of you did anything wrong." Freddy shrugged. "I'll go get Nova."

"And then you'll give us a ride back down to Unity?" I asked. "We all rode here in police vehicles, and Mom and Nova's cars are both parked at the port. I'll catch a ride home with Mom later."

"Oh you will, will you?" said Meredith.

It was good to hear a little animation in her voice. "You live in Ocean Crest. You'll be driving right by my door on your way home."

Merri gave me a squeeze. "Yes, dear. Of course I'm happy to give you a lift."

But first we had to go back to the port, and I don't think any of us were prepared for the amount of publicity that had been stirred up. There were two Portland television stations on site, and at least three regional newspapers were represented.

No one from the earlier cannery gathering was around,

and the reporters were milling amongst themselves, like sharks swimming along the beach, waiting for the sound of summer tourists splashing in the water. A missing crab fisherman, missing under suspicious circumstances, and a handicapped one at that, was apparently big news.

Microphones were stuck in all our faces the moment we arrived, and questions were shouted from everywhere, all at once. It was more than unsettling, and it caught Merri, Nova and me all off guard. What could we say, besides, "No comment." "No comment." "No freakin' comment!" What could anyone say under these circumstances?

Thankfully, Freddy came to our rescue.

"Ladies and gentlemen," he began, holding up both hands for attention. "There has been a terrible tragedy here today, and these women would just like some privacy to deal with their personal grief."

"Have any charges been filed?" asked one TV reporter.

"At this time," answered Freddy, "there is no reason to treat this incident as anything other than an accident. A horrible, heart-wrenching accident. No charges are pending."

That seemed to dampen the journalistic enthusiasm of the group, and in short order, they dispersed—all but Raven Coldwater, a recent high school graduate who was doing an internship at the local tri-weekly newspaper, the North Beach Peninsula Tribune.

Raven had been among the clamoring reporters when we arrived, but now she'd withdrawn back under the charter office eaves, and was busy scribbling notes. At this distance, I knew she couldn't hear anything we said.

Freddy left us then, and headed back to his car. He was, after all, on duty.

At the top of the ramp leading to the Estrella Nueva,

the yellow tape used to protect crime scenes proclaimed "Do Not Cross." Nova stopped in her tracks, pursed her lips, placed her hands on her hips, and looked hopelessly down the dock. We could see men on board her crab boat, but couldn't tell from this distance if they were Coast Guard or the county crime scene techs.

Rich walked up behind us, not coming up from his boat this time, but most likely from sitting in the "Can't Fathom It" upstairs bar, which had a clear view of both the walkway along the mooring basin and the boats in the marina beyond it.

"I wouldn't cross that tape if I were you, Nova," he said. "I'm not even allowed to go down to the Geraldine until I get the all-clear and the tape's officially taken down."

Nova's brow furrowed deeply. "Rich, I've got a load of crab on board. If I can't deliver it to the processor in the next couple hours, I'll lose payment for this run—on top of everything else."

Rich stuck his hands in his pockets and gave her a self-satisfied smile. He looked for all the world like a cat who'd swallowed a canary. "You're not going to lose any crab, Nova. Not a single one. I can promise you that."

"How can you be so sure, Rich?" asked Nova, tears in her eyes. "We don't know when they'll be finished down there. It could take hours—or days—for them to process the entire boat. Meanwhile, my delivery clock is ticking. The ice won't hold out forever."

Rich gave Nova a very tender look. I suddenly felt like Merri and I were intruding, and looked away, back up toward the charter offices. Raven had her camera out, and was entertaining herself by taking photos of the boats in the marina.

"Nova." Rich's voice was soft. "You've got to start

giving me a little more credit for my powers of persuasion."
He smiled. "I convinced the Coast Guard and the crime
techs to allow the cannery workers to offload your crabs,
which they did, under careful watch of both groups. Now
they can take all the time they need to go over the boat with
a fine-tooth comb if they want."

Nova gasped, then her overloaded emotions burst
forth. She spontaneously flung herself into Rich's arms and
hugged him tightly. "Oh thank you! Thank you, Rich! I
can't thank you enough! You're my hero!" Impulsively, she
gave him a quick kiss on the cheek.

Raven Coldwater got her first front-page headline news
story byline the very next day, complete with a photo of the
missing crab fisherman's widow, now quite possibly a
potential murder suspect, kissing a man already on
probation for unwittingly providing drug smugglers the
means to transport their illegal substances up the peninsula.

"She did the best she knew how," said Felicity
Michaels, my friend and Raven's former journalism
teacher, when I called her during her prep period at the
high school.

"Where do you think she got her alleged news from?" I
asked Felicity. "She didn't talk to Rich, or Nova, or Mom or
me."

Felicity didn't exactly answer my question when she
replied, "She's truly sorry for causing so much of a stir."

"You've talked with her?"

"Yes," said Felicity. "She was all excited and wanted to
share her first big story with me, but then admitted she
couldn't quite hear what you all were talking about on the
walkway, so she figured a picture said a thousand words
and just ran with it."

I shook my head and rolled my eyes, both unnecessary actions, considering we were talking on the telephone. "Felix..." I sighed. "There are a lot of lives at stake here. Nova and Meredith might both be charged, and if Rich is suspected of being involved in any way, his probation would be revoked, and he could go to jail for quite a while."

"I know," said Felicity. "I'm almost sorry I got Raven that internship." She sighed. "But she already plans to write a retraction, so we can all hope it will blow over real soon."

"So there will be a tiny little paragraph on page three in Friday's edition saying that the allegations in the missing crab fisherman story were highly exaggerated?"

"I think they might do a bit better than that."

"How so?"

"Raven said she's interviewing both Meredith and Nova tomorrow morning to find out what was really being talked about on the walkway yesterday. She's truly sorry and hopes she can clear this all up without losing her job over it."

"Her job—her *unpaid* job—covering an unfortunately fairly routine story at the port that nobody else at the paper wanted to cover that day, should be the least of her worries."

"What do you mean by that?" asked Felix.

"Nova and Rich are both understandably boiling mad," I began. "It wouldn't surprise me if they sued Raven, her parents, *and* the newspaper."

"Oh, Sylvia, I hope not," said Felicity. "Raven's a good kid. She was the first female on the wrestling team. I had thought she might go into the field of physical therapy, and she still might, but her folks don't have the money to send her to college right now."

Felicity knew she was touching a soft spot in my heart.

I'd worked for Child Protective Services for 30 years, and I'd seen firsthand what happens when parents fell on hard times and their kids suffered as a result.

"I'll talk to them," I said. "If they don't cool down, the Tribune has the deepest pockets. Maybe I can convince them to leave Raven and her folks alone."

"Thank you," said Felicity. "Now I've got students waiting." She sighed. "Guess I'll have to do all my prep after school today."

I was pretty sure she was talking to herself and didn't expect me to reply, so I signed off by simply echoing her thank you.

"And Syl?" asked Felix at the last second. "Please keep me in the loop about anybody getting sued."

"I will." Then I disconnected and smiled at Sheriff Donaldson. "She didn't even suspect I was calling her from your office."

"Good." Sheriff D tipped back in his chair and clasped his hands behind his head. "There are a lot of questions not yet answered in this case, and we don't need any more rumors printed in the paper to muddy the water any darker than it's already muddied."

"I couldn't agree more."

The sheriff continued, "What with the million dollar insurance policy, and a front page photo of Nova and Rich embracing the same day Mateo disappeared, the county prosecutor is putting some pressure on me to make an arrest—maybe several of them."

"Does that include my mother?"

Sheriff Donaldson sat up and ran his finger and thumb out along his mustache. "I don't know, Sylvia. It could. I just don't want to be too hasty."

"Now that I know there's going to be a retraction in the

next paper, I can stall the prosecutor a little while, while we continue hoping for a break in this case." He actually smiled a genuine smile at me.

I nodded. "It's times like this I'm very grateful the newspaper comes out every Monday, Wednesday, and Friday."

"Right," said Sheriff D. "And thanks for calling Felicity for me. I figured she'd be more forthcoming with you than with a formal visit to her classroom from the sheriff's department."

"I want justice served as much as you do, Carter. And I also don't want my mother being locked up for being in the wrong place at the wrong time."

I got the first and second inklings of further trouble when I received a text from my mother much too early on Friday morning. For one, Meredith very rarely texts. And for two, her cryptic message said only, "It's a good picture of me, don't you think?"

I fell for the bait, and texted back, "What are you talking about?"

And she replied, "Guess you haven't seen today's paper."

I didn't bother to answer her, but immediately left the house. I got into my car and headed straight for the home of the nearest friend I knew who had a newspaper delivered directly to his residence three times a week at the crack of dawn.

When I came through the manager's door of the Clamshell Motel, Jimmy Noble had 'that look' on his face. I was never sure just what 'that look' meant, but I set my phone and car keys on the counter, grabbed a mug from the cupboard, and poured myself some of his infamously strong coffee before asking any questions.

I stopped by the motel frequently on what I called my semi-regular "wellness check," and knew how to make myself right at home. Jimmy's mother and I had been close colleagues at CPS, and before she died of cancer, I'd promised to keep a watchful eye on her son—even though he was already pushing hard on 40.

This morning, Jimmy was sitting in his usual spot, which he called his 'command center'—a large, dark naugahyde recliner strategically placed directly in front of the biggest TV screen I'd ever seen in a private home. His calico cat, Priscilla, was settled comfortably on his lap.

"Don't get up," I joked, as I settled myself on the couch next to his chair.

"I can't get up," he replied amicably. "I have feline paralysis."

"Cat on lap disease?" I asked.

"Yep, it's a very bad case of C.O.L.," he replied, "and Miss Priss would not like it one bit if I even *considered* dislodging her during her early morning nap."

He reached down to the coffee table he'd pulled over next to his chair and picked up the newspaper. "And I'm afraid you're not going to like this one bit, either," he said, handing me the front section of the latest edition of the North Beach Tribune.

Raven had tracked down Meredith and Nova for clarification, all right, but never for one moment had anyone imagined it would be the cause of her second front-page photo and feature story inside of a week.

This photo, which was "above the fold," was of my mother, theatrically draped across one end of her couch in her living room in Ocean Crest. She was wearing a long, tie-dyed skirt and solid colored, but somehow matching, peasant blouse. Sitting next to her was Nova, dressed in her standard crabber's work clothes, well-worn blue jeans and sweatshirt, looking more than a little uncomfortable.

Meredith was smiling broadly at Nova, and handing her a cup of tea. I could guess it was tea, since there was a teapot sitting on the coffee table in front of them. There was a also a plate of cookies on the table, and Merri's three cats had taken up strategic positions, one on each lap, and one between them. It could have been a totally innocuous photo, destined for nothing more than the society page, if the Tribune had had a society page, except for the rather damning headline.

The headline, which appeared below the photo, and below the fold, boldly proclaimed in all caps: "Merri's Widows Add New Member."

I sputtered a mouthful of coffee all over the paper, and quickly used my sleeve to wipe it off before it blurred the words.

"What in the world?!" My breath started coming in rapid, shallow gulps. I looked over at Jimmy, as if I expected him to put the earth back on its axis or something.

"You better set down your coffee before you read all about it," said surprisingly-practical Jimmy.

I couldn't find the words to answer him; I suddenly felt frozen in time and space. It was as if I couldn't make my lips move at all, and there seemed to be some kind of weird buzzing between my ears while my heart pounded an irregular tattoo inside my chest.

Jimmy reached down and maneuvered the coffee table closer to me. "Set down your coffee, Syl," he said sternly. "Just set it down."

I did as I was told, but nothing else seemed to compute. Jimmy gently took the newspaper from my shaking hand,

and asked if I would like him to read it to me. Somehow, I managed a weak little nod.

He read the entire article, straight through, bless his heart, not even pausing to make any snide asides or editorial comments along the way. When he finished, he asked, "Would you like me to read it again?"

By now I had found my voice. "No. Thank you. That will not be necessary."

We sat in silence for a few moments, then I asked him to please bring me my phone.

"Your phone?" He seemed confused by my request.

"It's on the counter by the coffee pot. I'm not sure my legs are steady enough to walk that far at the moment."

This time Jimmy gave no thought to dislodging Priscilla and retrieved my phone for me. I immediately set up a group text to Meredith, Nova, and Felicity. Then I went back and added Freddy, just for good measure, or maybe just because I was pretty sure I was going to need some moral support.

I vocalized my message as I wrote: "URGENT. Meet at Clamshell, 2:30."

"Why here? Why wait until 2:30?" asked Jimmy.

"You got a hot date or something?" I snapped at him, then immediately regretted both my words and tone of voice. "Oh geez, Jimmy, I'm so sorry."

"It's okay, Syl. You're stressed."

"That's no excuse to be rude."

"It's okay, really. It's not the first time you've harshed my mellow, and I always manage to get over it."

I shot him a wan smile and took a deep breath. "We'll meet here, because it's both private and centrally located. Nova and Felicity are in Unity, Meredith is up north in Ocean Crest, and who knows where Freddy will be by then.

Two-thirty, so Felicity can get here after school, which gets out at 2 p.m. on Fridays."

Jimmy nodded. "Okay. That makes sense."

"Glad you approve." I smiled as I said it, stood, and ruffled his hair on the way by his chair as I headed for the door. "Meanwhile, I've got some damage control to do at the sheriff's office. I thought Raven was just going to write a simple retraction about the misleading photo in Wednesday's paper, not make everything so very much worse."

"No kidding." Jimmy had followed me into the kitchen side of his living quarters, and poured a few fresh kibbles into Priscilla's bowl. "See you at 2:30."

"Yes, we'll all see you at 2:30."

CHAPTER 4

I drove straight from Jimmy's to the Buoy 10 Bakery in beautiful, downtown Tinkerstown. I felt an urgent need to fortify myself with donuts, and I knew I could pick up my own copy of the Tribune there, too.

Then I spent the rest of the morning eating sugar and further digesting the contents of the front-page article. Consequently, the sugar rush threatened to put me into a coma by the time I felt strong enough to go face the lion in his den.

Understandably, Sheriff Donaldson was none-too-pleased when I walked around the corner and into his office shortly after lunch.

"Well, well, well," said Sheriff D, his cheeks puffing as he first inhaled, then blew out a big, deep breath. "I must say, I'm rather surprised to see you here today, Sylvia."

I dropped a white bakery bag on the desk in front of him. "Apple fritters still your favorite?"

"Trying to sweeten me up?" He looked like he was going to decline the pastry, then licked his lips, opened the bag, and took a big whiff. He smiled. "If it means anything to you, county officials cannot be bribed."

"Good grief and gravy, Carter, it was just a friendly peace offering. If you don't want it—" I reached out to take the bag back, but he shook his head and pulled the bag closer to his chest.

"I would have thought right about now you'd be busy

up in Ocean Crest, helping Meredith pack for Mexico."

"Not funny, Carter."

"No, it's certainly not," he agreed, and motioned for me to sit down. "So your mother is the designated ringleader of a band of Merry Widows, huh?"

"Still not funny, Carter." I didn't know where to begin, so I was letting him get it all out of his system before putting our heads together to look for a solution.

"Do you think, like the rest of us are beginning to think, that these women are a mite too merry to be poor little innocent widows?"

I didn't like the tone of Sheriff D's voice, and I stood to leave. "I came in as a courtesy, Carter, and I expected you to afford me the same."

"The prosecutor is breathing down my neck, Syl. If you want to keep Meredith, and Nova for that matter, out of jail, you'd better start talking fast." He opened the pastry bag, tore off a bite of the fritter, and popped it into his mouth.

"Raven didn't have all the facts," I began, "and what she did have, she exaggerated some, and withheld other information as she saw fit."

"So you're telling me she's a journalist who was purposely misleading the public? I'm shocked."

"Carter, she's 18. I don't know what she's doing on purpose, but I doubt she's doing it with malicious intent. She's probably thinking more about winning a Pulitzer Prize than she is about getting down to the truth of the matter."

Sheriff D pulled a sharpened pencil out of his cup holder and tapped the eraser end on the newspaper sitting on his desk. He turned his head this way and that, his nose reminding me of a parrot's beak as he considered which nut or seed to snack on next. "Can you tell me exactly what she wrote that isn't true?"

I shook my head. "I'm not sure. I know it's true that Mom has been widowed three times, of course, but I didn't know all her other close friends were also widows."

"Nova wasn't a widow until yesterday," the sheriff corrected me. "And both Nadine Larsen and Goodie Godwin lost their husbands within the past six months."

"But Orpha Starr has been a widow for decades," I said hopefully.

"That's correct." He sighed. "But at the end of the day, the final score still stands five for five."

I suddenly got defensive. "They're all a part of the dying generation," I proclaimed. "Statistics show that women in their 70s and 80s almost always outlive their spouses. They are part of the majority, Carter. There's nothing unusual about lonely women banding together for friendship and companionship. Don't make it sound like a criminal act."

Sheriff D tapped the newspaper with the pencil again several times. I could tell he was thinking hard about what I'd said, so I kept quiet to let him think. Finally he said, "I take it you've met all these women."

It was a statement rather than a question, but I knew he was waiting for me to say something. "Yes, of course. They get together regularly to play Pinochle, or Bunco, or go to the movies, or go bowling, or things like that. They all take fitness classes at the Senior Center, too." I was really rather proud of my mother and her aging "Merry Band" for getting out and doing things they enjoyed.

"How often does their club meet?"

"I don't know that you would call it a club..." my voice trailed off as I considered what information the sheriff might be digging for. "I guess they get together a couple times a week for their different activities."

"So no regularly scheduled meetings?"

"I don't think so. The Senior Center activities are regularly scheduled, of course, and all posted on a public monthly calendar." I frowned. "Just what are you getting at, Carter?"

"Maybe nothing," he replied. "Maybe nothing at all." He resumed his pencil tapping, and I resumed my silence until I couldn't take it any more.

"I'm getting together with Mom and Nova and Felicity over at the Clamshell this afternoon," I said, deliberately not mentioning Freddy's inclusion at the meeting. "Felicity is still unofficially mentoring Raven, so I know she has her ear.

"I want Mom and Nova to explain how and why Raven decided to take off writing another of her quasi-investigative pieces instead of just printing a simple retraction for jumping to conclusions when Nova hugged Rich."

The sheriff was suddenly all ears. "I'd certainly like to hear all about that, too," he said, nodding.

"Oh, no you don't! You, Carter, are not invited! I'm not going to let you turn this informal get-together into another opportunity for an off-site police interrogation!"

Sheriff Donaldson started to snap back, but held his tongue just long enough to find a way around my objections. "So, Sylvia..." he paused, ever-so-slightly, "would you have any objection to Freddy attending your little soiree this afternoon? In an unofficial capacity, of course."

I was annoyed that Sheriff D was using my relationship with Freddy, however we defined relationship, to get me to agree to police presence at the Clamshell. And I was further annoyed that I hadn't already considered that anything Freddy heard would have to be reported, whether he was there in an official capacity or not.

I shrugged. "Sure. Why not? Nobody's got anything to hide, Carter."

I arrived at the Clamshell first, with Nova pulling into the driveway right behind me. I waited while she parked her Outback next to my Mustang, and we entered the office together. Jimmy had the coffee going, but we both declined.

Next came Felicity, trailed by her ever-present shadow, Walter Winston. Walter had retired from his high school teaching career just a year or two ago, and divorced shortly after that, when his wife discovered there really was such a thing as too much togetherness.

Now Walter irregularly worked as substitute teacher, and lived in the same apartment complex in Unity as Felicity. If he'd been 30 years younger, there might have been something more between them, but Felix happily filled his bill as a friend, colleague, and surrogate daughter.

Both Walter and Felicity came through the inner office door carrying a bottle of the same kind of wine. "It's Friday, we've all had a tough week, and I thought a little wine might be appropriate," said Felix.

"And most welcome," said Nova, eagerly eyeing the bottles.

Jimmy reached up into the cupboard over the counter and set out three wine glasses. I don't drink, and he still had a motel to run, in case anyone came in to book a room, so I pulled two diet sodas from Jimmy's never-ending refrigerator stash while he got out his corkscrew and opened both bottles of wine.

Felix and Walter each poured from the bottle they'd brought, and Nova gratefully accepted the one Felicity poured for her. Then Jimmy put the corks loosely back into the bottles before placing them in his fridge.

Freddy arrived next. We could all clearly hear him coming up the driveway, around the motel office and Jimmy's living quarters, and into the parking lot. There's no denying the sound a Harley Sportster makes, no matter what the color.

Freddy turned down the offer of wine, poured himself a half mug of Jimmy's industrial strength coffee, then opened the fridge and filled the rest of the cup with milk.

The six of us gathered around Jimmy's yellow Formica table, and the room soon filled with pleasantries and polite chitchat. I looked around at the assembly and considered warmly the eclectic company I kept: teachers, crabber, motel manager, cop. I smiled a genuine smile, despite the circumstances that had led us to meet today.

There was a lull in the conversation while Felicity crossed the room to the fridge, retrieved one of the bottles of wine, then refilled Nova's glass before her own. She offered some to Walter, but he had barely touched his drink, and waved her off.

Felix shrugged, then finished off the bottle in her hand by filling both Nova's glass and her own clear to the rim. Then she looked around and asked the obvious question in the back of everyone's mind, "Where's Meredith?"

"Probably busy packing for Mexico," said Freddy.

We all knew he was trying to make a joke, but I also knew that the sheriff had used those exact words when we'd spoken just a couple hours ago.

Then it dawned on me that it was Friday afternoon, and Freddy was on duty, despite his casual attire and his arrival on the Harley. The sudden knowledge that he'd not come in his uniform because he'd been sent specifically to gather information for the sheriff irked me no end.

But before I could take him aside to chew his ear off, Mother turned into the parking lot at a pretty fast clip, spraying gravel out behind her red Saturn as she gunned it up the driveway. She flounced into the kitchen without bothering to knock, and she, too, carried a bottle of wine, which she thrust at Jimmy as she entered. "Be a dear," she said to him, as if he were the hired help, "and open this for me, will you?"

Then to the rest of us she exclaimed, "What a day I've had! And here I thought my 15 minutes of fame would be over 15 minutes after the newspaper came out this morning! All day it's been one phone call after another!"

Jimmy reached into the cupboard and pulled out another wine glass. The thought briefly flitted through my mind that I might soon be needing one, too.

Freddy stood and offered Meredith his chair, which she accepted with a smile of gratitude. Then he collected Jimmy's office chair from in front of the motel computer desk and squeezed in next to her at the farthest end of the table, but still within my direct line of sight. We made brief eye contact and I glowered at him, but no one else noticed the frosty chill between us.

Meredith was wiggling out of her long sweater-coat, and Freddy assisted her by holding her right sleeve while she pulled her arm out. Meanwhile, Jimmy used his corkscrew for a third time that afternoon and opened her wine bottle.

"So what's with the urgent text this morning?" Meredith asked, raising her eyebrows at me. "Hhmm?"

"Mom—" Although I'd had all day to think about how

best to approach her, I found myself at a loss for just the right words. Unfortunately, that seemed to be happening a lot lately.

"Mom," I began again, "do you know everyone here?"

Meredith had just succeeded in extracting her second arm out of the sweater, and she shook her head 'no.' She playfully pointed three times at Walter, seated to her left, then smiled brightly and said, "I don't believe I've had the pleasure of meeting this gentleman."

Holy Criminitly, I could swear she was batting her eyelashes.

My 'why is Mother acting so charming' radar went on high red alert as I introduced them, but I didn't have the energy right at the moment to follow up on that thought. Maybe later, if I thought I really needed to know.

"Now that we're all acquainted," Meredith returned to the matter at hand, "I'll ask again: What's with the summons, Syl?"

I hesitated, but Jimmy, bless his heart, jumped right in.

"Syl wants to know how in the world Raven got sidetracked from writing a simple retraction to composing another sensational feature article about your Merri's Widows," he said, cutting straight to the point. He handed her a full glass of wine, and set the bottle on the table in front of her.

He'd been a little more blunt than I would have been, but his statement aptly served the purpose.

"Oh, that!" Meredith beamed, waving her free hand as if to dismiss the whole matter. "That was all because of the cats!"

"Your cats?" I asked weakly, already afraid I knew the answer.

"You know my cats, Syl—Harlan, Chuckie, and Bob."

"Harlan, Chuckie, and Bob?" prompted Freddy.

Nova, obviously knowing what was coming next, reached over and poured herself a third glass of wine from the open bottle sitting on the table in front of Merri, not caring that it was totally different from the kind she'd already been drinking.

"Raven wanted to know how I'd chosen my cats' names, and I simply explained to her that I named each one after one of my three deceased husbands: Harlan, Charles, and Robert."

Freddy sputtered coffee down his shirt, and Jimmy choked on his soda. Walter leaned forward, apparently fascinated by every word that came out of Meredith's mouth, but the other three of us had seen this coming.

"After that, Raven asked Nova if she were going to name a pet after Mateo."

"And I told her I definitely had no plans to do any such thing," said Nova, who was beginning to slur her words. "Working fisherpeople rarely have pets."

"But then I told her our friend Nadine Larsen got a dog for protection after her husband died," continued Meredith.

"For protection?" I couldn't believe my ears. "Didn't Nadine get a toy poodle?"

"Well, yes," admitted Merri. "But she named it Claudette, after her husband Claude, who was about as much protection with his Alzheimer's as her new dog is now." Meredith shrugged, again minimizing how it all sounded.

"So after that, Raven asked if we had any other widowed friends with pets, and I told her that Goodie hadn't been able to have pets at home, because her husband Larry was allergic, so she volunteers at the Humane Society, and that Orpha just has a cat she calls 'Cat' because she'd forget the name if she named it anything else anyway."

Merri nodded enthusiastically. "But Raven was pretty excited about Nova being the fifth and final woman in our group of friends to become a widow, even if she isn't going to have a pet named Mateo."

Silence fell like the blade on a guillotine.

Felicity spoke first. "I hate to say it, and it may be the wine talking, but I'm kind of proud of Raven's investigative skills." She giggled.

"It's the wine," I said sternly, and nudged her with my elbow.

"So what about Raven's claim that Merri's Widows might all soon be very rich women?" asked Jimmy.

Meredith turned to Nova, who shook her head. Either she had nothing to say, or was warning Meredith not to say anything, and I couldn't tell which.

Freddy cleared his throat, and all eyes turned in his direction. "I believe she might have written that because, according to the sheriff, each of these women—with the exception of Orpha, whose husband died over a decade ago—had taken out online life insurance policies on their husbands within months of them passing," he said.

"So?" I challenged him.

Freddy shrugged. "Just sayin'."

"Well, you can just keep your 'just sayin's' to yourself, mister." I could almost feel my hackles, if people really do have hackles, coming into play.

"He's correct, dear," Meredith said softly. "Don't fault him for telling the truth."

This meeting was to clear things up, and I was getting more confused by the moment. "Mom? How come you happen to know so much about all their private insurance business?"

Meredith looked at Nova a second time, but apparently decided she'd get no help from her semi-inebriated friend, so she turned to Freddy. "What else does the sheriff know?"

Freddy didn't pull any punches. "He knows that you helped them fill out their online forms, Meredith, and that you're the secondary beneficiary on all the policies."

Holy Criminitly and good grief and gravy! I was aware I was wearing out my oaths saved for special occasions, but my astonished brain could think of nothing else. For one of the few times in my life, I was rendered speechless. And so was everyone else.

Turned out we didn't have to say anything, because before any of us could form a coherent sentence, Freddy held up his hand to signal he wished to continue.

"It's not a crime to help someone fill out online forms, Meredith. You're not in any trouble for that. But just how did you come to be second in line for the money on all those policies?"

Meredith lifted her palms in the universal gesture of 'who knows,' and rolled her eyes, a bad habit I suddenly realized I probably got from her.

"I was helping them at the computer," she said, "and when I came to the space on the form for beneficiaries, they all decided I should put my own name in there on the second line, just to hold the space for the time being, and they could change it later."

"And none of that is illegal either," slurred Nova.

I sat there, opening and closing my mouth, making some kind of guppy fish face when my cell phone rang, breaking the spell.

After taking a quick look at the display, I said, "It's Mercedes. I'll take it outside." I quickly left the kitchen and entered the office lobby, closing the door behind me. I sat heavily on the stool in there, glad to put a little distance between me and the rest of the crew while I sorted through my thoughts. "Hello Mercedes. What's up?"

I was only gone a few minutes, but when I re-entered the kitchen, the gathering was breaking up. Jimmy was setting cups and glasses into the sink, and Freddy was helping Meredith back into her sweater-coat. Felix was going to give Nova a lift back down to the port in her Camry, and Walter would drive Nova's car back for her.

"Before anyone leaves," I said, "Mercedes wants me to be sure to invite you all up to her big 'welcome back' party at the Spartina Point Casino and Resort tomorrow night. She's celebrating being back behind the piano keyboard, and promises lots of fun and surprises."

"We already know," said Felicity matter-of-factly. "Freddy just told us."

"And as for surprises," said Meredith, smiling broadly, "you don't know the half of it, my darling daughter, and it's going to knock your socks off."

At that moment, I didn't want to ask what, exactly, she thought could knock my socks off any more than our conversation this afternoon already had. On top of that, I was busy nursing a disappointment that I hadn't been the one to give us all something positive to look forward to, and wondering why Freddy hadn't already shared the information about the party with me, too.

The group was all leaving at once, and there wasn't an opportunity to privately resolve my mad with Freddy before the door closed behind them, and Jimmy and I were the only ones left.

"Oh, now don't go and get all pouty on me," said Jimmy, finishing up at the sink. "Just because you're dating the big bad casino boss doesn't mean he has to share everything with you first."

Jimmy was right, of course, but I had still had my feelings hurt, and I guess I was just looking for another reason to be mad at Freddy.

Jimmy, on the other hand, was all smiles about the upcoming party, and his joyous enthusiasm was downright contagious, making it hard to continue my pout. He dried his hands on a dishtowel and abruptly began clapping them in front of him like a trained seal. "Oh, goody! Goody! Goody!" he said. "I just love having an excuse to get all dressed up for a fun night out!"

CHAPTER 5

Saturday morning dawned bright and sunny, and settled my indecision over which of my vehicles to take for my drive up to the casino. I'd promised to help Mercedes finish getting ready for her big shindig, and was eagerly looking forward to spending some quality one-on-one time with her.

I smiled from ear to ear as I wheeled my bike out of the garage and strapped on my motorcycle helmet. Freddy isn't the only one around here who rides a Harley, but it is thanks to him that I now own a most beautiful cranberry red Sportster.

On the ride north, I traveled up Sandspit Road, which has a slightly lower speed limit, and much less traffic, than the main highway. The spring scenery was stunning, all green and gorgeous, with glimpses of Shallowwater Bay through the trees off to my right. I was alone in my thoughts. With no music to distract me, and my head tucked safely inside a matching cranberry-colored helmet, and I had a little time to think back upon the events of the past several months.

I thought about how I'd first come to meet Freddy, and the circumstances in which he'd ended up inheriting the Spartina Point Casino and Resort from his Uncle Harry, a known drug dealer, now deceased.

And I thought about Freddy's insistence on buying me this wonderful bike as an unofficial payment for helping the police force solve two murders during a television movie company's short-lived time on the North Beach Peninsula. No pun intended.

And that led me to think about my on-again, off-again romantic feelings toward Deputy Frederick Harold Morgan, which made me all queasy and mushy inside, as I wrestled with my conflicting emotions.

On one hand, Freddy was a fabulous guy—smart, good-looking, and now quite financially secure. On the other hand, he was so darn young, at least in comparison to me, and I wasn't sure I could ever get past that nearly 15-year age difference. It didn't seem to bother Freddy in the least, but I kept wondering what people thought when they saw us together, and it was hard for me not to care what others were thinking.

It was all quite mind-boggling, when you came right down to it, so I was actually glad my ride wasn't any longer this beautiful morning. I've found that too much time alone inside my head, or my helmet, isn't always in my best interest!

I pulled in and unashamedly parked in one of the four prime spots marked "Reserved" right next to the artificial drawbridge crossing the sturgeon-filled moat leading into the castle-themed casino's main lobby.

Those spaces had once held Uncle Harry's fleet of four big, black Lincoln Town Cars, but since Freddy had taken over ownership, those cars were no longer hogging the prime parking spots. Freddy had insisted that I could use any of those spaces anytime I wished, whether I came to see him, or even when I was there simply to visit Mercedes.

"You're lucky you didn't find me passed out on the floor," said Mercedes when I entered the main casino ballroom. She was doubled over, gasping for air. "We ran out of helium, and I've been having a heck of a time trying to get all these here balloons blown up for my big come-back party tonight."

"Merc—" I rolled my eyes, and briefly thought again how hard I'm trying to break this bad, and probably inherited, habit. "You were away from the piano bar less than a month. That hardly calls for so many balloons." I took off my leather jacket, and slung it across the back of one of the chairs near the dance floor.

Mercedes straightened up to her full five-foot, four-inch height, put her hands on her ample hips, tilted her bottle-blonde head, and glared at me. "You saying my public didn't miss me? You saying my peeps haven't been clamoring for my return? You saying I don't *deserve* a big, happy welcome back party?"

"No... I wasn't... I didn't mean... Here! Let me help you with those balloons!" I grabbed a red one from the package on the keyboard and pressed it to my lips.

"That's more like it," said Merc, nodding. "What I could really use around here is a little more practical help and a lot less dissing of my party."

Grateful that the balloon kept me from putting my foot into my mouth again, I quickly realized that blowing up balloons was a lot harder than it sounded. In no time at all, I was gasping for air the same as Mercedes had been doing when I arrived.

Freddy walked in, in full uniform, and if my breath hadn't already been taken away by my decorating efforts, the sight of him would have had much the same effect. Good grief and gravy! That man sure cut a fine figure—in or out of uniform!

He walked directly over to me, encircled my waist in his arms, and pulled me tight against him.

I didn't resist the hug, but I didn't want to appear too eager to be in his arms, either. "Hey!" I playfully pushed him away with both hands flat against his chest. "No PDAs, remember?"

He smiled, a sexy, almost-wicked little smile, and his mouth was just inches from mine when he softly said, "No public displays of affection. I got it."

"Who's saying this is public?" Mercedes abruptly broke into our moment, just a nano-second before I could cave in to his physical presence, and I wasn't sure if I were relieved, or upset with her timing.

"Casino singers are just the hired help," she said. "They're invisible, and they see nothing, nothing at all, ever." She discreetly turned her back, but over her shoulder she called out, "You can go ahead and give him a kiss if you want, Syl, I won't say a word."

Freddy chuckled, but the moment had passed, and he respected my hesitation for a smooch by releasing his grip. "When I saw that hot metallic cranberry Harley parked out there, I couldn't resist coming in for a minute to say hello to my hot girlfriend."

I resisted the urge to object to his use of the word 'girlfriend,' only because it followed the adjective 'hot.' Instead, I just smiled. "I'm really glad you did, Freddy. We need somebody to demonstrate the most effective way to get all these balloons blown up."

"Oh no you don't." He chuckled again. "You're not pulling that old Tom Sawyer whitewashing the fence scam on me! I can see that coming a mile away."

"That's too bad," said Mercedes. "I was hoping I'd get to see my new boss do a little honest labor around here. Never saw the old boss man do a single thing to help anybody else, ever."

We all laughed, but it naturally gave us pause while we reflected.

"I, for one, sure am glad that movie crew pulled the plug on their production," said Mercedes. "I can't wait for things to get back to normal around here. Believe me, I wasn't looking forward to seeing the whole sordid story of Uncle Harry using local kids to run drugs up the peninsula for him on primetime TV. Of course, if they'd hired J-Lo to play me, like I'd asked them to, well, then, I might be feeling different. A good actress who can sing can make or break a movie and—"

"Merc!" I put my hand on her arm. "You're babbling."

"I know," she said, bobbing her head up and down. "I do that when I get nervous."

"What are you so nervous about, Mercedes?" asked Freddy. "You've been playing piano lounges your whole life. Your opening tonight shouldn't give you anything to be nervous about."

"That part's true," Merc replied, "but I just realized that I haven't been so... uh... *familiar* with the guy who signs my paycheck before."

Freddy laughed at that. "Believe me, Mercedes, I haven't ever been in the position of signing anyone's paycheck before either, so we're just about even on that score!"

The radio on his collar buzzed, and Freddy quickly said, "I want to apologize again, Syl, for not being able to pick you up for the party tonight. Being the owner here, it's hard enough to keep up with my day job as a county deputy, much less have any time left to enjoy relaxing and socializing—yet.

"All that is going to change, though, once I get things delegated to some new staff I'm planning on hiring. I promise." He spontaneously leaned in to kiss me, but the radio buzzed a second time. He laughed and said, "Curses, foiled again!"

"No offense, Boss, but I think you're a lot more Dudley Do-Right than Snidely Whiplash, if you don't mind me saying so."

Freddy, already busy communicating on his collar radio, didn't reply, but gave Mercedes a quick wink and a thumbs up, and it made me strangely happy to see two of my closest friends developing such an easy rapport.

With all the static coming across the airwaves, I couldn't have eavesdropped on Freddy's radio call even if I tried, but I assumed it had something to do with the events down in Unity—events with which I was all too familiar. Personally, I have no idea how he's able to understand anything at all that comes over that radio of his, but after a few exchanges, he signed off and turned first to face Mercedes.

"Police work will keep me at the wrong end of the peninsula most of the day," he said, sighing. He glanced over at me almost apologetically, confirming my suspicions about the topic of his call, then back to Merc. "But don't you worry. I'm looking forward to being back in plenty of time to reintroduce you to your fans tonight."

Mercedes beamed. "And I'm looking forward to that too, Boss." She winked at him. "And that's the kind of professional support I appreciate—more than you know."

Turning back to me, Freddy said, "And as for you, my Sylleegirl, I'm looking forward to twirling you around the dance floor at least a couple times tonight, too."

Merc and I both watched him walk away, and he must have felt our eyes on him, because he looked back when he got to the door and blew two kisses in our direction, one from each hand, before going on out the exit.

My cheeks flushed red, but before Mercedes could tease me about it, her cell phone rang. She quickly checked the phone, which she kept tucked into the left side of her bra, to see who was calling, then involuntarily fluffed her hair before she answered it.

"Why hello, Carter," she gushed, actually batting her eyelashes. "How are you?"

I knew Mercedes and Sheriff Donaldson had been seeing each other, but to hear the flirtation in her voice made me just a little uncomfortable.

Technically, Sheriff D is married, but his wife has Alzheimer's, has been in a nursing home for a very long time, and does not recognize him when he visits. I haven't walked a mile in his shoes, so I tried not to judge. And most of the time, I succeeded in that.

We were finished with the balloons, so I put a few strands of purple crepe paper across the front of her keyboard, draped some from her side speakers, then put my jacket back on, zipped it up, and waved good-bye as I made my way toward the parking lot.

It was still before noon, but the sun warmed me as I pulled my key from my pocket and leaned down to unfasten my helmet from the bike.

But any warmth I'd had suddenly dissipated when I found a note tucked inside my helmet. It was written on a single sheet of small notepaper, the kind you'd find in any motel room, anywhere. The paper was folded in half, and my hands involuntarily shook as I unfolded it.

The neatly-penned message, written in all caps, read: "I am much too shy this day to say hello to such a beautiful woman in person, but I am most confident our paths will cross in the very near future, Ms. Sylvia Avery, and I look very much forward to it!"

Every hair on my body suddenly stood on end. I looked to the right and left, and then I spun around to look behind me, wondering if the person who wrote this note might still be near, watching my reaction. I was totally creeped out, but determined not to let my fear show.

While I could see no big, black Lincoln Town Cars anywhere in the parking lot, it was so crowded that a person could be hiding anywhere among the cars, or even in them, and my stomach desperately wanted to empty itself right then and there.

I checked the helmet again, thinking about dead salmon heads and the threatening events of the past few months, and shivered, head to toe. I couldn't help it, but I wasn't about to be intimidated by a note, either.

As I carefully re-folded the paper, I noticed it had a faint row of seashells running along the top, confirming my suspicion that it might have come from a local motel. Then I tucked it carefully into the back pocket of my jeans, and straddled the bike.

As the motorcycle rumbled to life, some of my confidence returned, and I decided to take a short cruise down the peninsula before going home. Of course I turned the bike south, since there was no road that went any farther north, but this time I chose to ride along the main highway, towards Tinkerstown.

The wind in my face—that which came under the half visor of my helmet—fortified me, and in no time I was feeling a lot less unnerved. It makes me feel almost instantly better to be out riding, and rides like this were better than therapy.

Although I had just seen Jimmy yesterday, my bike almost automatically pulled into the Clamshell parking lot so I could check on him. This time I decided not to leave my helmet clipped to the bike, but took it inside with me.

"Sylvia!" Jimmy enthusiastically greeted me. "I'm so glad you're here! You're just the person I wanted to see!"

I snorted and shook my head. "What do you want, Jimmy?"

"Oh! For shame! How dare you!" He put his hands on his hips and stamped his foot. "Can't I just be glad to see you?"

"Uh-uh." I nodded, skepticism oozing from my pores. "You saw me yesterday, and I didn't get a greeting anywhere near as enthusiastic."

"Well, yesterday I didn't need your opinion on my outfit for tonight's party!"

"See?" I teased, grateful it wasn't anything more serious than that. "You want something!"

Jimmy laughed and instructed me to sit over on the couch while he modeled a few outfits for me. I set my motorcycle helmet on the counter by the coffee pot, grabbed a diet soda from the fridge, and did as I was told.

"How do you like this one?" he paraded back and forth across the room in skin-tight lavender jeans and a long-sleeved white poet's shirt, the lacing hanging loose on his chest. For effect, he had on sunglasses, and when combined with his naturally pale skin and his still bleached-blonde hair, he gave the distinct impression that he suffered from albinism.

"I... Uh... What are the other choices?"

"Well, yes, of course, but I showed you this one first, because I have a purple beaded murse that goes perfectly with it," said Jimmy.

"A man purse?" I asked, searching my memory for a former mention of just such an accessory. "Did Mercedes give it to you?"

Jimmy nodded happily. "Yes, she did! She gave it to me when we were visiting the movie set down by the boardwalk, but I haven't had a chance to show it off yet."

"Well, then I think that settles it," I replied. "I'm sure Mercedes would love to see that her gift is being put to good use."

Jimmy perched on the edge of his gigantic Naugahyde command chair. "You don't want to see my other choices?" he asked, a little dejectedly.

"Why mess with perfection?"

When he jumped up, pranced over, and bent down to hug me, I prayed those tight-fitting pants of his would hold, and they did. Then he wisely started for his bedroom to change, calling back over his shoulder, "So what are *you* wearing tonight, Syl?"

When I didn't answer right away, he stopped in his tracks, backed up, and repeated the question. "Sylvia? I asked you what you're planning to wear tonight."

"I heard you. I just haven't quite decided yet," I told him honestly.

"You haven't decided yet?" Jimmy echoed, incredulous.

"Well, I thought maybe I'd wear that sundress I wore the last time I went to a party at the casino."

"You mean the time you and Freddy came home covered in chocolate from a little fondue mishap at the buffet table?"

"Yeah, that one."

"Sylvia, Sylvia, Sylvia," Jimmy wagged his head and clucked his tongue. "Haven't I taught you anything?"

When I made no reply, he continued, "You simply cannot wear the same thing twice in a row to the same venue, especially if you're dating the same man."

"Number one, Mr. Fashionista, Freddy and I are not dating. Number two, who came up with such a stupid rule? I'm not made of money, you know. I can't just go out and buy a new dress every time I have someplace to go, especially if you're telling me I should only plan on wearing it once."

"Who said anything about buying a new dress?" He looked just a little too smug when he said it, but I waited for him to explain before voicing my objections.

"Have you ever thought of asking Bim and Geri if they have something you could borrow for an evening?"

Bim and Geri, the baristas, roasters, and owners at the Sandy Bottom Coffee Cup, are cross-dressing aficionados, with closets chock full of Oscar-worthy party clothes from both sides of the aisle. Those two women looked equally fine in ballroom gowns as they did in tuxedos, and to top it off, they were generous to a fault.

"Jimmy! You're brilliant!" I got up and hugged him.

"Well, I just figured that since you're the casino owner's arm candy now, you ought to dress the part and glam up a bit."

"Don't push your luck," I retorted, then quickly changed the subject. "Would you like a ride to the party tonight? I know your Pinto's on its last legs."

"I sure would, thanks!" Jimmy beamed. "Then if I meet anyone interesting, I can always ask him for a ride home."

"Jimmy, you're incorrigible." I laughed.

It wasn't till I picked up my helmet that I remembered I hadn't mentioned the mysterious, and potentially threatening, note to him. It was just as well. Jimmy didn't need any reminders of the message we'd found tucked into a fish head tied to Priscilla's collar—particularly when he was so looking forward to a party tonight. I just didn't think his sensitive little soul was ready to handle another blow like that, so I decided not mention the note for the time being.

"I'll be by to pick you up at four-thirty."

"You mean four-thirty this afternoon?" he asked, incredulously. Then he blew out a quick breath, and I couldn't decide if he were pouting or disgusted.

"The party starts at five," I answered. "You got a problem with being on time?"

"Five o'clock is when old people's parties start."

I laughed. "You want a ride, or not?"

"Yes, of course I do. I'll be ready at 4:30, but geez, Sylvia, it's not even going to be dark when the party starts."

"Don't blame me, Boy George," I said as I opened the office door to walk through the small lobby to the parking lot, "you know old people aren't so good at driving at night."

I was still chuckling when I got onto my bike, fired it up, and turned south on the highway, toward Tinkerstown proper.

Although my stomach was rumbling louder than my Sportster, I passed up the High Tide, and despite the fact that I was drooling at just the thought of their wonderfully delicious tsunami burgers, I kept going—straight to the Sandy Bottom—eager to ask for access to the most glamorous closet on the peninsula.

CHAPTER 6

Bim greeted me with a smile and an acknowledging nod when I walked into the coffee shop, but then she just stood there, eyeing me warily, looking from me to the wall clock and back again several times, obviously perplexed.

"You're making it tough on me today," she finally said, smiling again, but not immediately moving to bring me any coffee.

I unzipped the top half of my leather jacket and perched on one of the stools at the coffee bar rather than taking a seat at my usual spot at the larger octagon table near the roaster. "How so?"

"Well, normally, it's either morning, or it's not, and I can tell by the time of day whether to bring you regular or decaffeinated coffee." She laughed. "You don't usually come in so close to noon, and I'm undecided."

"Decaf, please." I smiled. "And I'm here at this time of day because I need to ask you for a really big favor."

Bim set a steaming cup of joe down in front of me and automatically wiped her hands on the towel stuck into her waistband. "I bet you're going to ask me not to be talking so much about you behind your back."

I paused with the cup halfway to my lips, and set it back down. "Well, no, that wasn't what I came here to ask you, but now that you bring it up, what have you been saying about me, and to whom?"

Although there was no one else inside the Sandy

Bottom at the moment, Bim leaned in and whispered, "He was just so darn good-looking, you know?"

"Who was?"

"This guy..." Bim trailed off. "He was so... exotic, I guess you'd call him."

"Bim—" I paused, not sure what was politically proper in this situation. "I... uh... I didn't think you or Geri ever looked at men."

"Oh, no, no, no, no, no, no, no. We're both fine, our relationship is fine, and we're both quite happily gay, thank you." She laughed. "But neither one of us is dead. We're allowed to *notice* good-looking people, whether male or female, you know?"

I wasn't really sure I understood, but I nodded anyway. "So what were you saying about this guy?"

"He came in at the crack of dawn," said Bim, enthusiastically. "In fact, he was waiting for us when we opened the front door. Real sharp dresser. He ordered a Chai tea."

"Bim! I don't need every single detail of your encounter with this fellow, I just want to know how my name happened to come up!"

"Oh, right!" She laughed again. "But first I got to tell you, I think he might have been Indian, if I'm not guilty of profiling or something."

"I honestly don't know—" I took a sip of my coffee, resigning myself to the fact that Bim was determined to tell her story her way, and there was nothing I could do to speed up the process. "Isn't profiling a term reserved exclusively for Muslims?"

"Muslims? I don't follow you." Bim tilted her head and looked like she was trying hard to figure out why we weren't effectively communicating.

"You said you thought he was an Indian." I tried again. "Which we now refer to as Native Americans, although I don't think the term Indigenous Peoples would be particularly offensive to any of them."

This time when Bim laughed, she completely doubled over, hanging onto the coffee bar and gasping for air. When she managed to straighten back up, she said, "Oh Syllee, I didn't think he was a cowboy and Indian type of Indian, I meant that he might have actually been from India!"

I'm sure my face turned scarlet. Hanging around one-eighth Native American Freddy had made me hypersensitive to the political incorrectness of the word 'Indian,' and I had just assumed that's what Bim had been talking about.

Bim continued, "He was tall, dark, and handsome—if you happen to like the type." She winked at me. "And when he ordered Chai tea, I kind of put two and two together and came out with a strong four."

"Chai tea! Of course! I can't believe I missed that."

"And, to answer your question," said Bim, finally getting to the point I'd been waiting for, "he said he'd seen a woman who lived in this area on the national news last month. He said he didn't remember her name, but that she was about his age and had helped the sheriff solve a double homicide on a movie set."

"Where's he from?" I interjected. "I mean, where does he live now?"

"I'm not sure." Bim scowled, then brightened. "But he's thinking about moving to this area, if he can find a house in his price range, and he said he definitely wanted to personally meet such an interesting woman, graced with such great intelligence and beauty."

I choked on my coffee. "What was he selling?"

"Oh, Sylvia, don't be so cynical. He was gallant and charming, and I didn't think it would hurt anything if I told him your name. He would find out sooner or later, anyway. Everybody around here knows you, and you are the only woman his age that helped solve those murders. So don't be mad—he could have gotten his information from anyone."

Inside my jacket sleeves, I was pretty sure the hair on my arms was waving a warning. "Did you happen to tell him I'd be up at the casino this morning?"

Bim nodded. "Yes, I believe I did. It isn't very busy here that early on a Saturday, and I kept talking to him so I could listen to his beautiful accent. I'm serious, Syl, when he spoke, it was like lyrical music filled the room, and—"

I held up my hands in front of me in the universal sign for "STOP!" and miracle of all miracles, she stopped talking. "So you basically told him where to find me."

"I told him there was a big public party up at the casino tonight, and that you were probably not coming in for your usual morning coffee here today because you'd be up north helping decorate the hall."

I nodded. It all sounded very plausible, and not very threatening, but there was one more thing I needed to know. "Did you mention I might be riding a motorcycle?"

Bim thought about it before answering. "No." She shook her head. "I'm sure I didn't. I don't think the subject of cars or trucks or bikes came up at all.

"A stream of people started coming into the shop about then, and I left him to finish his tea alone. Gee, Syl, I didn't do anything wrong, did I?"

"Well..." I drew out the word, making it sound like I might be considering what she'd done, but I wasn't upset with her in the least. I'd just immediately seen her accidental indiscretion as an opportunity to exploit the situation to my advantage. "I'll tell you what— You can make it up to me if you have a shimmery cocktail dress that I can borrow for tonight's festivities."

"Oh boy! Do I!" exclaimed Bim, bouncing with excitement. "I've been wanting to get you all gussied up in something besides jeans and sweaters for years!"

"For years?" I queried. "Seriously?"

"You've got a great figure, girl! Why you want to go hiding it is beyond me!" She quickly spun around and pushed open the slatted saloon doors behind her.

"Geri!" Bim called to her partner in the back room. "Can you take over the counter for about an hour? Sylvia and I are going to go play dress up!"

I got up from the bar stool, zipped up my jacket, and gulped the last swig of coffee. No time like the present to get this over with.

Promptly at 4:30, I honked the Mustang's horn outside of the Clamshell Motel. Jimmy appeared, put the standard "Be Back Soon" sign in the office window, and hopped into the passenger seat.

His first words to me were, "Wow, Syl, can you drive like that?"

"Nice to see you, too, Jimmy."

"But... But... You're barefoot!"

"Technically, I have pantyhose on. My shoes are in the back seat. I didn't want to mar the heels trying to drive in them."

"So you didn't want to drive in a skirt, either?" he asked.

I wheeled the car out of the motel parking lot and headed north. "It's all pulled up around my waist. I'm just not used to wearing anything so constricting."

Jimmy snickered. "You wear a *bra*, don't you?"

"Not around my knees, smarty." I shook my head. I'd known I'd get some ridiculous reaction from him, but he really shouldn't look his free taxi driver in the mouth—or some other equally messed up phrase like that.

I shot him a look, and turned the subject to his choice of fashion eyewear. "I'm glad you opted not to wear your dark glasses tonight," I said. "Those are much more... uh... eye-catching."

Jimmy flipped down the visor and peered into the mirror, turning his head from side to side. "The lavender bedazzled sparkles on the frames match both my pants and my murse. Did you notice?"

"Of course I noticed, Jimmy, and they look great."

He nodded happily, then lapsed into silence for the majority of our trip. But when we passed through Ocean Crest, he suddenly sat up and took notice of his surroundings. "Boy, this town is sure growing. Oh! Look at that—a two-story pharmacy!"

"A pharmacy *and* a full clinic, Jimmy. This end of the North Beach Peninsula is gaining a lot of retirement-age population."

Jimmy nodded. "Just what we need. More old fogies."

I let his young and uninformed assessment slide, and we pulled into the Spartina Point Casino and Resort a few minutes later.

Without giving it a thought, I parked in the same space I'd parked my Harley in earlier, and as I did, I remembered the anonymous note I'd tucked into my clutch purse. Although I was sure it would only upset Jimmy, I thought if there were time and opportunity, I'd show it to Freddy after the party.

Jimmy got out and ran around the car to hold the door

open for me. By then, I'd retrieved my strappy heels from the backseat, so when he opened the door, I swung around in my car seat and put them on. He held out his hand, I gratefully accepted the help standing, and wiggled my dress down to its full length.

"I gotta say it Syl," said Jimmy, shaking his head, "you look really, really fine."

I kept a hold on his arm crossing the drawbridge and on into the main lobby. "No sense tempting fate on these heels until I get more used to them." I didn't feel quite like myself, and I know I didn't look like me, either. I was decked out from head to toe in burgundy taffeta and sequins, and wasn't too sure if I felt more glamorous or silly.

A strategically placed red carpet guided us from the lobby to the main ballroom, and for a split second I got an image in my head of some not quite over-the-hill movie star, let's call her Sandra Bullock, walking the red carpet at the Oscars. I shot a look at my escort's poetic lavender and white attire, and the spell was shattered.

"Ok, Jimmy, let's find a table to park me up close to the bandstand."

Jimmy, not suspecting I was trying to dump him, said, "Great idea! You can hold down the table, and I can go scouting for my peeps. People are filing in, and I might get lucky enough to be the first in line to call 'dibs' on some hunk."

I tried to contain my smirk, and thanked him for being my temporary escort.

"I see Felicity and Walter," said Jimmy, scanning the room before he decided which direction to go. "They're sitting with some of their other teacher friends."

I looked in the direction he was pointing, caught

Felicity's eye and waved. The last time I sat at "the teachers' table" the evening had quickly turned into an off-site faculty meeting, so this time I decided not to join them.

Jimmy first told me to save him a seat, but then he amended his statement to "Don't wait up," in case he got lucky. I chuckled to myself and wished him well.

Then I entertained myself by watching Mercedes make her last minute sound checks. "Check, check, check," she said into her headset, and adjusted a dial in front of her. "Check, check, check." Then she looked up at me, grinned, and wiggled her fingers.

I wiggled my fingers back, and continued to watch her as she finished preparations for her first number.

"A beautiful woman such as yourself should not be sitting here alone."

The accent was distinctly foreign, lilting, definitely intriguing, and downright sexy. I looked up into dark brown eyes that certainly matched the voice, and if I hadn't been seated, I might have swooned. No doubt about it, this man was hot!

"And, if I may be so bold," he continued, "I'll bet you did not dare to ride your motorcycle here in that outfit tonight."

"I— Um— Uh—"

I hate it when words fail me, but my inability to articulate at the moment did not deter the gorgeous tuxedo-clad man standing next to my chair. "I was told by the bartender that your preferred beverage is diet ginger ale, rather than champagne." He was holding two glasses in his hand. "May I sit down?"

I nodded, and he set one of the glasses in front of me. Bless the bartender for remembering me and my beverage of choice. I knew the casino had begun stocking diet ginger ale just for me, thanks to Freddy, and it suddenly made me feel all warm and fuzzy, like I was safe here, and someone would always have my back.

The mystery man pulled a chair uncomfortably close to me before he sat down, saying, "So we do not have to shout to each other after the music begins." He smiled a smile that was guaranteed to make most women's hearts melt, and I wondered if I would soon be counted among the group of "most women."

"I am most pleased to finally make your acquaintance, Miss Sylvia Lee Avery."

The mention of my full name snapped me right out of the spell I'd been under. "Who are you? How do you know my name? Have we met before?" I could hear my voice go up at least one octave as I spoke.

He chuckled, and held out his hand. "Forgive me, and please allow me to properly introduce myself. My name is Kanjirappally Kumera. But my friends call me Ken."

I shook his hand. It was warm, tender yet strong, and very inviting. Although I'd never experienced this particular type of sensual rush before, and never really believed it existed outside the pages of trashy romance novels, I could swear I felt a tingle.

"Mr. Kumera." I acknowledged him politely with a small nod of my head.

He released my hand and placed it over his heart. "I was hoping we might become friends," he said, feigning injury, "and that you would be pleased to call me Ken."

As if the moment weren't awkward enough, Mercedes chose that moment to launch into her first number of the evening, and her enchanting rendition of "Strangers in the Night" filled the room.

I tore my eyes away from the attractive man sitting

next to me and shot a glance at Mercedes, who wore the most angelic look of sweet innocence. That sealed it. She didn't miss a thing from her post behind the keyboard and she'd purposely selected that song.

But during that brief distraction, my senses returned, and when I spoke again to the man next to me, I was back on top of my game. "We may yet become friends, Mr. Kumera, once we get to know each other a little better." I barely refrained from batting my eyelashes. No doubt about it, flirting ran in the family.

He smiled. "What about me would you like to know?"

Man! I could get so lost in those eyes!

I cleared my throat. "First, tell me if you are the one who left this note in my motorcycle helmet this morning." I pulled the paper out of my handbag.

"Yes, of course," he replied without hesitation. "Please forgive me for my boldness, I am normally quite shy."

"But how did you know it was my bike?" I asked. The words came out of my mouth a little harsher than I intended.

Ken glanced down at his hands then back up. "I arrived in my car as you were fastening the helmet to the motorcycle. It had been my intention to introduce myself to you right away, but I lost my nerve. My note was well intentioned, believe me. I hope it did not frighten you."

Who me? Frightened? It had nearly scared the bejeezus out of me, but I wasn't about to let him know that.

"Why did you want to meet me?"

Ken took a sip of his ginger ale, contemplating his reply. "I have been a fan of yours," he began, "since I learned of your sleuthing and intelligence on the national news, and I knew one day I must come to meet this bright and beautiful woman."

Of course I knew he was just trying to flatter me, but darn it, it was working. Thankfully, my 'sleuthing and intelligence' skills were also working.

"What city did you come from?"

"Chicago," Ken replied. "I recently retired from a very long and boring career in accounting, and decided it was time to strike out on an adventure, to travel to see the west coast, the Pacific Ocean—and you." He lifted his glass in salute before taking another sip.

Wow. This guy was certainly playing hardball in the charming department, but I decided to give him the benefit of the doubt, chalk it up to a cultural thing, and take him at face value. And oh boy, what a face that was!

We chatted amicably for several more minutes, and he never hesitated to answer any of my questions. Not wanting it to totally sound like I was doing a 60 Minutes investigative interview, I directed the conversation, if you could call it that, back toward gentle questions of a more personal nature.

"Kanjirappally," I said slowly, hoping I was coming close to pronouncing his name correctly. "That's quite a name you've got there."

"I was called Kanji throughout public school, but I somehow became Ken in college, and then in the business world."

"Is Kanjirappally a family name?"

His deep dimples showed dramatically when he smiled. "My mother always wanted me to remember where I came from—my roots—so I'm named after the town in India where I was conceived."

I almost choked on his answer, bordering on being TMI—too much information. "And were you born in India?"

"No. I was born in New Jersey. I guess that technically makes me an anchor baby, as my mother and father immigrated here to continue their collegiate schooling shortly before I was born."

I considered his statement, along with his age. From my work with Child Protective Services, I was well acquainted with the term 'anchor babies,' and its derogatory and offensive implications, but it was a term coined fairly recently. "Did your parents both have F-1 Student Visas?"

My question caught him momentarily off guard. "Yes. Yes, of course. They were not here illegally, if that is what you are implying."

I tilted my head and considered how uncomfortable the current political tide might have made this man, who had lived and worked in no other country than the United States his entire life. "I am implying no such thing. There is no need for you to ever apologize for your birthright, or your heritage." I knew I was in danger of climbing up on my soapbox, but I couldn't help it.

Ken took my hand and pressed it to his lips. "Beautiful, smart, and a champion of children," he said softly.

I couldn't remember if I'd mentioned my prior affiliation with CPS, and it threw me for a moment. But then, I must have, or why would he have said such a thing?

"So—" I said, "I want you to be honest—by which name would you prefer I call you?"

Ken's face went through a series of emotions, and he did not immediately answer. "I do not believe anyone has ever asked me that question before," he said, reflectively.

"Now that I am retired from the predominately Caucasian American business world, I think I really do prefer Kanji over Ken."

I reached over and lightly touched his left forearm. "Then I shall call you Kanji. And I shall introduce you to my friends as Kanji. And Kanji it shall be." I nodded and grinned.

Kanji put his right hand on top of mine. "Thank you, dear lady."

Our eyes locked, and although I'm ashamed to say it, I was the one who looked away first.

CHAPTER 7

"There you are!" Freddy sang out as he approached the table. He looked absolutely delicious in his tuxedo. Without stopping to consider who was or wasn't watching, he casually slung an arm across my shoulders, leaned down, and gave me a big kiss on the cheek. "You look absolutely stunning in that dress, Syl," he said.

"Thank you." I smiled. "It's a Bim and Geri special."

Freddy laughed. "The way you look in it, Syl, I would have thought you had had it made special, just for you," he gushed.

What was going on with him? I'd never known Freddy to be so... so... demonstrative and complimentary. Ordinarily, he never commented on anything I wore. But then, as Bim had so ungraciously pointed out a few hours ago, I rarely wore anything but a simple sweater, or hoodie, and jeans.

"Won't you join us?" I asked, motioning to an empty chair on the other side of me. Oh, wow. The thought flitted through my head that I'd feel just like Cinderella if I ended up sitting between these two most handsome men. My, oh my, what bookends they would make! I almost blushed at the thought.

"Afraid not," Freddy said, destroying my fantasy, "with ownership comes responsibilities." He shook his head. "I'm really very sorry I won't be able to keep you constant company tonight, my Syllee girl, but duty calls."

Although he was speaking to me, his eyes were on Kanji, and I suddenly felt like I should lift my feet from the floor to avoid getting any of that overflowing testosterone on Bim's good shoes. Good grief and gravy, was it my imagination, or was Freddy posturing to get my attention? I glanced at Kanji, and confirmed my suspicions: I was now a piece of US Prime, precariously poised between two lions hungrily licking their lips.

I cleared my throat and pulled out my best Scarlet O'Hara—minus the southern accent. "Goodness! Wherever are my manners? Frederick Morgan, I'd like you to meet Mr. Kanji Kumera. Kanji is a recently retired Chicago accountant and is thinking of moving to the North Beach Peninsula."

At the mention of his name, Kanji had stood, and extended his hand. "It is my infinite pleasure to meet you, Mr. Morgan."

Given that Freddy wasn't wearing his cowboy boots with his special occasion tux, Kanji was a good two or three inches taller.

Freddy grasped Kanji's hand with a great deal of firmness, and it occurred to me they might be about to arm wrestle. It must have occurred to Mercedes, too, who now reached into her bag of musical editorial commentary and began playing Paul McCartney's rather obscure, but at this moment certainly spot-on, "Tug of War."

The song wasn't exactly dance music, but the guests didn't seem to mind, and many of them toddled by our table to hug and sway on the ballroom floor.

"So you're thinking of moving here?" Freddy echoed my introductory words.

"This is definitely one of the areas I have under consideration for my retirement," said Kanji. His eyes went from Freddy's to mine. "There are many quality enticements here, and a realtor will be showing me some properties next week."

Freddy nodded thoughtfully, sizing him up. "Might you be looking for part-time work, Mr. Kumera?" he asked, catching both Kanji and me completely off-guard with such an abrupt segue.

"Am I to understand you are offering me an employment opportunity?" asked Kanji.

"I own this resort." Freddy let his words sink in for just a beat, then added, "I could use a mature man with a grip as strong as yours."

Neither Kanji nor I had seen that coming, either.

Kanji hesitated just a moment, then released Freddy's hand and replied, "Yes, indeed. Although I had not considered it until this moment, I am quite interested in working a few hours each week. What is it you have in mind?"

"I'm looking for a part-time Hospitality Specialist," said Freddy. He smiled. "That's a meet-and-greet guy that they used to call a bouncer. It's an upscale resort, and there's plenty of actual security personnel, but it's always nice to have a face up front—without a uniform—that keeps an eye out for any potential trouble." Freddy shrugged. "I can't be everywhere at once."

"No... Of course not." Kanji briefly considered the offer. "And yes, I believe working here at the resort is something that would allow me many fortuitous opportunities to 'meet and greet' as you call it."

I wasn't quite sure what Kanji meant by that, but Freddy seemed genuinely pleased.

"Terrific," said Freddy. "Stop by the front desk and ask for an application before you leave."

There had to be some ulterior motive to Freddy's idea, but I couldn't get a firm hold on it. For a moment I thought he was politely offering Kanji an olive branch, but he ruined that comforting thought with the very next words out of his mouth.

"So Syl— I saw you were riding that bike I bought you this morning. How's it running?"

My face flamed scarlet, and I wanted to adamantly refuse to play his territorial war games. Who did he think he was fooling, anyway? It's a new bike. Of course it was running perfectly, and I struggled for formulate some kind of reply.

Fortunately, I was saved from having to answer. Unfortunately, I was saved when Kanji threw an expert zinger that hit Freddy right between the eyes.

Kanji had also seen right through Freddy's attempt to establish a proprietary relationship. He sat back down, looked up at Freddy and said softly, in that gorgeous lilting accent of his, "Such a beautiful lady naturally commands the attention of many suitors, but I doubt that she will be swayed for long by material objects."

It was Freddy's turn to blush. He wisely ignored Kanji's not-so-subtle challenge, reminded him to pick up that application, and excused himself to greet some other guests—but not before telling me to save him a dance or two.

Without missing a beat, Kanji seamlessly continued our previous conversation right where we'd left off. "So now let me return the favor," he began. "By what name do you wish for me to call you?"

"Most people call me Syl. It's less formal than Sylvia."

Kanji frowned. "Yet I believe I heard Mr. Morgan refer to you as Syllee?"

"Mr. Morgan? Is he here?" I looked around. "I don't remember seeing Rich come in."

"Rich?" asked Kanji, his eyebrows drawing down. "Who is Rich?"

"Oh!" I flushed again with added embarrassment, but managed a chuckle. "You were referring to Freddy!"

"There are two Mr. Morgans?"

"Rich is Freddy's father. He runs a charter fishing boat out of Unity." I refrained from telling Kanji all about Rich's probation status after he unknowingly helped run illegal drugs up the peninsula from the port to the casino. It wasn't my story to tell.

"Hhmm," said Kanji. "That is very interesting information, but at this moment, it is essential that I keep you on one topic, if that is possible."

I smiled, but demurely kept my mouth shut, and Kanji smiled back, showing his gleaming white teeth.

"I also saw the name Syllee on the license plate of a Mustang convertible in the parking lot," he continued. "Might that also be yours?"

I nodded, briefly wondering who else on the peninsula would be driving a car with my name on it. "That Mustang is my one extravagant retirement present to myself. And Syllee is a nickname for Sylvia Lee."

I took another sip of my ginger ale. "So why did you choose to consider North Beach Peninsula as a possible place to retire?"

"I do not believe you have answered my question yet about what to call you," said Kanji. "But if you will do me the honor of this dance, I will momentarily forgive you."

Mercedes suddenly announced she was about to play the last number of her first set. I followed her eyes and saw that Sheriff Carter Donaldson, in full uniform, had entered the back of the room, and was standing there, Stetson in hand, watching the proceedings. More power to them, I thought.

Under normal circumstances, Mercedes always played "Band on the Run" when she was about to take her first break, but when she saw Kanji stand and take my hand, she launched right into Mazzy Star's slinky-slow "Fade into You."

I shot her a glance, and she silently mouthed, "Thank me later."

I wanted to concentrate on not stepping on Kanji's toes, but the lyrics of the song began to haunt me: "I want to hold the hand inside you, I want to take a breath that's true, I look to you and I see nothing, I look to you to see the truth..." sang Mercedes.

Lucky for me, Kanji was an excellent dancer, very skilled and easy to follow, and I allowed myself to relax and enjoy the moment—until I caught Freddy scowling from the sidelines. I could only imagine his expression when Kanji initiated a very practiced and elegant dip at the end of our dance.

With his hand lightly across my lower back, Kanji guided me back to our table, where we found Jimmy, all bubbly with excitement.

"Wow, Syl!" He breathed the words in admiration. "I had no idea you could dance like that."

I laughed as Kanji held my chair for me. "Neither did I, Jimmy." I sat and smiled up at Kanji. "It's a lot easier to follow when there's someone who knows how to lead."

Kanji returned my smile and made a small bow. "It is my good fortune to find a beautiful and strong woman who is not afraid to let a man lead."

To cover my blush, which I seemed to be doing a lot of

this night, I pretended to suddenly remember my manners for a second time. "Jimmy, have you met Kanji?"

"Kanji?" Jimmy looked around, confused. "Who's Kanji?"

"When we first met, I introduced myself as Ken," said Kanji to Jimmy, "but Sylvia has encouraged me to be proud of both my birth name and the land of my conception."

"Huh?" said Jimmy, pushing his lavender bedazzled glasses up with his middle finger.

Trust Jim to have such a snappy comeback.

"I was born in America," explained Kanji, "just like you. But my parents were in college and about to leave India to study in America when I was conceived. I am happy to have someone like—Ms. Avery—" he looked at me pointedly, "tell me I have nothing to be ashamed of, and to celebrate my heritage."

"Syl's like that," Jimmy agreed. "She always tells me to be true to exactly who I am."

"Indeed," said Kanji, his eyes filled with mirth as he took in Jimmy's flamboyant lavender evening attire. "It is most welcome to have such unconditional friendship."

I was distracted from asking where Kanji and Jimmy had met before by Mercedes' voice booming over the microphone from the bandstand.

"Ladies and gentlemen," she began. "Are we having fun yet?"

Her statement was met with much clapping and cheers of support, and I was glad "her peeps," as she called them, had come out in force tonight.

"Thank you! Thank you for welcoming me home after my absence this spring." She took a theatrical bow to more applause. "And I know I promised an evening of fun and surprises, so brace yourself, cause here comes a first at

Spartina Point.

"Instead of playing generic background elevator muzak while I take my break, I'm very pleased to be able to introduce to you a geriatric—oops," she giggled, "I mean 'mature'—belly dancing troupe to entertain you. These lovely local ladies, making their public dancing debut right here on our dance floor tonight, are known as 'The Veiled Rainbow,' and I'd like you all to give them a big Spartina Point welcome!"

"Oh no!" I buried my face in my hands. "No, no, no, no, no!" I shook my head without looking up.

Mercedes pressed the button on her CD player, and Middle Eastern music filled the room. Five elderly women emerged from the ballroom exit nearest the restroom and shimmied their hips as they swirled onto the dance floor, amid much applause, and a few cat calls, from the assembled audience. Each of the five women wore variations of just one color of the rainbow: red, orange, yellow, green, and blue.

Jimmy clapped enthusiastically, bounced in his seat, and threw in several raucous wolf whistles, much to my dismay.

Kanji had applauded politely, and was now studying the movements of the women on the dance floor with rapt attention. His expression was indecipherable, and I wondered just what this guy from India thought of our local talent.

Meanwhile, Mercedes went to the back of the room and warmly greeted Sheriff D with a lengthy hug, then pulled him by the hand to our table.

I smiled at Carter. He certainly looked relaxed and happy, despite being in his uniform. Spending time "on the north end" to allegedly keep an eye out for casino riff-raff, was obviously agreeing with him.

We sat at a table for eight, so there were plenty of chairs. I introduced Kanji to Mercedes and Carter, and then I asked Mercedes a question that was burning a hole in my brain. "Merc, how did you find these women to perform here tonight?"

"Oh! Aren't they wonderful?" She beamed. "And I didn't find them, Sylvia, they found me, and offered to participate, at no charge, in my homecoming party!"

I had a feeling that would be the case.

"Aren't they the most delightful troupe of dancers you've ever seen?" Mercedes continued.

Delightful was not the word I would have used, but before I could say as much, Jimmy cut in with a burst of his encyclopedic trivia.

"Did you know," he asked of no one in particular, "that troop, spelled t-r-o-o-p, refers to a group of soldiers or a collection of people or things, and troupe, spelled t-r-o-u-p-e, refers specifically to a group of actors, singers, or dancers?

"No, Jiminy Cricket," replied Mercedes, rolling her eyes, "I had absolutely no idea."

We all laughed. All but Kanji, who was clearly surprised by Jimmy's interjection. He looked to me for an explanation. "Jiminy Cricket?" he asked. "Like in Walt Disney's movie Pinocchio?"

"It's complicated." I laughed and patted his hand. "You'll get used to it."

Kanji asked for no further explanation, and we all turned our attention back to the troupe, t-r-o-u-p-e, dancing before us.

Red, Orange, Yellow, Green, and Blue flipped their hips in unison, sending off a round of jingles from their coin belts. Their 'mature' bodies were definitely not well-toned or tanned, but I gave them big points for being brave enough to expose their lily-white midriffs in public.

Nevertheless, as their first, and, as it turned out, their only, and very lengthy number concluded, and while everyone was applauding, and a few were trilling their approval "la-la-la-la-la-la-la" in high-pitched voices, I was visibly squirming in my seat.

Kanji leaned over and whispered, "I could not help but notice that you were not pleased to hear these delightful ladies were performing for us tonight."

It was a statement, not a question, but I felt he needed an explanation, and it was always best to do these things sooner rather than later. I took a deep breath. "You see the woman in red?"

"Yes." Kanji nodded. "She seems to be the leader of this group."

"She is. Her name is Meredith. She's my mother."

Kanji scowled, and he paused a long moment before he spoke. "Your mother and her friends of advanced age are still dancing and celebrating femininity in a highly appropriate way. Why are you not proud?"

I was still considering his question when I heard my mother's voice on the microphone. "Thank you! Thank you so much for that warm welcome! Now while we catch our breath, I'd like to introduce you to the individual members of The Veiled Rainbow.

"My name is Meredith, and I wear red—the color of passion!" She did a rambunctious shoulder shimmy, which set off her hip bells and inspired many enthusiastic hoots from the crowd.

She winked and grinned, enjoying every hoot and whistle. "Next we have Orpha, the oldest of our troupe, who wears orange."

Orpha did a demur twirl with her veil and called out, "Orange is the color of rust, you know!" which, understandably in this crowd, got her a huge laugh.

"Goodie wears yellow, the color of sunshine!"

Goodie rotated in place, doing a kind of snake arm wave. I couldn't help but smirk when she turned her backside toward us, and wondered if she knew her calligraphy "Carpe Diem" tramp-stamp tattoo showed above the harem pants of her costume.

"Green is worn by Nadine, our favorite retired Greenpeace activist!"

Nadine flipped her scarf around her body, then up and over and back around her head in a dizzying display of aptitude.

"And finally, wearing blue for the open water, we have the lovely Nova!"

Nova, understandably, wasn't so much into being lovely or in dancing tonight. I was sure she was only there because she didn't want to let the others down on their big debut night, but her face looked drawn, and she barely mustered a little parade wave to the crowd with her azure chiffon scarf.

I looked over at Sheriff D, and I could tell he was more than a little surprised to see Nova out there on the dance floor. He must have felt me looking at him, because he turned, his eyes caught mine, and he stage whispered, "Merri's Widows."

Kanji had caught our interaction, but asked no questions. I gave him bonus points for that. He was not a local, he did not know these women, and he wisely understood that what Carter and I shared with each other was clearly none of his business.

The Veiled Rainbow then shimmied off, and Merc sighed heavily. "That's my cue," she said. Sheriff D and Kanji both stood as she prepared to leave us, but I could tell Jimmy was clueless as to why they were all getting up.

Sheriff Donaldson gave Mercedes a quick peck on the lips.

"I take it you're wearing your uniform because you have to go back to work?" she asked him.

"We're going to make a detective out of you yet, Miss Mercedes." He laughed. "Since Freddy's at this end tonight, I can't leave the whole other end of the peninsula unprotected."

"But what about Bill and Bob?" asked Merc, looking like she was about to pout.

"They both have kids who play soccer," said Sheriff D, "so I try to give them weekends off whenever the games are played out of town."

"Of course." Merc nodded, but her disappointment was evident. "I totally understand." Then she turned to Kanji and powered up the charm. "It was so very nice meeting you," she said. "So very, very nice."

Kanji took her hand and pressed it to his lips. "It was my pleasure to make your acquaintance, Miss Mercedes."

"I hope you do decide to move to the North Beach Peninsula," said Merc. "We could certainly use a few more gentlemen like you around here."

Mercedes had resorted to using what I referred to as her 'southern accent for convenience,' voice so I didn't have to look at her to know she was batting her eyelashes.

Now was as good a time as any to visit the little girls' room, so I excused myself and walked out with Sheriff D. As soon as we hit the hallway, he became all business.

"Don't you think it a little odd for Nova Johanssen to

appear here tonight? Her husband has only been missing since Tuesday, and she's out here dancing up a storm."

"You just hold it right there, Carter!" I could almost feel the steam coming out of my ears. "What's Nova supposed to be doing tonight?"

"It wouldn't be so bad if she were here as an onlooker, but out belly dancing? That's a little much," huffed Sheriff D.

"You'd rather she were isolated from the very people who love and care for her most, sitting at home, all alone tonight, drowning her sorrows?" I asked.

I was dancing dangerously close to saying something in anger that I would regret forever. It was right on the tip of my tongue, and yet I managed not to say it. I didn't have to. The ashen look on Carter's face said he'd already made the connection.

His own wife was isolated tonight from the people who love and care for her, sitting all alone in a nursing home, while he was out playing footsie with Mercedes.

I reached out and gently touched the sleeve of his uniform. "It's not the same, Carter," I said softly. "Mary Ann has Alzheimer's, and there's nothing you can do for her. You're not doing anything wrong."

Sheriff D met my eyes for a long moment. I could almost see him mentally wrestling with his thoughts. He sighed deeply. "Then, if I accept your line of thinking, Nova is not doing anything 'wrong' either. She has a perfect right to find comfort where she can—" he paused, and his face returned to its normal, ruddy, all-business appearance.

"Unless, of course, we find out that she did, indeed, murder her husband."

CHAPTER 8

By the time I returned from the restroom, all five women of The Veiled Rainbow, thankfully now in their regular street clothes, had pulled up chairs at the table with Kanji, and Jimmy was nowhere in sight.

I slid back into my recently vacated chair, and allowed myself to feel the admiration I had for this group of active senior women. It seemed to be a night filled with owning who you are, and who you love, and I had to admit I was quite fond of them all.

Mom—Merri to her friends—was 20 years older than me, but she took good care of herself and still turned many men's heads. I wasn't too happy when she insisted upon wearing hot pants and tank tops in public, but she always smiled and told me, "when you've got it, flaunt it."

It was rumored that Goodie Godwin, the most religiously devout of the group, had married her husband Larry just to get his last name: God-win. My favorite thing about GiGi, besides her insanely wonderful "Carpe Diem" tattoo, were her strappy sandals, and I often wondered how many bejeweled pairs she owned.

Nadine had extremely sensitive eyes, and wore progressive sunglasses, indoors or out, night or day. I loved Deenie's car—a black and white smart car on which she had added long, curled eyelashes above the headlights. What I didn't love about her was her yappy little poodle, which she claimed was a service dog for her poor eyesight. I was surprised, and relieved, that she hadn't brought the little ankle-biter with her tonight.

Outspoken four-foot, ten-inch Orpha, with her over-permed, Brillo pad hair, was always a hoot to be around. She felt she had lived so long that she'd earned the right to get away with saying anything and everything that occurred to her, and often did, with no filter whatsoever. Sometimes age really does have its advantages.

Last but not least was Nova, a confident, take-no-prisoners kind of woman who had stormed into the man's world of commercial crab fishing and flourished. Crabbing is one of the most dangerous occupations in the world, and Nova had always fearlessly faced the risks to work alongside her husband Mateo.

Naturally, through my mother, I was fairly familiar with their individual stories, but it was interesting now to observe the way in which they each presented themselves to someone from outside the peninsula.

Goodie and Nadine, best friends for decades, were playfully bickering among themselves. Nova was understandably withdrawn. So that left only Meredith and Orpha to compete for Kanji's attention, and I couldn't tell, from my casual observation, who was commanding the greater portion of his interest.

The waitress came with a tray of champagne flutes, and two glasses of ginger ale. She placed the ginger ale in front of Kanji and me, then went around the table offering the ladies a "complimentary beverage" for their performance, noting that "the boss" thought they all must have worked up quite a thirst. All of them eagerly accepted.

"So, as I was saying," said Orpha to Kanji, "we took up belly dancing at the Senior Center just a few months ago." She grinned. "We used to take their kick-boxing class, but after a few minor injuries, those pansy-wansy ER doctors insisted we all try something a little more tame in order to get our exercise."

I knew this particular story inside and out, but I chuckled once again as Orpha explained it to Kanji.

"The docs suggested we try chair yoga, or tai chi, but those were just too boring, and besides, those classes were all filled with *old* people."

Orpha's punch line got the desired reaction, and Kanji's hearty laugh was a delight to hear. How was it possible he also laughed with a charming accent?

Kanji reached into his breast pocket and retrieved a ballpoint pen, which he used to tap against his glass. Then he lifted it high into the air. "To the most beautiful and inspiring women of the North Beach Peninsula," he said, his eyes definitely including me as he spoke. "May you all enjoy many, many more years of healthful fitness!"

They all drank to that, then Kanji, bless his heart, asked 'Mrs. Starr' if she would do him the honor of a dance.

"Mrs. Starr?" Orpha looked around the table as if he were not speaking to her. "Is my mother-in-law here?" Her eyes were wide open in surprise. "She better not be, cause she's been dead for over 40 years!"

That got another big laugh from everyone.

"Oh!" She exaggeratedly batted her eyelashes. "You mean me!" She pointed to herself. "Well, certainly, I'd love to dance with such a handsome young man, but you'll have to do me one small favor first."

"A favor?" asked Kanji.

"You'll have to promise to call me Orpha," she replied. "O-r-p-h-a. It's the same letters as Oprah, but people are such dimwits, they call me by the wrong name all the time." She huffed. "Really. You'd think they be able to see right off that I'm not black."

Kanji's smile extended from ear to ear, as he stood, took her by the hand, and helped her to her feet.

"Young people hold hands for love. Old people hold hands for balance," she quipped as Kanji led her out to dance. Orpha was certainly on a roll tonight.

We all watched in awe as Kanji created magic once again on the dance floor. Mercedes had seen them coming, and began playing the instrumental version of "Try to Remember."

I knew we were all familiar with the words, so most likely we were all singing it quietly inside our heads. I know I was. "Try to remember, the kind of September, when life was slow, and oh so mellow..." Discreetly, I wiped a few tears away.

As the couple swayed tenderly on the dance floor, I glanced at each of the women's faces in our small group. There wasn't a dry eye among us. My heart simultaneously swelled with love and sadness. We all knew that dear Orpha was beginning to show definite signs of senility, though we all pretended it wasn't so. Without ever formally talking about it, we all found ways to cover for her as circumstances allowed.

Kanji guided Orpha back to the table at the end of the dance and held her chair for her. Then he put out his hand to me. "Ms. Avery? Would you care to dance?"

"Hold on a minute!" said Meredith, waving her hand in the air. "I'm also Ms. Avery!"

As expected, everyone laughed.

"Forgive me," said Kanji, pulling me to my feet, but speaking to Meredith, "but I can only dance with one lovely Ms. Avery at a time."

As he took me into his arms, I shook my head. "You

made your point," I said. "It will be fine for you to call me Sylvia, or Syl, but never Sylvia Lee, cause that's reserved for my mother when she demands my full attention."

Kanji grinned again. "That is more than fair enough," he said. "For now."

For now? I wondered exactly what he meant by that, but I didn't have time to dwell on it. We'd danced only a few measures when Freddy suddenly appeared, asking to cut in. Kanji graciously released me, and bowed slightly. I'd have been upset if I hadn't known he had a full table of potential dance partners eagerly waiting their turns.

Freddy was not nearly as smooth a dancer as Kanji, but then, I thought ruefully, Kanji had probably had at least a decade and a half longer to practice.

We danced in silence for a few minutes, then Freddy said, "So... what's with the foreign guy with the mumbo-jumbo eyes?"

I wasn't sure if that was an ethnic slur or not, but it got my blood boiling just the same. "So what's with your obvious green-eyed jealousy?"

Freddy pulled me tight against him. "I have no idea what in the world you're talking about, my Syllee girl," he said into my hair, nuzzling near my ear.

I pulled back a little. "And what's with you offering him a job here, anyway?"

"You know the old saying," said Freddy, with a strange look of cunning superiority. "Keep your friends close, and your enemies closer."

"Kanji is not your enemy!"

"No, but apparently he's my latest competition." Freddy looked deep into my eyes for confirmation or denial. "Isn't he?"

I knew he wanted me to say otherwise, but I couldn't.

"You and I are not dating exclusively, Freddy. We both agreed to that."

"No," said Freddy, pointedly meeting my eyes, "*we* did not agree to that, *you* agreed to that, all by yourself."

"Now is not a good time to discuss this," I said from behind a phony smile.

"I agree," said Freddy, with an equally fake grin plastered on his face. "But rest assured, we *will* be discussing this further."

"Don't threaten me."

"Wouldn't dream of it." He paused, then his eyes twinkled mischievously. "I'm too busy dreaming of you."

My laugh was genuine as he returned me to the table of women. I noted that Kanji's and Meredith's chairs were empty, and I turned and saw them coming off the dance floor behind us. I laughed again. Mother had certainly wasted no time.

Kanji held Merri's chair for her, then slid in next to me, despite the hopeful looks on three of the other four women's faces.

"I must pause to catch my breath," he explained. "I am not in so fine a shape as your company of lovely dancing women."

That seemed to appease them for the time being.

"Do you remember me?" asked Goodie, looking thoughtfully at Kanji. "You came into the Humane Society a few days ago when I was volunteering. I am the one who processed your adoption application."

Kanji nodded. "That is correct. I do remember you, now that you mention it. Forgive me for not recognizing you sooner, but you did not look the same when you were in your dancing costume."

Goodie seemed please by his acknowledgment of their

previous connection. "So what have you named your new puppy, Kanji?"

Boy, oh boy, this guy was just full of surprises. He's brand new in town, and here he's taken a giant leap and adopted a puppy before he even has a home to bring it in to.

"I regret that I have not yet named him," said Kanji. "I am waiting for him to choose his own name." He smiled. "It is a custom in my family that a pet's personality will let us pick an appropriate nomenclature. And so far, he hasn't told me what I shall call him."

Goodie smiled. "I've never had a pet of my own, but I've heard of all kinds of ways people determine their pets' names."

"You have never had a pet?" asked Kanji in surprise. "And why is that, Mrs. Goodie Godwin?"

Goodie sighed. "My husband Larry—he died a few months ago—he was allergic to all animals, and I just love them, so that's why I began volunteering at the Humane Society. If I couldn't have pets at home myself, at least I could help match abandoned pets with their new forever homes."

"My condolences for your loss," said Kanji with sincere compassion, "and my kudos to you for finding a way to compensate for not having a pet of your own. Now that your husband is gone, do you think you will bring a cat or dog home?"

Goodie smiled and shrugged. "I hadn't really thought much about it. I spend so much time at the Humane Society, a pet at home might begin to feel neglected."

Kanji nodded. "I understand. And, if I am not being too insensitive, just how was it that your husband died?"

I thought that question was a little abrupt, and quite a

bit forward of him, but perhaps in his culture it's more socially acceptable to talk about such things openly. Fortunately, Goodie did not seem to mind his question, and did not hesitate to answer.

"We're not sure," she began.

Kanji looked from one face to another. Obviously, he was the only one confused. "You are not sure how he died?" he prompted.

"Well, we're sure it was a poison called abrin, which is similar to ricin, but we're not sure if he swallowed it or got it from a needle," said Nadine, trying to be helpful.

"Oh dear," said Kanji, "I'm afraid I still do not understand."

Jimmy chose that moment to return to the group, announcing that the buffet table had been brought out and was filled with yummy-looking hors d'oeuvres. "Who wants to go help me reduce the world's food supply?" he asked, oblivious to the serious nature of the conversation in progress.

Meredith and Nova both took him up on that, while Nadine stayed put next to her best friend Goodie, who continued to explain what had happened to Larry.

"It's all my fault, really," she began.

Kanji's eyes opened wide. "Your fault?" he prompted. "How could that be?"

Goodie nodded thoughtfully. "Larry used to like to make jewelry, and I told him what I really wanted for my birthday was an authentic Italian rosary."

"You are Catholic?" Kanji sounded surprised.

"You probably saw her tattoo when she was dancing," interjected Nadine. "She got that 'Carpe Diem' tat when her dad decided to keep her from joining the hippies and enjoying all that 'free love' by sending her off to a nunnery."

I nearly spit ginger ale clear across the room. This was a part of Goodie's life I had heard nothing about. So her tattoo was the result of a teenaged rebellion!

But Goodie was not to be sidetracked and continued to tell the original story. "So I went online and ordered some seeds of the Abrus Precatorius plant. They call it a rosary pea, but it's really a very pretty seed. Some are white or green, but I wanted the ones that are bright red with a black end—the ones that kind of look like a ladybug."

When no one interrupted her, Goodie continued, "Sometimes these seeds are used in percussion instruments, but mostly they are for jewelry. The problem is, they are very, very toxic, but we didn't know just how toxic until it was too late." She sighed. "So it's all my fault."

Kanji began, "I fail to see—"

"I wasn't home when he was making the rosary," said Goodie. "And he must have been holding a part of it in his mouth or something while he was looking for his jewelry pliers or some other tool.

"Anyway, he accidentally swallowed some seeds. Then my guess is that he must have tried just to wash them down with coffee, which was about the same as crushing them, so they got into his system faster, but he wouldn't have gone to the hospital or anything because he wouldn't have felt the symptoms for hours."

"That," said Nadine, "or he could have simply poked his finger with the needle he was using to string the seeds together. When they did the autopsy, they said that abrin is so toxic, it can kill you either way."

"Either way," echoed Kanji. "That is quite unfortunate."

"So," continued Goodie, wiping her eyes with the back of her hand, "we'll never be sure if he died by ingestion or injection."

Kanji reached across the table to pat Goodie's hand. "You must not blame yourself," he said sympathetically, "I am sure it was all just a tragic accident."

"Yes," said Nadine. "Just like when my husband Claude died a few days later."

"Oh!" said Kanji, visibly startled. "I am so sorry for your loss as well!"

"It's okay," said Nadine, brushing off his condolences, "he had Alzheimer's. He thought he could walk out to Elk Island, across the Shallowwater Bay mud flats when the tide was out." She shook her head. "Who told him he could do that? Everybody knows you can't walk across there no matter how solid the land looks.

"But before he left the house that day, he'd told me he wanted to go pick flowers for me, and he said he was sure he knew where the prettiest ones grew, and wanted me to have a big bouquet of them.

"So the poor dear got stuck in the mud and drowned when the tide came back in. Horrible way to go, but much easier on all of us than if he had hung around for years in a nursing home like Sheriff D's wife."

Wow. I hadn't known the specifics of Claude's death either, only that the two husbands of the two best friends had died the same week.

Jimmy, Meredith and Nova returned with plates loaded with finger food "for the table," and Nadine immediately helped herself to the tempura shrimp.

I looked longingly at the crab puffs, then asked if anyone knew how many calories were in them. Jimmy told me not to be such a killjoy and suggested if I did some more dancing I could burn off the calories in no time.

"That sounds like my cue to ask you to dance again,"

said Kanji, and immediately led me back onto the dance floor.

The current song ended before we got a chance to dance, but we stood there and waited while Mercedes took her time starting the next tune.

"So your mother and her friends are all widows?" asked Kanji. "Is that what Sheriff Donaldson was referring to when he called the dancers 'Merri's Widows'?"

I knew Kanji had overheard Sheriff D's crack about the belly dancing group, but thought maybe he'd forgotten by now. I hesitated to answer. Something was making me a little uncomfortable that he'd continued the morbid topic from the table, but I decided to dismiss his interest as idle curiosity.

Mercedes began another number. Thankfully, this time the tune had no particular point behind the selected music, and Kanji and I continued to talk as we danced.

"Yes, unfortunately. Since Nova's husband Mateo has been missing since Tuesday, we have to assume that's true." I sighed. "My own mother has been widowed three times."

"Yes, I read that in the North Beach Tribune," said Kanji. "And she honors her deceased husbands by naming her cats after them. That was most interesting to me."

I couldn't help it, I had to ask him why.

"In some cultures," said Kanji, "speaking the names of the departed spirits keeps them from resting in the afterlife."

That was exactly what Native American Freddy had said, so I answered Kanji the same way I had answered Freddy. "I think she secretly hopes that is true."

Kanji chuckled, then grew serious. "Is your father one of those three deceased men?"

"No. At least I don't think so. Meredith says my father

was a 'tweener,' because he was a two or three night stand between the husbands."

"And he did not want to marry her?" asked Kanji.

I managed a small smile. "She said he was gone from her life before she knew she was pregnant."

"And you do know his name?"

"Sylvester." I actually laughed. "And since there was already a famous cartoon cat named Sylvester, Mom didn't name a cat after him, she named *me* after him!"

Kanji chuckled politely, but said nothing.

It was at that point I realized Mercedes had been playing "Sentimental Journey," and it was nearly over. Kanji had expertly maneuvered us right over to the table as the song ended, but before I could sit down, Freddy appeared.

"I'm taking a well-deserved break from hosting," he said cheerily. "I hope you have enough stamina for two dances in a row."

Kanji handed me off, promising to save me a crab puff.

"What was that crack about stamina supposed to mean?" I asked when we were far enough away from the table to talk privately. Once again, my voice had come out a little harsher than I'd intended, but it didn't matter, since Freddy chose to ignore my question.

He pulled me tight against him, preventing me from making an escape when I realized Mercedes had launched into "September Song." Were they in cahoots together? She wouldn't dare musically underscore our age difference—or would she?

I made a face at her over Freddy's shoulder, and in retaliation, she sang the longest version ever, with several instrumental bridges interwoven between verses, and I thought my aching feet were going to swell right out of

Bim's shoes before it was over.

Freddy, of course, was enjoying every single minute of my tight-shoe torture.

CHAPTER 9

"Let me just say again how much I admire your determination to stay fit in your retirement," Kanji was saying to the ladies as Freddy and I finally returned from the dance that seemingly would never end.

Freddy, having previously observed Kanji's manners, now remembered his own. He politely held the chair for me before pointedly kissing me on the cheek, then headed off to attend to the casino's other guests.

"Don't you want to know how old we are?" Orpha asked Kanji. "Everybody always asks."

"A gentleman would never pose such a query to a lady," said Kanji.

Meredith looked directly at me and stage whispered, "He's a keeper."

I mentally patted myself on the back for not acknowledging her comment in any form, not even with one of my all-too-frequent eye rolls.

"I'm the oldest," said Orpha, undaunted by Meredith's interruption. "I'm 85." She pointed to the women around the table. "Goodie's 79, Nadine is 78. Meredith won't admit her age, but she's next. And Nova is the baby of the group at 68."

"Funny how she can't remember what she had for breakfast, but she can nail our ages every time," said Nadine under her breath to Goodie.

Goodie nodded. "She even gets it right the day after

one of us has a birthday."

"I'm right here, you know," said Orpha, glaring at them. "And I can hear you."

"Thanks in great part to your hearing aids," replied Nadine.

"So I wear hearing aids, big deal. I'm an old lady, and proud of it."

Meredith reached over and patted Orpha's hand. "Don't you go getting your pretty little gray head all worked up, Honey. We're all friends here."

"And speaking of gray hair," Orpha quipped, "I just read in a magazine that if you color your hair," she looked pointedly at Nadine, "you have to remember to dye it *down there* too. Otherwise, if you have close gentlemen friends, you're going to be found out."

I snorted ginger ale out my nose and grabbed for a napkin. The others all seemed to take Orpha's comments in stride, including Kanji, although the crinkles around his eyes significantly deepened.

"Where in the world did you get ahold of an article like that?" asked Nadine.

Orpha shrugged. "I get around."

"Well, it certainly wasn't something you'd find lying around at the hearing aid clinic," said Goodie.

"I don't recall," said Orpha. "But whatever it was called, it had a picture of Tom Selleck on the cover. Now there's heck of a hottie I'd sure like to get my hands on." She looked at Kanji and grinned. "Present company notwithstanding."

I considered crawling under the table, but mostly because I wondered which of these women I'd end up emulating in just a few short years. Given my genetic make-up, I was pretty sure I wasn't going to act my age without a fight.

There was a brief lull in the conversation when the waitress came around with another beverage tray, this one filled only with glasses of ginger ale. "There's still plenty of food on the buffet table," she said. "Please help yourselves."

This time, nobody moved. Was it because nobody wanted to kill their buzz by soaking up the bubbly champagne with food, or because each of them were afraid if they left, the rest of us would be talking about them while they were gone?

Kanji restarted the conversation when he said, "I have come to understand that all five of you are widows."

Orpha, Goodie, Nadine, and Meredith enthusiastically nodded in unison. Nova immediately teared up and wiped her eyes again on her napkin.

"But we weren't all widows when we met," said Goodie.

"No," said Nadine. "Orpha had been widowed for at least a decade, and Meredith had been widowed twice when we first got together playing pinochle at the Senior Center."

"Yes," said Merri, agreeing with them. "I was on husband number three."

"I'm so grateful we met when we did." Nova's eyes met Meredith's. "I don't know what I would have done without your friendship this past week."

Nadine nodded. "Meredith has saved all of us," she said solemnly.

"I'm sorry," said Kanji. "I fail to understand."

"At our very first meeting," said Goodie, "Merri insisted we all take out large insurance policies on our husbands."

"She said it was prudent for us to prepare for our futures," said Nadine.

"Merri said the statistics were stacked against us," said Goodie, "and since we'd all eventually end up being widows, there was no reason not to profit from it."

Kanji was suddenly all ears. "Please tell me more about that."

"Meredith even helped them fill out their online insurance applications," said Orpha, happy to have something to contribute. "I wish I'd met her a lot sooner. Then there'd be five millionaires sitting at this table instead of me being left out of the money grab."

Ginger ale came out my nose for a second time, and without a word, Kanji handed me a clean napkin. He seemed oddly cool, calm, and collected after Orpha's disclosure, but it had shocked the bejeezus out of me.

"Mother! You insured Robert for a million dollars?"

Merri shrugged and tucked a strand of hair behind her ear. "I'd lost two husbands already, and each time I was left a drawer full of bills and barely enough cash on hand to cremate them for all my trouble." She sighed. "And as Goodie has already explained, the actuary odds were in my favor for outliving the third one too, so I hedged my bets. No way did I want to be left poor a third time."

Aghast, I looked from one to another of four smiling, aging, cherubic faces, and then to poor Nova, who was hunched down in her chair, quietly crying her eyes out. Nothing in the world could have stopped me from asking, of no one of them in particular, "So where's all your money?"

"Sylvia Lee!" Meredith exclaimed, "Didn't I raise you better than that? It's none of your business what anyone has done with their insurance money!" She glared at me. "And Nova's in mourning, remember? She hasn't even gotten her check yet."

"Nova's still under investigation," said Freddy, returning to our table with his father in tow. "She has to be cleared of any wrongdoing before there's any chance of some actual check cutting going on."

I wanted to punch him in the arm for being so... so.... so "practical" about Nova's insurance claim, but I knew he was just being true to his day job, as he called his time in a county uniform.

There was only one empty chair at our table for eight, and Freddy grabbed it and repositioned it next to Nova. "I brought you another friendly face to talk to," he said with a great degree of compassion, motioning for Rich to take the seat.

"How you holding up?" said Rich, placing a hand tenderly on her shoulder. He wasn't just saying that, he looked genuinely concerned.

Nova took a long, steadying breath, and looked up at him. "You clean up well," she said, and almost smiled.

"Sorry I missed your belly dancing debut," said Rich. "Can I make it up to you now by asking you to dance with me?"

I would have bet my life savings that Nova would turn him down flat, but she surprised us all when she nodded and slowly got to her feet. "I think it would help me get my mind off other things."

Rich took her hand, and when he put his arm around her back, he kept his body at a very respectable distance. We could see they were talking constantly as they danced, but the music was too loud for any of us to be privy to the contents of the conversation.

I quickly looked around the room for Raven. She had been there earlier, taking photos of Mercedes at the keyboard, and then a few shots while The Veiled Rainbow performed, but now she was nowhere to be seen. I breathed a deep sigh of relief.

I knew a photo of Nova participating with the belly dancing troupe was damning enough in the public's eye, but a picture of Nova and Rich waltzing less than a week after Mateo went missing would put Sheriff Donaldson's blood pressure over the moon.

Before Nova and Rich could sit down when they returned to the table, Orpha piped up, "I'm not looking for a one-night stand, but I sure wouldn't mind taking another spin around the dance floor, Captain Morgan."

Rich froze in place, then grinned. "Well, then, Mrs. Starr," he volleyed a shot right back at her, "how about tonight and Wednesday?"

We all laughed, even Nova, and I could tell having Rich's shoulder there to cry on was probably the best medicine she could have asked for.

Mercedes was having so much fun back behind the keyboard that she'd played right through her second scheduled break. I suppose not having Sheriff D there to flirt with had something to do with it—that, or the fact that the bandstand was the best seat in the house when you wanted to watch what everyone was up to.

But now Mercedes paused briefly to thank everyone for coming to her "par-tay, y'all," then announced to the dancers that they had one last chance to "polish those belt buckles" as she played the final song of the night.

I expected Freddy to want the last dance, but I saw him already standing next to the ballroom door, shaking hands and thanking everyone for coming. Kanji saw that too, and seized the opportunity to dance with me once again.

We didn't as talk much while we danced this time. I thought for sure Mercedes would play her customary

"Goodnight Sweetheart" to close the party, but once again, she went rogue.

Had I not already been on the dance floor when Merc started singing, I might have begged off, but there I was, hugging and swaying to the strains of "Can't Help Falling in Love." She wasn't Elvis, but she was pretty darn good. I just hoped neither Kanji nor Freddy were listening too closely to the lyrics.

It took so much concentration to follow Kanji on the dance floor that I didn't notice who else was dancing until we were all standing still, clapping for Mercedes.

Jimmy and Orpha, Rich and Nova, Freddy and Felicity, and Mom and Walter all stood around us, and for the life of me, I wasn't sure which of these pairings caught me the most off guard!

"Guess I'll be snagging a ride back home with you, if that's okay," said Jimmy when we returned to the table.

I nodded. "Of course." I didn't bother to tell him I had already planned on that when I picked him up—no sense adding insult to his lack-of-relationship injury. He stood on one foot, then the other, impatiently waiting for me to hurry it up, so I handed him the keys to the Mustang. "I just need to say goodbye to a few people and I'll be right out."

It turned out that "a few people" was quite a large number, and by the time I was actually ready to leave, Freddy was nowhere to be found. Kanji, of course, was Mr. Johnny-on-the-spot, and gallantly asked if he could walk me to my car.

Just for spite, I accepted his offer and took his arm. I waved goodbye to Mercedes as we went through the exit, and she gave me a double thumbs up. Thankfully, no one else—meaning neither Kanji nor Freddy—saw her do that.

And then there was that awkward moment when we

parted. I was grateful Kanji didn't try to kiss me, as there was a known blabbermouth sitting right inside my car. But on second thought, I wondered if I were more relieved or disappointed.

Instead, Kanji lifted my hand to his lips, pressed it there for a brief moment, and asked if I might be available to meet him for coffee the next day.

"Oh, I'm so sorry," I replied sincerely. "Felicity and I already have plans for tomorrow. How about Monday, instead?"

As soon as the words came out of my mouth, I wanted to rip my tongue out. Mondays were Freddy's sacred days off from both jobs, and we'd made a recent habit of spending them together. Well, we wouldn't be getting together this particular Monday, as Kanji had eagerly accepted my not-too-well-thought-out counter offer to his initial suggestion.

I got into the car and watched Kanji as he headed back inside the casino, perhaps to pick up that job application for part-time "Hospitality Specialist." I involuntarily shuddered as I started the car, remembering Freddy's declaration that he intended to keep his friends close, but his competition closer.

"Well, well, well," said Jimmy, as we pulled out of the casino parking lot. "And here I thought I was the only one out on a man hunt tonight." I could tell he was miffed. "It's a little greedy of you to have two when I have none, don't you think?"

I hoped he was teasing, but I couldn't play along. Not right now. I needed time to process what in the heck had just happened. Two men? Interested in me? At the same time? Good grief and gravy!

"Unless you want to walk home," I said to Jimmy in

the sugary-sweet voice I reserved for especially sticky situations I was trying to get out of, "I suggest you keep your thoughts to yourself on the trip home." I turned the radio on and set the volume a little higher than necessary, and refused to engage in further conversation.

Late Sunday morning I picked Felicity up at her apartment in Unity, and we headed across the Columbia River to the city of Fort George for some "quality girl time." It was an annual tradition—a planned afternoon get-away as another school year hurried to a close. Yet every year it was hard for me to convince Felix that taking a break to have lunch and a matinee movie was the ticket to keeping her sanity as her anxiety ramped up.

"I don't know if I really have time for this," she said as she got into the car. "There's just so much still left to do before graduation."

I smiled. Just like clockwork, we danced this dance every May. Felicity would fuss about taking a little time for herself, and I would insist that a little time to herself was just what she needed before heading into the final weeks of the school year.

Felicity was in charge of senior graduation, and although she'd done it for several years, she hadn't yet learned the full power of the word "delegate."

The drive across the Columbia River to Fort George on the Oregon side always puts me in a fresh frame of mind. Somehow, just placing four miles of water between me and any problems or worries I might have had "back home" in Washington is just enough distance to get a fresh perspective.

Crossing the 'Bridge to Nowhere,' as the ambitious construction had been dubbed back in the 1960s, worked its magic on Felix today, too, and I could almost feel the tension draining from both of us as we motored south.

"You said you'd found a new place to have lunch?" Felicity asked as we swooped down from the highest point of the bridge to the land below. ·

"Well, it's not exactly 'new,' but it's new to us," I told her. "It's built right on the docks in the industrial part of town. It's a great spot to watch the ships go by, and there's even a window in the floor where you can see some sea lions napping."

"So you've been there before?" she asked.

"Nope." I laughed. "This will be a first for me, too. I only know about it from the reviews I've read."

"Fair enough." Felix nodded. "For a minute there, I thought you'd been holding out on me."

I shot her a look as I pulled into the parking lot tucked in between old relics of buildings where once thriving cannery businesses had resided. "But since I haven't been here before, I can't vouch for the food."

I needn't have worried. The menu immediately set our mouths to watering, and our meal lived up to the glowing descriptions. We each had a delicious bowl of clam chowder and split an order of cod fish and chips while watching the world float by outside the immense windows all along one wall.

The restaurant also housed a craft brewery, and the beers all had very interesting names and looked very enticing, but neither one of us imbibed.

While we ate, we chit-chatted about the warm weather, where the ships moored in the river might be heading, the cargo they carried, and the problems the fishermen were having with the sea lions we could hear below us. In fact, we talked about just about everything except the metaphorical elephant on the table.

Then we headed to nearby Fort George Cinema, got our tickets, passed on having any theater popcorn, and found our seats. We both preferred sitting in the highest rows, so fewer people could sit behind us and talk.

But just as the previews began, when I thought we were home free, Felix brought up the topic we'd carefully avoided throughout our drive and the meal on the water.

"Aren't you ever going to ask me about dancing with Freddy?" Felix leaned over and whispered in my ear.

"It's really none of my business," I whispered back. "You two are about the same age. It's only natural that you'd enjoy spending time together."

"Syl! Don't go getting all crazy jealous on me! Freddy and I haven't been spending time together! I'm not the least bit interested in him!" She elbowed me in the ribs. "He was headed for your table, saw you were already dancing with Kanji, and you should have seen the look on his face. So what could I do? Walter was already out there with Meredith, so I jumped up and helped Freddy save face. That's all there was to it. I swear."

I thought for a moment that the lady did protest too much, but decided to take what she'd said at face value. Oddly enough, I felt a great deal of tension residing between my shoulder blades, tension I hadn't even realized I was holding, begin to dissipate after her reasonable-sounding explanation. By the end of the matinee, which was a very funny comedy, I felt genuinely upbeat.

But as the lights in the theater came up, Felicity leaned over again. "Would you look at that?" she whispered.

"You don't have to whisper now, Felix, the show's over."

"Oh no it's not," she whispered back. "Not by a long

shot." She pointed to a couple sitting far down below us in the theater.

My eyes nearly popped out of my head. His arm draped across the back of the theater seat next to him, Walter, with a big sappy smile on his face, was chatting through the credits with none other than Meredith Avery—my dear, sweet, three-times-a-widow mother—who seemed to be hanging onto his every word.

"What should we do?" Felicity continued whispering.

"Do?" I echoed stupidly.

"Should we duck down so they won't see us?"

I couldn't decide if that was a good idea, or a bad idea, so I sat frozen, like the proverbial deer in the headlights, and said nothing, staring at them as if they were the next Coming Attraction. And maybe they were.

The credits ended, and the crew with brooms and dustpans came in. Walter stood up, held his hand out to Merri, and they left the room still holding hands, oblivious to us at the back of the theater, watching them.

"Wow," breathed Felicity, standing up. "That was close."

"Sit back down," I replied. "We can't leave yet. We have to wait for them to have time to clear the parking lot, and mother will want to 'freshen up' before they leave the building, so it will be a few minutes."

Felix plopped back into her seat.

"There's nothing wrong with them dating, you know." She touched my arm. "Neither of them are married, and I'm sure they both get lonely. At least I know Walter does."

I nodded, then leaned forward, squished my eyes closed and pinched the place between them at the top of my nose.

"Are you going to faint?" asked Felix.

"No," I chuckled. "I'm just trying to figure out what Meredith is going to do when she sees my Mustang out there. With my custom purple and green chameleon paint job, it's the only car like it in the entire world."

Felicity laughed. "And I was just thinking that Walter knew I had a play date with you today, so he'll know we're here together."

I stood and picked up my purse. "So much for being discreet. We might as well go out and face the music."

But a happy surprise was waiting for us in the parking lot. Walter and Merri were nowhere to be found. For the time being, we had dodged a bullet.

CHAPTER 10

Monday morning I took a lot longer than I usually do getting dressed, taking care with both my makeup and hair, which turned out to be ridiculous, because I put the top down on the Mustang as soon as I got into the car.

But Jimmy sensed something was different right away when I realized I was way too early to meet Kanji at the coffee shop and swung into the Clamshell lot to kill a few minutes hanging out with him.

"No coffee?" His eyebrows arched. "And it's still morning? What's up, Syl?"

I leaned against his kitchen counter and made an attempt at nonchalance. "I— Uh— I'm meeting someone for coffee at the Sandy Bottom in about half an hour. He's new to the community. I don't think you know him." I would have babbled on and on, digging myself a much deeper hole, but I suddenly realized that Jimmy *had* met Kanji, and only two days ago—or even before that.

"Someone?" Jimmy's eyebrows arched. "Hhmm. I wonder who that could be?" He feigned innocence, then quickly looked disgusted and shook his head. "You're not usually such a terrible liar, Syl."

He was right. I was totally flustered. But before I could answer, he asked if I would mind bringing him back some ground coffee from the Sandy Bottom. Relieved that he'd changed the subject, I told him I'd be more than happy to do that. He wrote down the specifics on the notepad by his phone, tore off the top sheet, and handed it to me.

Everything in me suddenly went queasy. Even without putting them side-by-side, I knew this notepaper exactly matched the notepaper Kanji had written on when he'd left the message in my helmet. It had the same small row of seashells running along the top.

"Of course!" I said aloud. "This is notepaper from the Clamshell Motel."

Jimmy looked genuinely concerned. "Syl, are you alright?"

"Jimmy, I tried to introduce you to Kanji during Mercedes' party, and he said he had already met you, but that he had introduced himself to you as Ken. It was right when Merc was announcing The Veiled Rainbow, and I never got around to asking you where and when you and Kanji first met."

"Oh," said Jimmy, pouring some fresh kibbles into Priscilla's bowl. "I thought he must have already told you about that, and that's why you stopped in this morning."

"What?" I tipped my head and peered at him quizzically. "Why I stopped—" I looked out Jimmy's kitchen window to the parking lot. Jimmy's split-pea green Pinto was in its usual space, then my Mustang, then a little farther out was a dark blue Scion xB, which I assumed was the vehicle of someone renting a room.

"Jimmy..." I felt color rising up my neck and into my face.

"I thought you knew!" Jimmy laughed. "Honest, Syl. I wasn't hiding anything. Ken—I mean Kanji—is renting Unit 6 by the week, and he has the cutest little puppy, and the Clamshell is pet friendly, and the pup gets along really well with Miss Priss, and—"

I held up my hand to silence him. "And now he's going

to think I'm stalking him or something." I plopped into a kitchen chair. "I cannot believe you failed to mention your newest tenant." I scowled at him.

A knock on the outer office door saved Jimmy from any more of my venom. I hadn't heard a car pull in, but before that thought could fully register, Jimmy and Kanji entered Jimmy's living quarters.

"A very good morning to you, Miss Sylvia," said Kanji, with just the slightest suggestion of a bow. "It is most fortunate you have stopped here to visit your friend Jimmy this morning."

I considered making some type of lame explanation, but it turned out to be unnecessary. Kanji's pup, a gangly yellow lab mix, bounded into the room and went straight to Priscilla's bowl to help himself to a snack.

Jimmy took this in stride, and even Miss Priss seemed undisturbed by the intrusion.

"What a cute puppy!" I exclaimed, bending down to pet it. "What's his name?"

Both Jimmy and Kanji laughed.

"I told you a puppy was a natural chick magnet," said Jimmy.

A chick magnet?! I started to protest, but I could see the silliness in that. After all, it had certainly attracted me, hadn't it?

"Jimmy has kindly consented to watching my pup while I am away today, so I do not have to leave him in his kennel," Kanji explained.

"I was just getting to that," said Jimmy.

I started to give him my best 'sure you were' look, when I realized he was telling me the truth. I had cut him off right when he'd been telling me how well Miss Priss and Kanji's pup got along.

"Now may I ask if we can carpool to the coffee shop together?" asked Kanji. "And then, perhaps, if you are not too busy, I would certainly enjoy a tour of the south end of the peninsula from someone who is not trying to sell me a house."

All three of us chuckled, and the fuchsia color in my cheeks started returning to normal as we climbed into the Mustang.

At the Sandy Bottom, Bim was all a bustle. Kanji's presence, especially arriving with me, had thrown her for a loop. She asked him far too many questions about his Chai. I know this, because Bim has a bartender's memory for drinks, and I'm sure she could have fixed his tea without asking him anything at all.

Perhaps she really did enjoy his accent so much she couldn't help herself, and it really was fun just to see how far Bim would go with all her silly questions.

Kanji paid for both our drinks, and without thinking, I sat at my usual spot at the large, octagon table by the roaster. Moments later, we were joined by an uninvited third member to our private party.

"Mr. Kanjirappally Kumera!" exclaimed Freddy, shaking Kanji's hand as if they were long-lost brothers, and sliding into the seat next to him as if I weren't even there. "Everything is in order, and all I need now is your signature here on the W-4."

Freddy handed Kanji an IRS W-4 Employee Withholding form and a pen, watched while he signed it, and shook his hand again. "Welcome aboard."

When Freddy did not immediately get up to leave, Kanji excused himself to use the restroom. That man was a gentleman clear down to his toes, and my esteem for him kept growing as he discreetly gave Freddy and me a few minutes alone.

As soon at the bathroom door clicked shut, Freddy reached out and gave my hand a quick squeeze.

I was all but spitting nails. "Did you put a tracking device on my Mustang?"

"What would make you say that?" asked Freddy.

"Don't you dare answer my question with a question!"

Freddy laughed. "You watch too much crime TV."

"Then how did you know we were here?"

"Oh, that." Freddy waved it off. "Kanji told me where to find him this morning when we spoke on the phone yesterday." He shrugged. "No big deal. And I told you I was going to hire some new part-time staff to give me more time away from the casino."

I saw right through his ruse, and I was plenty miffed, but I knew it wasn't the time or the place for this discussion.

As Kanji returned to the table, I asked Freddy how the investigation of Mateo's disappearance was going.

Freddy shook his head. "We don't know anything more today than we knew on Saturday," he said, "and even if we did, I probably couldn't tell you." He smiled. "What I can tell you is that at this time, the evidence isn't there to charge either woman, and the sheriff is thinking he's going to go with the accident theory."

"If you don't mind me asking," began Kanji. "I am most curious as to why Sheriff Donaldson, or the Coast Guard, or even the Department of Fisheries, has not retrieved all of the crab pots set out by the Estrella Nueva the night Mr. Rodriguez disappeared."

I looked at Freddy, who looked at me, but neither of us said anything.

"I know it is gruesome to imagine such a thing,"

continued Kanji, "but wouldn't it be a good way to dispose of a body—to cut it up and put the pieces into the crab pots for bait?"

"Oh my gawd!" I exclaimed, my hand flying to my mouth. "You think someone would use a human corpse as crab bait? What kind of a monster would do such a thing?!"

"I am most sorry to have upset you," said Kanji, putting his hand on my lower arm and leaving it there. "But I have been following this story in the newspapers, and have wondered why the investigators have left that particular stone unturned."

Freddy cleared his throat. "That particular question, I *can* answer.

"Although it's true that soft tissue is devoured rather quickly by the scavengers in the sea, it takes quite a bit to completely destroy the bones. Just a couple years ago, crabbers up in Westport discovered a skull in one of their pots."

"Oh! I remember that," I interjected. "The skull had apparently washed into the crab pot during a big ocean storm. It was sent to Quantico, and the DNA identified it as a young, female, Native American. Carbon dating placed it at 2,300 years old."

"Hey," Freddy said to me, "who's telling this story?"

Our eyes met, and my anger suddenly dissipated. "Sorry."

"Maybe you don't know this, since you're new around here," said Freddy to Kanji, "but if anyone were going to try disposing of a body by stuffing it into a crab pot, they for sure would not leave their buoys attached to mark the pot's location."

"It is true, I had not thought of that," said Kanji. He looked at me and squeezed my arm, which his hand was still resting upon. "Forgive me."

"Of course," I replied. "Nova's no dummy. If she were going to do something like that, she would have made sure the pots would stay on the ocean floor forever."

Kanji's eyes narrowed, and he looked pointedly at Freddy. "And are the number of crab pots normally found on the Estrella now all accounted for?"

A shiver ran up my spine. Just what was Kanji implying? And why was he so darn interested in all the possibly-gruesome details of this incident?

Thankfully, Freddy took Kanji's question in stride. "As I told you, it's an ongoing investigation. Crab pots come loose from their buoys all the time. That's why you see so many buoys hanging from trees and fences and porch railings all over the peninsula. Beachcombers often find them after a storm, and use them to decorate. It's not unusual for a crabber to lose several pots each year."

"So you are telling us that there are fewer crab pots accounted for than would normally be in the possession of Nova Johanssen?" said Kanji.

"I said no such thing," said Freddy, glaring at the man sitting between us.

"Anybody ready for a refill?" asked Bim, standing beside our table.

I almost laughed. There was a half-full Chai tea sitting in front of Kanji, I was taking my time with my one cup of regular coffee for the day, and Freddy had not gotten anything to drink when he'd arrived.

"We'll hold it down, Bim," I said. "Sorry if we disturbed your other customers."

Bim smiled. "No problem." She nodded with her head toward the young woman seated at the counter, hunched over a notepad. "Raven only just arrived, and she's getting her coffee to go."

'Thanks, Bim," said Freddy. "I owe you."

"Leave your thanks in the tip jar, Honey," said Bim, wiping her hands on her ever-present dishtowel. "I just figured nobody needs any more bad press today."

"Uh... Bim...?" I was afraid to ask, but I asked anyway. "What do mean by 'today'?"

Bim sighed. "Oh. Then I take it you haven't seen Monday's edition of the Tribune."

"Oh, no. What now?"

She retrieved her personal copy of the North Beach Tribune from behind the counter, flipped to an inside page, and folded it back. The photo, a modest three columns wide and three inches long, was in black and white, which didn't do it justice, but the headline made me see bright red: "Millionaire Widow's Club Dance Up a Storm."

"Your mother and her friends are very photogenic," said Kanji, diplomatically.

I shot a quick glance in Raven's direction, but she had already left the coffee shop. Nice timing.

Freddy and Kanji scanned the article, and Freddy's head came up first. "There's some good advertising in there for the casino," he said.

I wanted to kick him, but my legs weren't long enough.

"It's okay, Sylleegirl," he said tenderly. "It's no worse than anything that's already been printed." He paused, then brightened, "And see?" He pointed to the page number. "It's already old news, not good enough for the front page, even here on the North Beach Peninsula."

I took some small consolation in that.

Kanji, sensing my distress, hurriedly finished his tea, and said he was now ready whenever I was for the south end peninsula tour.

The newspaper article had taken some of the wind out of my sails, but the ride out toward the Foggy Hollow overlook with the convertible top down restored much of my positive attitude. It always does.

After we spent a few minutes enjoying the view from the overlook, I drove Kanji farther up into Pacific Bluff. It still irked me something fierce that Harold Rodman the Third, a.k.a. Uncle Harry, had clear cut that entire area to make room for his high-end housing development, but I had to admit, the views from the homes there were stellar.

We took our time meandering through the maze of roads, and I did my share of oohing and aahing over the diverse and attractive houses up on the hill.

"I am afraid these homes are quite a ways out of my price range," said Kanji, "but I enjoy seeing them, nevertheless."

"I didn't think you'd be looking for a house up here," I told him, "but no tour would be complete without taking a swing through Poker Bluff."

"Poker Bluff?"

"It's what the locals call it, but I'm not sure of their reasoning. It was a gamble for Uncle Harry to build such expensive homes on speculation up here, considering the peninsula is such a low socio-economic area, but it's also quite risky to build in a steeply-sloped area that now has no vegetation stabilizing the hillside."

"Those are both gambles, indeed." Kanji nodded. "But what of the forest animals who used to call this area their home?"

"Good question. There were quite a few deer and bears who had to go looking for another place to live." I chuckled. "Nadine—the woman in the green veiled costume on Saturday—has been all up in arms about that for years. She used to work for Greenpeace in Seattle, and she's still quite the advocate for our environment."

I pulled out of Pacific Bluff, drove less than a mile farther south, and parked next to some state park restrooms in a small paved parking lot. I hung my Discover Pass from the rearview mirror, and we both got out of the car.

"How about taking a little walk this morning?" I asked Kanji. "I promise, the view out at Swiftstone Lighthouse is well worth the short walk."

"I would be most honored to take this walk with you," said Kanji, "and I would love to hear more about Nadine, too."

It crossed my mind that it was kind of an odd request, but I dismissed it as simply Kanji wanting to know more about the people of the peninsula. After all, I'm the one who had brought up Nadine's name. And as we headed down the wooded, but vehicle-wide trail, I was only too happy to share Deenie's most recent "Save the Bears" escapade.

"Nadine lives over on Sandspit Road," I began, "about a mile or two south of where I live. Technically her address is in Tinkerstown. I doubt the leveling of the forest on Poker Bluff has anything to do with it, but there are a lot of bears in both those areas. In fact, bears have become a pretty big problem all over the peninsula."

Kanji looked nervously to each side, and then over his shoulder to scan the area behind us, as if expected to see a bear materialize right then and there.

"I am a city boy from Chicago," he explained. "The only place we ever see Bears is out on the football field."

We both laughed at his joke, but I knew it was quite possible to run into wildlife while walking this trail. I had seen deer out here dozens of times, but never a bear.

Nevertheless, I always carried pepper spray when I walked any trails, to ward off aggressive dogs, bears, raccoons, and whatnot. I pulled the spray from my pocket to show him, in the hopes that he could then relax and enjoy our stroll.

"I am fine now," he said, after I explained I was prepared to defend us from wild animals. He smiled, and his eyes twinkled. "But I would feel even better if you held my hand while we walked."

His request caught me by surprise, but I didn't hesitate to accept his hand as we strolled down to the lighthouse.

"Nadine got into some trouble with the law last fall for feeding the bears," I said, returning to the story. "She was putting out big bowls of dog food for them on her back deck, and the neighbors were complaining about her activities, because the bears were becoming a huge nuisance."

"She was feeding wild bears?" asked Kanji, with a mixed expression of surprise and horror. "She wanted to invite them to come to her home for dinner?"

"Oh, yeah. Nadine's such a softie. She and Goodie became best friends over their love of animals." I momentarily stopped walking, as we were about to round the final curve before coming to the lighthouse, and I wanted Kanji not to be so distracted by the story that he missed the wonder of the scenery right in front of us.

In silence, we took a few more steps, and almost by magic, the massive Swiftstone Lighthouse filled the sky.

"Wow," said Kanji under his breath.

"Wow, indeed," I replied, happy that he was as awestruck as I always am. "I never get tired of coming to this sacred place."

Since it was Monday, and still slightly before noon, there was nobody sitting on the bench at the overlook, so we eagerly took "the best seats in the house," and breathed in the peace and solitude.

"Thank you so very much for bringing me here," said Kanji. "As you promised, it was most worth the walk."

I looked toward the lighthouse and sighed. "For most of my time here, that lighthouse had a red top," I told Kanji. "But during restoration, it was decided to return the roof to the original black, and I can't say that I'm all that fond of it."

Kanji smiled, put his arm around my shoulders, and pulled me a little closer. "Change is often difficult and unsettling," he said. "It takes time for one to adjust."

I leaned comfortably against him and looked out over the water. There was no need for further conversation as we sat in contemplative silence.

After a time, my stomach growled, and I took that as a sign to continue our journey. I stood, dusted off my bottom, and automatically took Kanji's hand for the return walk.

"You were telling me the story of Nadine and the bears," he prompted.

"Yes, I was!" I laughed. "But right now it seems like that was weeks ago!"

Kanji smiled. "Yes, it was a fine place to meditate and be present in the moment, but now I would enjoy returning to the story."

I nodded. "So Nadine drives a little black and white smart car—"

"I saw one in the casino parking lot with big, black eyelashes over the headlights," said Kanji. "Would that be her car?"

"Uh-huh. And it's too little to do any major shopping at Costco, so Nadine got Goodie to pick up two 40-pound bags of dog food for her every week."

"Oh my," said Kanji. "That's a lot of dog food. And does Nadine have a dog?"

"Well, yes, I guess you could call it that. After Nadine's husband Claude died, Goodie, the woman you first met at the Humane Society, convinced her to adopt an obnoxious, yappy little French poodle that nobody liked. We have a no-kill shelter, but this dog had been there for a very long time, especially in dog years, and Goodie really wanted to find it a home in the worst way. So Nadine adopted it and named it Claudette."

"Do these ladies all name pets after their deceased husbands?" said Kanji.

"No, just Meredith and Nadine, but let's get back to the bears." I quickly redirected the conversation before it became all about the Merri's Widows.

"There are laws against feeding wild animals in our state," I explained. "And Nadine had been given several warnings. Finally, she was arrested and went to court last fall. She was fined $500 and told that if she ever did it again, she'd be spending time in jail."

"And she has been a law-abiding model citizen since then?" asked Kanji.

I shot him a look, but I couldn't read his expression. "I certainly hope so," I replied, "but she's Nadine, a dyed-in-the-wool Greenpeace rebel, so—" I sighed heavily. "I really can't say for sure."

CHAPTER 11

Kanji and I made a brief stop at the Lewis and Clark Interpretive Center. It's a steep, but paved climb up from the main parking lot, and the view from the railing out in front of the building was one of the very best waterscapes the peninsula has to offer.

"This time of year, most of the gray whales have already migrated north," I told Kanji, putting my metaphorical tour guide hat back on. "But the females with calves come along at a slower pace, and there might yet be a few passing by."

I pointed out the southern and northern jetties marking the river mouth, and told him about the need for bar pilots to navigate the large international ships through the shipping channel.

"Sylvia," said Kanji, squeezing my hand. "You have brought me to see the best and most pristine scenery I could imagine today. Thank you! I did not think one would be able to see so far from shore at the mouth of the Columbia River." He breathed a deep sigh of appreciation. "Where you live is a truly spectacular place."

I would have loved to stand and watch the ships come and go over the Columbia River bar for hours, but my continuously growling stomach commanded too much of my attention and I knew I needed to get some food into it soon.

"How about we save touring the inside of the

Interpretive Center for another day?" I asked Kanji. "The exhibits are amazing, and to do it right, it takes several hours."

"I am most willing to do that," he said, smiling, "especially since it means I will be spending more time with the peninsula's most beautiful tour guide."

I have got to learn to take a compliment without blushing. I'll put it on my bucket list. But this day I decided I just wanted to enjoy the flattery without worrying about my flaming red face. Who was I to object being called beautiful?

We headed back around the southern lighthouse loop road to the port of Unity. Fortunately, I knew the perfect place to go for a quick and delicious meal.

I pulled the Mustang into a small parking area between Captain Morgan's tiny little deep-sea charter office and the Can't Fathom It bar, where you can sit upstairs and eat and drink while watching the boats come and go in the harbor. But the Can't Fathom It wasn't my current destination this day. This day, Kanji was in for a real surprise.

Just east of the cannery was my favorite place for lunch at the docks. Pier 103, a repurposed commercial fishing boat, was a wonderfully eclectic floating takeout-only restaurant. It was named for the highway rather than an actual pier number, which often confused the tourists trying to find it by using their GPS.

Pier 103 was a modified "fast food" spot that served only one thing—tuna fish and chips. You could get a full order, a half order, or an order without fries, but you were going to have the tuna fish and chips or nothing.

Fortunately, they made the very best fish and chips in the entire region, so no one cared about the lack of other options on the menu.

We got in line with a few cannery workers on the later lunch shift, and Kanji took note of the uncommonly reasonable prices written on a chalkboard nailed to the side of the restaurant boat.

"I didn't think to ask—" I said as I mentally crossed my fingers. "Do you like seafood?"

Kanji smiled. "Yes, I am very fond of your fish and chips, although it is quite different from those one would order in India—or anywhere in the United Kingdom of Great Britain and Northern Ireland."

"How so?" Having never been to either India or the UK, I was curious.

"Most often, the fish is cooked as one large filet, which includes the entire side of the fish. In the United States, it is served as several smaller pieces."

Kanji and I got two full orders, a couple sodas from their ice chests sitting nearby on the wharf, and found a nice spot in the sunshine on the grassy hill above the port docks.

"Fish and chips are an everyday meal in the UK," Kanji continued the conversation we'd started while waiting in line, "but in India, it is a delicacy. Most often in India it is made from any white fish, such as bhekti, which is also known as Barramundi, or Asian sea bass, and dipped in a chickpea batter."

I couldn't wrap my mind around such a foreign thing as chickpea batter, so I said nothing. I was too busy digging into my yummy tuna for any more talk at the moment.

Most of the charter boats were lined up in the first row, as close as they could get to their tiny land offices. The majority of them were backed in, with their names painted in large letters across the sterns. Right below us in the marina was Rich's boat, the Geraldine.

Farther out along the dock running perpendicular to the land was Nova's boat, the Estrella Nueva, since it was used for commercial crabbing, and not sport fishing. Ironically, the Kriselle, which was going up for auction soon, now that Dennis Evans was in jail for murder, was just down from Nova's boat, on the same pier. Both were still shrouded with "Do Not Cross" yellow crime scene tape.

I continued to eat in silence as I mentally reviewed the events of the past few days and months, but then it crossed my mind to wonder why Kanji was also so quiet. "Is the fish okay?" I asked.

He nodded, swallowed, and wiped his mouth. "Yes. It is excellent."

"Oh, you were so quiet, I wasn't sure if you liked it..."

Kanji smiled. "In my culture, we do not talk as much as you do in America during meals. It is a time of quiet reflection and appreciation of the food before us."

"Oh. I'm sorry. Should I just be quiet and let you finish eating?"

He laughed. "I have been raised to be an American in public, so you have not offended me in the least."

I chuckled at his tactful response. "So how does tuna compare to the type of fish and chips you're used to?"

"It is a denser fish than I have previously enjoyed cooked in this manner," said Kanji. "It is very tasty, but very much more like halibut than cod, which is flaky."

"I agree," I said, after taking a swig of soda. "Of course," I laughed, "some might say that many of the people in America are just like fish and chips—either dense or flaky."

Thankfully, Kanji understood that I was making a joke, and he laughed heartily, the sound of his laughter rang out over the marina.

Rich emerged from the cabin of the Geraldine, perhaps looking for the origination of the laughter, and spotted us sitting on the lawn above him. He waved.

"Come join us!" I called out before I gave it a second thought. I quickly turned to Kanji. "You don't mind, do you?"

"Any friend of yours is a friend of mine," he said gallantly.

There was certainly a lot to like about this guy.

Rich washed his hands with the hose on the Geraldine's back deck, wiped them off on his jeans, and retrieved his giant stainless steel coffee mug from the boat's cabin. Then he climbed the ramp nearest us. The tide was mostly out, so the ramp was quite steep.

Kanji stood up, wiped his greasy hands on his napkin, and extended his hand as Rich approached.

"I am Kanji Kumera. I am sure I saw you at the party at the Spartina Point Casino and Resort on Saturday evening, but we were never formally introduced."

Rich switched his coffee mug from his right to his left hand and gripped Kanji's hand, pumping it up and down several times. "Richard Morgan," he said. "Captain Richard Morgan. But I'd prefer you call me Rich."

"Pleased to meet you, Rich." Kanji dipped his head in his customary nod/bow. "Would you now care to share some grass with us?"

I laughed, Rich laughed, and finally Kanji laughed, but I'm not sure he knew why we thought it was so funny for him to offer Rich a seat on the ground.

Marijuana is legal now in Washington state, and whether you call it pot, weed, dope, Mary Jane, cannabis, or grass, being "420 friendly" is no longer a big deal. Even my mother and her merry belly-dancing band imbibed in the stuff once in a while.

Rich sat down next to me, and I held my cardboard lunch container out to him. "There's another piece of fish in there, and a few fries, if you'd like some."

He waved the offer away. "Already had lunch," he said. "I took a small group out on the water at dawn this morning, so both breakfast and lunch came earlier than usual."

"Did you catch any fish?" asked Kanji.

It was a fair question, given that Rich runs a sport fishing boat, but Kanji didn't have all the necessary information to ask the *right* question.

"The salmon fishing season hasn't started yet," I explained. "Rich supplements his income by taking tourists out sightseeing, or bird watching, or *whale* watching, and even once in a while for special occasions like birthdays and weddings."

"And my boat's been modified so I can accommodate special needs kids and adults," added Rich. "I teach high school kids all about boating safety and a little about sport fishing when the seasons line up with the school year."

I fondly smiled at him. "That has worked out well for you, hasn't it?"

Rich nodded, then said to Kanji, "Taking special needs kids out on the river to study the history of the lower Columbia region was court-ordered."

"Court ordered?" asked Kanji. "Were you guilty of a crime?"

"Well, yes and no," said Rich. "I had no personal knowledge of crimes that were being committed, so I was an unknowing accomplice. I'm just grateful the judge decided I could work off my sentence doing community service."

"Which you love doing," I interjected.

"Which I love doing," Rich echoed, smiling.

"Then, if I may ask, what was the purpose of the boating group you took out today?"

Rich sighed. "It's been seven days since Mateo Rodriquez went missing. The Coast Guard is no longer looking for him. For all intents and purposes, he died working out on the ocean. Several of his friends at the cannery wanted to release a wreath and some flowers outside the mouth of the river before their shift today."

Kanji nodded solemnly. "Is that a tradition of this community?"

"Yes," said Rich. "The first Saturday in May is our annual Blessing of the Fleet. That's when most of the charters go out together to receive a religious blessing to ensure a safe and bountiful season. But it's also an annual remembrance that the ocean is to be respected at all times, and that there may be fishermen who do not return each year. Today, Mateo's friends wanted to honor him specifically."

"Was Nova with them?" I asked.

"Of course," Rich replied. "And in the beginning she was hanging in there real well, but then we got out into the ocean and she saw a fish spotter flying a grid, and she just broke down and lost it."

"Oh, Rich, that must have been hard on all of you."

"It was," Rich agreed. "The ocean giveth, and the ocean taketh away."

"Excuse my ignorance," said Kanji, "but could you please explain what a fish spotter is, and why it would upset Nova to see it flying something called a grid?"

Rich smiled. "There are six or seven pilots over in Fort George who are hired by fishermen on both sides of the river to locate signs of salmon or tuna or sardines so that they don't have to waste fuel fishing in areas that have no fish.

"There are all kinds of visual clues out there—rip lines, slicks, weed lines, birds, and surface activity.

"Birds usually feed on bait fish, as do some larger sport fish, such as salmon and tuna, which are both surface feeders, as opposed to bottom feeders."

Rich took a swig from his coffee mug. "Tuna often run in the company of porpoises, and porpoises are easy to spot, because they do a lot of jumping. Often the tuna are just beneath the porpoise pod.

"Today the fish spotters were looking for a sardine carpet stain—it's like a giant teardrop under the water. They can spot a school of sardines, which is a giant bait ball, at three or four thousand feet. It looks like a teardrop if they are on the move."

"This is all very interesting," said Kanji. "But I do not understand why it would so upset Miss Nova."

"I'm sorry," said Rich. His face flushed. "Sometimes I talk too much."

I had already smelled the distinct odor of booze on his breath, and had wondered just what ratio of bourbon to coffee he was toting with him in his travel mug.

"Nova saw the plane and got a crazy idea to put up the Estrella Nueva as collateral so she'd have enough money to hire all the fish spotters at once to fly patterns along the current to continue looking for Mateo."

"Oh..." said Kanji, nodding. "Now I think I understand."

We briefly sat in silence, then Kanji asked, "I saw you dancing with Nova at the party Saturday. Was she asking you then to take your boat out for her today?"

It was an innocent enough question, but Rich narrowed his eyes and glared at Kanji for a long moment before answering. "Everyone on the docks is like family. Nova and Mateo and I have known each other for years. I even helped Nova modify the Estrella so Mateo could have access in his wheelchair."

Rich took a deep breath. "And for your information, it was Miguel, from the cannery, who asked me to take my boat out today. Nova had nothing to do with it."

I studied Rich's face. Yes, I knew they'd all been friends for years, but it felt like he might be over-explaining his relationship with Nova just a tad. And I wondered, not for first time, if maybe they really did have something going on in private.

My fish and chips were gone, my soda can was empty, and there seemed to be little left to say, so we gathered up our trash and disposed of it in a garbage can set out for the purpose of collecting such picnic trappings. I whistled to get their attention, then gave a "two thumbs up" to the folks in the Pier 103 boat, hugged Rich goodbye, and Kanji and I were on our way.

But shrugging off the thought of Rich and Nova conspiring to get rid of Mateo was easier said than done, and our return trip north was rather quiet. Amicable, but quiet.

That silence was immediately shattered when we pulled up into the Clamshell driveway. Kanji's puppy was tied to the commercial dumpster at the far end of the parking lot and he was barking up a storm.

The lid to the dumpster was closed, and there was a two-step stepstool standing next to it. I recognized the stepstool from a previous visit to Jimmy's residence. It was the one I had used to get access to his living quarters

142

through his bedroom window when he thought someone might be trying to kill him.

Kanji had the door open, and jumped from the car almost before we had come to a full stop. He ran to the puppy to comfort him, while I was worried much more about what we might find inside the dumpster.

"There, there," he sat on the ground, and held the wriggling pup on his lap. "It's okay. Daddy's home."

Before I could say anything, there was a rapping from inside the dumpster. "Hello? Who's out there? Can somebody help me?"

Kanji stood up and lifted the dumpster lid high overhead, where it balanced on its own, aimed toward the sky. Jimmy timidly looked over the rim of the opening, his hands on each side of his face, like in the old "Kilroy was here" graffiti.

"Are you alright?" I asked. "You haven't broken anything, have you?"

"I'm fine," said Jimmy, sighing.

"Then perhaps you'd like to explain how it was you came to be trapped inside the dumpster?" said Kanji, who was now holding his dog in his arms.

"I'd really rather not," said Jimmy. "If you could just hand me the stepstool, I can climb out and we can all just go on about our own business."

I folded my arms across my chest. "Oh no you don't." I shook my head. "No story, no stepstool."

Kanji looked at me, horrified. "Are you serious that you will not assist him in getting out of there without him first telling us how and why he got in there in the first place?"

I was bluffing, but Kanji didn't know me well enough to know that. Jimmy, the world's worst poker player, might have known I wouldn't make good on my threat if he'd paid closer attention when we played cards.

"That's right. No story, no stepstool," I repeated, deadpan.

"Oh geez, Syl..."

Jimmy looked uncomfortable, Kanji looked aghast, and I stood my ground.

"Okay, fine!" said Jimmy. "Whatever! Just get me out of here!"

"Story first."

I'm sure by now Kanji must have thought I was some kind of heartless monster, but I knew that if we retrieved Jimmy first, any hope of hearing why he'd climbed in there in the first place would be long gone.

"Ok. Fine." Jimmy pushed his glasses up with his middle finger. "Well, you know sometimes I rent a room just for a couple hours, right?" he asked, I suppose for Kanji's benefit more than mine, since I occasionally babysat the motel for him and already knew his rental rules.

"Right."

"So a couple came in this morning, not long after you left, and they spent a few hours in Unit 5."

I nodded. "Go on."

"And after they left, I decided I'd better get with it and clean that unit. It was the only one not all ready to rent." He took a breath. "So I changed the sheets, and replaced the towels, and scrubbed the bathroom, and vacuumed, and—"

"Jimmy! Unless you want to be left in there the rest of the afternoon, just get to the point!"

"Well, I got all done with the cleaning, and I went back into my apartment, and there was a message on the answering machine from the guy who'd rented the unit, telling me not to empty the wastebasket because he'd—he'd accidentally dropped something in there and—and he needed to get it back."

"That sounds quite reasonable," said Kanji, nodding.

"Only I had already emptied the wastebasket into the dumpster," said Jimmy.

"So you climbed in to find it for him." It was a statement from Kanji, and not a question, but Jimmy nodded.

"Now will you please hand me the stepstool?"

Kanji set the pup down and picked up the stool, but I put my hand on his arm to delay him from handing it to Jimmy.

"If that's all there was to the story, you wouldn't have hesitated to tell us right away." Even though I could only see half his face sticking up above the rim of the dumpster, I'd swear I could see him squirm. "So tell us, Jimmy, exactly what was it that the guy had 'accidentally' thrown away?"

"Geez, Syl, do I have to?" I think he already knew the answer to that.

"Fine! Fine! Fine! Geez! You drive a hard bargain," Jimmy began. "I'm getting claustrophobic in here, you know." He paused, perhaps hoping I'd relent, then sighed and said, "Well, the man had, uh... he had a, uh... he had brought a certain type of... uh... *appliance* with him."

"Appliance?" I asked. "You mean like an electric tooth brush?"

"Not exactly."

"Be more specific, Jimbo, unless you want to spend the rest of the day in there." I held my ground.

"Ok, well maybe you'd call it a device," said Jimmy.

"My curiosity is also piqued," said Kanji. "Please explain this appliance device further, and why it is so important to this man."

"*Whatever!*" Jimmy's voice was high-pitched and squeaky and I knew if he'd been standing on firm ground he would have been stamping his feet in a full-blown temper tantrum. "It was a male member enhancement appliance-type device, and when he was through using it, he set it in the wastebasket next to the bed instead of putting it on the nightstand or on the floor or something, and after they both showered and got packed up, he forgot to collect it before they left."

Jimmy's explanation left me wide-eyed and speechless, but Kanji's brow was still furrowed.

"I beg your pardon," said Kanji, "and I do not mean to be intentionally obtuse—"

I'm sure I blushed a color far beyond scarlet, and Jimmy totally lost it.

Beyond frustration, Jimmy yelled, "It was his dick, Kanji! He had a strap-on dick! *The guy accidentally threw his dick away!*"

The silence was deafening, and I couldn't risk even a quick look at Kanji. Talk about Too Much Information!

Kanji, bless his heart, was the first to partially recover. He quietly handed the stepstool to Jimmy, who climbed out, with an ominous paper bag clutched in his hand. "And will you be mailing this man's—personal item—to him?" asked Kanji.

"No," said Jimmy, stomping off toward the motel office. "I'll just give it to him the next time they check in. They're both locals." He stopped at the top of the office steps and turned to glare at me. "It's a hotel manager's job to be discreet, so don't ask me any more questions. I've said all I'm going to say."

I'd learned my lesson, and pressed him for no additional information.

CHAPTER 12

I roared into the back casino parking lot on Tuesday, parked my bike next to Mercedes' motorhome, hooked my helmet to the handlebar, climbed the two metal steps to the front, and only door, and banged loudly. "Open up, Merc. It's after noon."

I could hear Mercedes padding around in there, but she certainly took her sweet time coming to the door. Finally, she opened the door a crack and peered out. "Holy Mother Forklift! Are you some kind of sick sadist or something? That much sunlight without warning could blind me!"

"You're not a vampire, Merc, and a little vitamin D won't kill you."

She pushed the door open a smidgen wider. "Come on in, but be on the look out for Brutus. He's hiding. I guess we both had kind of a hard night last night."

After my experience in the Clamshell parking lot the day before, I didn't want to know what she considered a hard night, even though I briefly wondered if it had anything to do with Sheriff Donaldson.

"Go get dressed," I told her. "I need a wing woman, and I choose you."

Mercedes trotted back to her bedroom while I stepped into the motorhome living room, if you could call it that. I headed straight for the miniature couch, clear across the room, but just two and a half steps from the door. Putting one knee up on the seat, I grabbed the back of the orange love seat with both hands, and peered behind it.

Yep, there was Brutus, all 10 or 12 quivering pounds of him. He looked up at me with his big, brown eyes and I felt almost sorry for the little guy. Brutus is a long-haired dachshund, which Mercedes insists she got "for protection," but as far as I can tell, all he is interested in protecting are the dust bunnies behind the couch.

I didn't even try to coax him out. No telling what the poor guy had witnessed last night. He was probably traumatized. Of course, if I mentioned that to Mercedes, she might want to sign him up for doggie counseling or something.

"Mercedes! Come on! Hurry up!"

Merc re-emerged from her bedroom dressed head to toe in something that looked like a cross between a tie-dyed kimono and a neon sarong. In other words, she looked just like she always looked—overdressed and accessorized to the hilt, with dozens of arm bangles and bracelets, and massive multi-colored earrings dangling to her shoulders.

"What's the rush? It's Kanji's first day at work. No doubt Freddy will be showing him the ropes and neither one of them will have too much time to talk."

"Actually, Freddy had him come in last night to get the lay of the land," I told her.

"The lay of the land?" asked Mercedes. "I hear through the grapevine that you may be in contention for that particular title, Syllee."

I froze with my hand on her doorknob. "Who's been talking about me? What have you heard?"

Mercedes smiled her most enigmatic smile. "Why do you suppose Freddy had Kanji come in last night?"

"I have no interest in playing guessing games with you

today."

"Freddy called Kanji to come in last night to make sure he wasn't spending a little too much time with you yesterday, if you get my drift. And you know what they say—keep your friends close, and your competition closer."

"Only Freddy says that, Merc, so you've obviously been talking to Freddy."

"He's worried, Sylvia. He knows a good thing when he sees it, and he's afraid you'll throw him over for some guy a little closer to your own age with a crazy-great accent."

"So now Freddy's confiding in you, huh?"

"Hairdressers, bartenders, and lounge singers make the best therapists."

I was hardly in a position to argue. I needed Mercedes to be my reason for hanging out at the casino lounge today. Or so I thought.

I left my motorcycle parked next to Merc's motorhome and we walked the short distance across the back lot, and on into the main parking area.

"Don't you ever carry a purse?" asked Merc, exaggeratedly swinging her sequin-studded handbag as we walked.

"I've got everything I need in my pockets," I replied, tapping each of my pockets as I talked. "Car keys, money, driver's license, cell phone. If I carried a purse, I'd always be forgetting where I set it down. And besides," I asked rhetorically, "what kind of a gal who rides a motorcycle carries a handbag?"

"So where do you keep your heat?"

"My what?!"

"Your heat—your gun. And your pepper spray. And condoms—condoms are another form of protection, you know. Seems to me you're a few pockets short, Syl."

A half dozen caustic replies flew through my mind, but I stuck with a more generic response. "Mercedes, you're one of a kind."

Although it was early afternoon on a Tuesday, there were quite a few cars parked out front, and I didn't think all of them belonged to overnight hotel guests at this time of day.

"Hey," said Mercedes, "isn't that Meredith's red Saturn over there?"

I looked where she was pointing, and confirmed that it was indeed a red Saturn, but that I thought Tuesday afternoons were belly dancing practice days at the Senior Center.

"Well, look what's parked next to it," said Merc. "Nadine's smart car, the one with the cute little eyelashes over the headlights."

I froze in my tracks. Good grief and gravy! If I wasn't mistaken, the next three cars after that were Goodie's Toyota Corolla, Orpha's Crown Vic, and Nova's Outback.

"Are they here to practice their dancing? Are they going to be a part of the regular entertainment at the casino?" I could hear the tone of my voice rising.

"Beats me," said Mercedes. "I suppose the boss can have anyone he wants entertain on occasion, but I got a contract. If he thinks he's going to bump me out of the spotlight, for that veiled geriatric dance troupe, he's got another think coming!"

I might have laughed if I hadn't seen the look on her face. "It's probably nothing," I told her, trying to smooth her ruffled feathers. "Maybe it's a bar mitzvah or something, and they're all just here as witnesses."

I had tried to make a joke to lighten things up, but Mercedes was not to be placated. "Those broads better not be trying to take my place, cause I might forget that I'm a lady and do something definitely unladylike."

I couldn't imagine what that might be, and for just a moment, I was almost looking forward to it. "Let's not jump to any hasty conclusions."

We paused on the drawbridge spanning the sturgeon-filled moat, and Mercedes threw in a couple coins "for luck." She was one superstitious old gal, that's for sure, but then I decided it couldn't hurt, and threw a few in for myself.

There was no one rehearsing for anything in the ballroom, and Mercedes breathed a huge sigh of relief. "Guess I won't be having to punch anyone's lights out today after all," she muttered under her breath.

We walked on into the bar, and found the ladies of The Veiled Rainbow, thankfully dressed in their regular street clothes, all lined up like birds on a telephone wire. Perched on consecutive barstools were Meredith, Orpha, Goodie, Nadine and Nova—Red, Orange, Yellow, Green and Blue. I wondered if they'd sat that way on purpose.

Behind the bar were Kanji and Freddy, laughing and talking with the gals like it was some kind of party. And maybe it was.

Mercedes and I sat down at a table for two, and I loudly cleared my throat. Either no one noticed us, or else everyone pretended not to notice us.

"I got this," said Mercedes. She reached inside her little sequined handbag and retrieved her police whistle, another of the items she insisted were "for protection." I caught her arm just as she was raising the whistle to her lips.

"Merc! Don't you dare!"

Apparently my voice carried much better than my throat clearing, and Kanji hurried over to wait on us.

"I didn't know you were going to be a bartender here," I said, shooting a look past him and over at Freddy.

"A Hospitality Specialist must fill many shoes," Kanji replied. "The regular bartender called in sick with an abscessed tooth, and I offered to fill in. I tended bar to help pay my way through college, and the skills I learned then have served me well."

Mercedes was smacking her lips. "What do you recommend today to quench our thirst?" she asked. "We've both got a mighty powerful thirst."

Kanji smiled, his perfect teeth lighting up the room. He spoke directly to Mercedes when he said, "May I recommend you try a Spartini? It's our signature drink."

"A what?" I asked, even though I was sure there was nothing wrong with my hearing.

"A Spartini," Kanji repeated. "It's new today; I created it myself."

I'll bet Freddy just loved that. One day on the job, and the new guy had come up with a signature drink, aptly named after the Spartina Point Casino and Resort.

"How do you make it?" asked Merc.

"First," said Kanji, "I fill a cocktail shaker with ice. Then I add vodka and just enough jalapeño juice to give it a little kick. I cover the shaker and shake it until the outside of the shaker has frosted. Then I strain it into a martini glass and garnish it with a blade of Spartina grass, woven back and forth onto a swizzle stick."

"Just like putting a worm on a hook," volunteered Mercedes.

"I will have to take your word for that," said Kanji. His brow furrowed, then relaxed. "Would you like to try one, Miss Mercedes?"

"You betcha!" said Merc enthusiastically. "It sounds

absolutely yummy!"

"And for you," said Kanji, speaking to me this time, "may I suggest a club soda with a splash of cranberry juice and a lime garnish? We shall name it after you and call it Sylvia's Signature Cranberry Splash, and it will be our non-alcoholic offering in honor of all the cranberries produced on the peninsula."

"That's perfect. Thank you." I nodded dumbly. "And will it have a Spartina Swizzle Stick in it as well?"

"I hadn't thought of that, but it might be a good idea. I'll run it by the boss and see what he thinks."

I smiled up at him. "And will you also be adding Chai Tea to the beverage list?"

Kanji smiled back, and the sizzle between us was almost palpable. "If you, dear lady, would be interested in drinking Chai Tea with me, I shall make it a top priority of the new and improved bar list."

As soon as he left the table, Mercedes leaned over to whisper, "Where do you suppose they get the Spartina grass they use for the garnish?"

"Why? Shallowwater Bay is chock full of the stuff. What difference does it make where they get it?"

"I'm just hoping it isn't some that Brutus has gone wee-wee on," said Merc. "That's a little more 'signature' than I'd care to taste."

If I'd been drinking anything at that particular moment, I would have sprayed it all over the table. "Perhaps that's a question you should personally ask Kanji," I said.

But it was Freddy, and not Kanji, who delivered our beverages, both of which contained Spartina Swizzles. "Club soda and cranberry for the lady looking quite fine in her leathers today, if I may say so, and one very special

Spartini for the equally-fine looking Mercedes," he said as he set our drinks in front of us.

Without asking our permission, Freddy pulled another chair up to our table and sat down. "The Spartina Point Casino and Resort has a signature drink! How about that?"

"Tell me the truth," I said. "Did you even know what a signature drink was before Kanji came up with it?"

Freddy grinned like a Cheshire cat, and recited from memory: "A signature drink is any unique or original drink that expresses the nature of the person or establishment creating it. Signature drinks often incorporate local ingredients and culture."

"Did you look that up on Wikipedia?"

Freddy clutched his hand over his heart, feigned momentary indignation, then winked at me. "Of course I did!"

Mercedes and I both laughed. It was tough not to love a man who embraced his vulnerability. Whoa! Hold on a minute! Love? Who said anything about love? My neck and cheeks began to feel uncomfortably warm.

"So what brings Merri's Widows out today?" I asked, abruptly changing the subject.

"You told me not to call them that," said Freddy.

"It's different when I say it. It's my mother and her friends we're talking about."

Freddy sighed, started to challenge my way of thinking, then wisely thought better of it. "None of the ladies like to drive at night, so they came up in the middle of the day to give Kanji some moral support."

"That was awfully nice of them, don't you think so, Sylvia?" said Merc.

"Yes," I said when I found my voice. "Awfully nice." And for just a moment, I wondered which of those old barstool buzzards had set their sights on Kanji. To them, he might be seen as nothing more than a piece of fresh peninsula meat, dropped from the sky solely for their entertainment.

I instantly heard how shallow that sounded when it went through my mind and I realized I was no better than any of them.

My unflattering self-talk was interrupted when Meredith looped by our table on her way out the door. "I'd love to stay and chat, but I've gotta run, kids," she said, fluttering her fingers in our direction. "I've got places to be." She blew an air kiss and kept right on walking. Well, at least that ruled her out as the old broad with her cap set for Kanji.

While Mercedes was talking to Freddy about her new work schedule, I looked back and forth between Kanji and Freddy. Any woman in her right mind would be in Seventh Heaven to have the attention of just one of these fine men. How did I get so lucky as to have them both come a-courting?

"We can certainly check the master entertainment calendar in my office," Freddy was saying to Mercedes when my ears checked back in to their conversation. "Would you like to do that now?"

Mercedes stood up. "Yes, I would. That way I can do some long-range planning in case I might want to take a little vacation somewhere or something."

Mercedes? Take a vacation? That was the first I'd heard of her wanting to take a trip anywhere. What was she up to now? And, more to the point, where was she thinking of going, and exactly whom did she think would be going with her? Oh, never mind on that last question. I was pretty sure I could guess.

Taking her Spartini with her, Merc followed Freddy from the room, and I decided to move up to the bar instead of sitting there at the table all by my lonesome. I picked up my Cranberry Splash, and slid onto the empty barstool next to Nova.

"Sylvia!" Orpha called out, from the far end of the group. "We were just talking about you!"

"Me? Why me?"

"We're looking for Violet."

"Uh, Orpha?" I laughed. "Perhaps you need to call the florist."

"Not Violets," said Orpha, speaking across both Goodie and Nadine. "A Violet. Singular. We only need just one."

"I'm afraid I'm not following you." I looked to the other gals for a clarification, but no help was immediately forthcoming.

"Meredith is red, then orange," Orpha pointed to herself, "then yellow," she pointed to Goodie, "then green and blue," she pointed to Nadine and Nova, "and you! Sitting on the end there! Violet!"

"Oh no you don't!" I finally got the gist of what she was implying and started to feel a wave of panic coming on. "I'm not nearly old enough to join your Veiled Rainbow! Whatever gave you the idea I'd be interested in such a thing?"

"You could at least pretend to think about it," said Nadine.

"You're a already a member of the Senior Center," said Goodie.

"And you like to stay in shape," Nova chimed in.

They were ganging up on me. I looked in desperation at Kanji, but he was leaning back against the back counter by the cash register, arms folded across his chest, with an amused smile on his face. I could tell he wasn't going to be any help.

"I— Uh—" My mind raced for an escape. "I'm pretty busy."

"Doing what?" asked Orpha.

Leave it to Orpha to pin me against the wall.

"You're retired, just like us," said Goodie.

"Are you afraid you can't keep up?" asked Nadine.

"I'll bet she doesn't want to compete with Meredith," said Orpha.

Compete? That didn't make any sense. I met Nova's eyes. "Help me."

Nova shook her head. "Not a chance," she said. "I'm tired of being the baby of this group. We could use some younger blood."

It was a long shot, but I suddenly thought of an alternative. "Are there male belly dancers in the middle east?" I asked the group.

"Why yes. Yes, there are," said Nadine.

"I think I know where you're going with this," said Goodie, "but Kanji already turned us down."

Kanji? I hadn't even thought of Kanji! "No, I was thinking that maybe Jimmy would be interested. He likes to get out and about on the peninsula."

The women representing orange, yellow, green, and blue all arched their eyebrows. Kanji's smile widened.

"You all saw Jimmy at the party here Saturday night. He was the one wearing a white poet shirt and lavender slacks. Lavender slacks! Remember? And lavender bejeweled eyeglasses and a matching sequined murse. So you see, he'd be a natural Violet for your troupe! Lavender is already halfway there!"

There was a momentary pause while they all seemed to consider it, then Orpha smacked her hand down on the bar. "Let's ask him!" she declared, looking down the row of her compadres. "After all, who loves rainbows more than gay people?"

I really wish I hadn't been taking a sip of my drink when she'd said that, but Kanji was quick to my rescue with a handful of cocktail napkins.

"So what do you think of the people on the peninsula so far?" I quietly asked him as he wiped the bar in front of me.

He smiled. "I am very much enjoying getting to know all the beautiful women here," he said, meeting my eyes, "*including* your mother and her friends."

He really was charming. I wondered if that was due more to his culture, his upbringing or if maybe—and I instantly hated myself for thinking such a thing—maybe he was some kind of ne'er-do-well gigolo kind of guy and was looking for a woman to support him.

I wasn't sure where that thought had come from, exactly, but in my experience, if something, or someone, seems too good to be true, then you'd best check it out before your heart, or your wallet, got in too deep.

"Isn't that right, Sylvia?" Orpha was asking when I pulled myself back from my crazy thoughts and checked into the conversation at the bar.

I leaned across Nova and gave Orpha a little smile and a shrug. "I'm sorry, would you repeat the question?"

Orpha nodded. "Of course. I'd be happy to. But first I want everyone here to know that I'm not the only one whose mind drifts from time to time." She beamed at the other women at the bar. "Sylvia is more than 30 years my junior, and you've all just witnessed that she sometimes has trouble following the drift of a conversation, too."

I wanted to protest, but kept quiet on that point. "Your question, Orpha?"

"I was just asking you if you'd agree that a nice young man as Kanji would have no trouble at all finding an eligible woman around here to keep time with," said Orpha.

Good grief and gravy! I should have left well enough alone and not encouraged her to repeat the question. All eyes looked at me as my face flamed, and it was all I could do to keep from taking a quick look at Kanji.

Fortunately, before I had to give Orpha an answer, Nova's and my phones both rang simultaneously with a text message. I pulled my phone from my pocket, glanced down, and the hair on my arms stood up. I looked at Nova, who held her screen so I could read it. We had received the same text—from Meredith.

"911! Come quick! I need your help!

CHAPTER 13

Nova and I hit the ground running, as best as middle to senior-aged women in fairly decent but not decathlon shape could, and we were already across the moat before it dawned on me that A, I didn't know where we were going, and B, my motorcycle was parked clear over by Mercedes' motorhome in the far lot.

"Nova! Where is she?"

"Get your bike and follow me!" said Nova, not slowing her stride one bit.

I did as she directed, and wheeled my Harley toward the main exit. Nova was waiting with the motor running in her green-over-gray Outback, and she took off the moment she saw me coming.

Just south of Ocean Crest, where the highway speed limit increases to 50, Nova starting passing cars right and left. Right and left is a figure of speech, of course, as there are no double lane passing zones anywhere along that highway.

Suffice to say she was driving like a maniac, and it was a good thing she had a car top carrier on her vehicle, or I might not have been able to keep track of her.

Nova really had her "pedal to the metal," as we used to say, and under other circumstances I might have teased her about her lead foot. But right now, all I wanted to do was get to my mother—wherever she was—and find out what was wrong.

I don't think Nova ever slowed her car at all until we started nearing the northern city limits of Tinkerstown. Then she abruptly stomped on her brake pedal, and without bothering to signal, took a hard right—right into the driveway of the Clamshell Motel.

Gravel flew in every direction as we both careened around the motel office and came to a stop in two available parking spaces in the line of cars in the back lot. Cars that included Jimmy's split pea green Pinto, Meredith's red Saturn, and a blue, non-descript, late-model Chevy sedan that looked vaguely familiar.

Jimmy came out on the stoop of the office and motioned for us to come inside. "I'm the one who sent you the texts," he began. "Meredith's in no shape—"

"Where's Mom?" I interrupted. My voice was at least an octave or two higher than normal. I quickly pushed my way around Jimmy and continued inside as he held the screen door for Nova.

"Meredith's on the couch. She's fine."

"Fine?" I was confused. "Then why the 911? Nine-one-one is only for flat out, bona fide emergencies!"

Meredith was indeed on the couch, but she was far from fine. Her hair was a mess, her mascara was streaked down her face, and both her hands trembled as she tried, unsuccessfully, to hold a cup of coffee without sloshing it all over the place.

I sat on one side of her, and put my arm around her back. Nova sat on the other side. Jimmy took his usual seat in the oversized Naugahyde recliner. Priscilla, oblivious to anything being out of the ordinary, jumped up into his lap without waiting for an invitation, as did the no-name pup, who had apparently been left in the custody of Jimmy Noble's doggie day care while Kanji was at work.

Knowing Merri was not hurt was some consolation, but she was visibly shaking from head to toe, and that was no exaggeration. I wasn't sure how long I could quietly sit there before climbing out of my skin and jumping all over her—symbolically speaking.

Finally, I couldn't take it the prolonged silence any longer. "Jimmy?" I turned to look at him.

"*Me?! Why me?*" There he was, caught in the headlights again. He bit on his lower lip and his eyes told me that he wasn't going to say anything more.

"Meredith?" Nova said so softly I barely heard her. "Is it Walter?"

"*Walter?!*" I looked from Nova to Mom to Jimmy, who squinched his eyes shut, hoping, I presume, that if he couldn't see me, I couldn't see him.

"What's Walter got to do with—" And then I remembered. I remembered them dancing Saturday night. I remembered them laughing and talking at the movies on Sunday. I remembered Jimmy telling me on Monday that his job as a motel manager was to be discreet. And I remembered whose blue Chevy sedan that was in the parking lot.

"Mom?"

Meredith didn't answer. She just continued to sit there and tremble.

I looked around her and tried again to get some information. "Nova?"

"It's not for me to say," said Nova.

"Jimmy! Please!" I started to stand up, but Priscilla hissed and the puppy made a half-hearted attempt at growling. "Will somebody please tell me what in the blue blazes is going on around here?"

Meredith's eyes finally focused. "Sylvia..." She said my

name like it was a soft sigh. "Sylvia..." She sniffled. "Sylvia, Walter's dead."

Jimmy kept his eyes shut. Nova didn't look all that surprised by the news. As for me, I thought for a moment I was going to throw up all over the coffee table.

A long minute or two passed while I tried to soak it all in. Or wake up. I kind of hoped I'd wake up and— But no, I didn't need to pinch myself to prove I was awake.

Meredith was still looking in my direction, but her eyes didn't quite seem to focus. "You have to help me fix this." She turned to Nova. "Both of you."

"I don't see how," said Nova, frowning. "You're the nurse."

"We have to take him back to his apartment in Unity," said Meredith.

"*What?!*" I looked around. "No! What we have to do is call the police." Was I the only one who thought Merri was talking total nonsense?

"Look, Syl, we have to protect Walter's teaching reputation. Even though he retired a couple years ago, he still has a legacy in the community. If any of his students found out he'd been fooling around, he'd just die..." She suddenly heard what she'd said, and sucked in a hiccup of a sob before continuing.

"Walter simply cannot be found here. There's no way he'd want his ex-wife to discover he'd been meeting anyone in a seedy motel."

"Hey!" said Jimmy, opening his eyes. "This motel is neither sordid nor disreputable. If it was good enough for you two to rendezvous here, then—"

I held up my hand to stop him. "Not now, Jim."

"And..." Meredith hesitated, then refocused on me. "And there's that little matter of me already being under investigation in Mateo's disappearance. How would it look if I were under investigation in *two* middle-aged men's deaths this week?"

Oh geez, that little bit of information hadn't even crossed my mind.

"What do you want us to do, Merri?" asked Nova.

Meredith weakly nodded. "Thank you."

I didn't remember ever saying I'd go along with her plan, whatever it was, but I knew I had to hear her out.

Merri took a big gulp of coffee and swallowed hard before she spoke. "Nova, I'm very sorry to drag you into this, but you're the only one who's got a coffin top on your car," she began.

Nova stiffened. "It's called a car top carrier."

"Roof-rack, luggage rack, rooftop carrier, car top carrier, coffin top—" Jimmy was happy to have something to contribute, but this time it only took one harsh warning look from me to silence him.

"And Jimmy told me he's got a mummy sleeping bag," continued Meredith. "You know, the kind that zips up over the top, all the way closed?"

When no one said anything, she plunged ahead. "We can put Walter in that, then after dark we can hoist him up into—" she looked pointedly at Nova— "the car top *carrier,* and take him back to his own place."

Nova looked puzzled. "Even with the four of us, I don't think we can lift Walter that high, Merri. He must weigh a good one-eighty, one-ninety."

Meredith nodded. "I figured we could back your car up next to the motel office steps, then it wouldn't be so far to lift him from the top of the stoop to the carrier."

The ringing in my ears was getting so loud I was afraid everyone in the room would soon hear it, so I opened my mouth to let the growing noise out.

"If you're going to zip him into a full-body sleeping bag, why do you have to put him up in the coffin top? Why can't Nova just fold the back seat down so we can slide him into the rear of the car?"

Everyone froze for the count of 10. Or maybe 20. Then Merri exhaled with an "aahhh," and hugged me tight. "Honey, you're so smart. I never would have thought of that. I guess I'm just too frazzled to think clearly. That's a wonderful idea. Now all we have to do is wait until dark."

I knew I had plenty more to say on this cockamamie idea, but for some reason, I couldn't get the words to form. I couldn't get past the pounding noise in my ears—Walter was dead. Walter was dead. Walter was dead and he'd been with my mother in a motel room when it happened. Walter was dead. Walter was—"

"Would anyone like to play some cards while we wait?" asked Jimmy, abruptly breaking into my obsessive thought loop. "I could get out my poker table and chips."

"Chips sound good," said Nova, looking back toward the kitchen side of the room. "Do you have anything to eat around here?"

"Whoa! Whoa! Whoa! Now wait just a darn minute," I began. "Let's not be so cavalier about this. Walter is dead. Dead! And I never actually said I would help you keep the location and circumstances of his passing a secret."

"Sure you will," said Merri. "You have to help. You're the one who thought up the plan in the first place."

As the twilight deepened, Meredith and Nova took Jimmy's sleeping bag over to Unit 5 to prepare Walter's body for transport. I didn't ask if they would have to dress him first; I didn't want to know.

I looked at Jimmy, who had remained uncharacteristically calm throughout the late afternoon. "I'm proud of you for not freaking out," I told him.

He looked chagrined. "But I did freak out," he said. "I freaked out real good when Merri came to the door and told me that Walter was dead. My heart started pounding so hard I thought my chest would explode, and for awhile I was hyperventilating and semi-hysterical, and wringing my hands until they hurt."

"So what changed?" I narrowed my eyes and studied his face.

"Meredith gave me a little something from her medical go-bag. Apparently she had a spare kit, cause the police still have the one she had on the boat with Nova. She said what she gave me would calm my nerves." Jimmy smiled. "And it worked."

"Better living through chemistry?" I wasn't sure if I were grateful, or angry with her for dispensing prescription medication without a prescription. Was that woman never going to learn?

Jimmy shook his head. "Don't blame your mother. I was really freaking out, Syl. Really bad. Really, really, really bad. And so was Merri."

"Did she take some of the pills herself?" Until then, I hadn't thought to ask.

"Of course! She said they help her relax, so she can sleep. But—" he said sadly, looking toward the door, "she didn't need them to get to sleep this time."

Good grief and gravy! My mother was a walking pharmacy!

I watched from the kitchen window until Nova gave us the high sign, then turned and told Jimmy they were ready for our help. He donned a baseball cap over his bleached blonde hair and added a pair of sunglasses as we headed out the door.

Unfortunately, the sunglasses took away his depth perception in the growing darkness, and he tripped going down the office steps. Before I could grab him to stop his fall, he was flat on his face in the parking lot. At that moment, his motion sensor porch light, as well as the full array of parking lot lights, came on.

Jimmy apologetically looked up at me. "Oops. I guess I forgot to turn all those outside lights off."

"Oops is right," I said, relieved that he appeared to be unhurt. I gave him a hand up. "Go throw the breaker."

I waited for him next to the stoop, then together we walked solemnly over to Unit 5 in the semi-darkness.

On the motel bed was the sleeping bag, and I tried not to think too much about its contents. "Before we go," I said, "I think we should check for anything that might be left behind. Anything that would indicate Walter had ever been here. Anything that might be missed at home when he's... uh... discovered."

"You mean things like his glasses and his cell phone," said Jimmy.

"You mean things like his socks and underwear," said Merri.

"Whatever you mean," Nova cleared her throat, "it's already been put inside the sleeping bag, but you can double check all you want."

It only took a couple minutes to find nothing more, including anything that might have been accidentally left in the bedside wastebasket, and I was greatly relieved to find it empty.

Nova went out and started up her car. She backed in as close as she could to the door of Unit 5, but a picnic table and portable barbecue grill prevented her from getting as close as we'd hoped.

"Help me move the table," I said to Jimmy, stepping back outside.

"Can't," he replied. "Somebody stole a table from the motel a few years ago, so when I replaced it, I cemented it in place."

"Swell." I went back inside. The evening chill, or perhaps the ominous nature of what we were about to do, was beginning to seep into my bones, and I started shivering.

Nova parked as best she could, got out and opened the hatchback. She joined us inside, and stood with Meredith on one side of the bed while Jimmy and I took our places on the other. Then we solemnly picked up the sleeping bag like pallbearers and started out the door. We stepped down the one short cement platform step and went around the picnic table.

I tried not to think about what—or rather who—was inside the bag. Walter and I had known each other for many years, and I considered him a good friend. Good enough, I rationalized, that allowing his body to be found in his own apartment seemed the right and noble thing to do. Good old Walter would certainly not want Merri to be implicated in another scandal, I told myself, blinking back tears.

Nova's Outback was just a step away when a car suddenly wheeled up the driveway and into the darkened parking lot. And there we were, all four of us—five if you count Walter—totally illuminated by the Scion xB's headlights.

There was nothing we could do, no time to rush back inside, and no place to hide if we did. We were all caught dead to rights, certainly no pun intended.

It took Kanji only a few seconds to take in the scene and figure out exactly what was going on. "I'm calling the police," he said, and without waiting to hear us out, he punched in 9-1-1 on his cell phone, went into his own unit, and closed the door.

There was nothing the rest of us could do but carry the sleeping bag back inside Unit 5 and trudge over to Jimmy's apartment, which we did in total silence. Jimmy flipped the breaker back on for the parking lot, and we all resumed our previous places in his living room—three on the couch, and Jimmy in his command chair.

I was shaking so hard now that I considered asking Meredith for some of her feel-better drugs, but knew I'd need to keep my head as clear as I could for what was surely to come once the sheriff got there.

True to form, Sheriff Donaldson was the first to arrive, followed closely by John Stark, the coroner, and a pair of CSI guys. The scene was horrifyingly reminiscent of what had taken place a few months ago in Unit 4, right across the parking lot from Unit 5, but only Jimmy and I were painfully aware of that.

Time seemed to stand still, yet I knew we'd been sitting there for well over an hour when Freddy pulled in, driving his Inceptor sedan, blue lights flashing. But instead of immediately joining the other investigators, he strode straight through the motel office and into Jimmy's living quarters, still dressed in the same clothes he'd been wearing at the casino this afternoon, despite arriving in the police car.

"Freddy!" I said, genuinely relieved, "I'm so glad you're here."

But Freddy was not there for moral support. He was all

business, which I would have known if I'd seen the clipboard in his hand when he came in. "The sheriff radioed for me to come in and start taking statements," he said. "But by now," he said, glaring at Meredith, "I suppose you've all practiced getting your stories straight."

Meredith, bless her heart, wasn't about to be intimidated. "There has been no crime," she began. "Nobody has done anything wrong. There's no need to take statements from anyone."

Jimmy jumped right in. "A witness statement is a formal document containing your own account of the facts relating to the issues arising in a dispute. The purpose of the witness statement is to provide written evidence to support a party's case that will, if necessary, be used as evidence in court."

Freddy sighed. "Thank you, Mr. Wikipedia." He looked around the room. "Since you've had plenty of time to collaborate your stories," he said, "there's really no point in isolating each one of you. Just remain here in the living room, and stay silent from now on." He looked at each of us in turn. "I'm quite serious when I say you will stay silent. No talking at all. None. And while you're busy doing that, I'll meet with each of you individually at the kitchen table to take your statements."

Somehow we all managed to mutely nod.

"Let's start with you, Meredith," said Freddy, motioning for her to take a chair at the dinette set. "I take it you were the only one present at the time of Mr. Winston's demise?"

"He died of natural causes," insisted Merri, sitting down at the table and crossing her arms. "This is all such a waste of time."

Sheriff Donaldson, trailed by Kanjirappally Kumera,

entered the building just as Meredith was re-explaining her position.

"Sheriff!" exclaimed Merri, "I was just telling your deputy here that there's no need to take anybody's statement. Walter had a heart attack, plain and simple. It was probably brought on from taking Viagra, but nobody forced him to do that. Believe me, Sheriff, there was plenty of foreplay, but no foul play."

I could tell from their expressions that it was obviously too much information for everyone in the room. Including me.

"Is it really important where Walter died?" continued Meredith. "Couldn't that particular detail be left out of the formal record? He'd be embarrassed enough as it is." Then she pulled her trump card. "Just imagine, Sheriff," she said just as sweet and smooth as buttermilk pie, "how you would feel if you unexpectedly died and your body was recovered inside a certain motorhome up in the casino parking lot."

It was the lowest of low blows, but by that time, Meredith must have figured she had nothing left to lose and had pulled out all the stops.

I'm sure we all held our breaths as a torrent of colors and emotions flew across Sheriff D's face. I, for one, was just grateful he paused before saying anything.

Then, without a word to any of us, he pushed the brim of his Stetson back a little on his head and pressed the tactical mic clip on his shoulder strap. "Dispatch, please send Bill and Bob to give the news of Walter Winston's passing, in his sleep, of an apparent heart attack, to his ex-wife, Mrs. Nancy Winston."

He waited while the dispatcher repeated his instructions. "And tell them to tell her she may view his body when she arrives at the mortuary to make arrangements." Then he signed off, and he, like the rest of us, all released the air we'd been holding.

To Freddy he said, "We're still going to need statements. Moving a body, even when no crime has been committed, from one location to another, but still within Washington state, is a gross misdemeanor and carries a penalty of up to 364 days in jail and/or a fine of up to $5,000."

He looked pointedly at all four of us. "And even though the coroner's preliminary examination on cause of death initially agrees with Ms. Meredith Avery's very personal declaration, an official investigation may still be required."

CHAPTER 14

"It's well past my usual dinnertime," said Sheriff D, creating an abrupt segue from the bombshell he'd just dropped to the very mundane topic of food. "Has anyone else eaten?" He rocked back and forth on his heels, waiting for someone to answer him.

I was pretty sure he knew we had not, and wondered what he might have up his sleeve with his seemingly innocent question. In my association with him, Sheriff Donaldson never said or did anything without some sort of ulterior motive or agenda.

Nova shook her head and spoke up for all of us. "Jimmy only had poker chips in his cupboard." She sighed. "I hate to admit it at a time like this, but I'm starving."

"Crime or no crime, we're all going to be here awhile," the sheriff continued, "so we're going to need to eat." He looked at me. "Sylvia, would you mind picking up an order of burgers for us at the High Tide?"

"Why me?" I asked in surprise. "I'm on my motorcycle. I can't carry anything as big as a order of burgers for all seven of—"

Sheriff D held up his hand to silence my protests, then he used his fingers to tick off his reasoning. "One, Freddy and I are in official county vehicles, which must only be used for official county business. Two, Merri and Nova aren't going anywhere at the moment, and neither are their cars. Three, Jimmy can't leave, because it's his motel, and he has a right to be here until we clear the premises. Four, we all know that Jimmy's Pinto is not the most dependable, and I wouldn't be so foolish as to send anyone anywhere in it."

Jimmy made a face, but a fact is a fact, and he did not interrupt.

And..." without missing a beat, the sheriff looked at Kanji, "five, I'm pretty sure Mr. Kumera doesn't even know where the High Tide is located, much less what to order."

"You can call in the order," I countered, "and I'm pretty sure Kanji can find the High Tide with his GPS."

Sheriff D nodded. "You're right."

"I am?"

"It's a very good idea for us to call in the order, but you're still the obvious choice to go and pick it up."

Kanji smiled and gallantly handed me the keys to his Scion xB. "My vehicle is not equipped with Global Positioning," he said, "but I would be honored to have you drive it to retrieve our nourishment."

I took his keys, but something was niggling at the back of my brain. "But— Wait— Do you even eat beef?" I asked Kanji. "Aren't cows sacred in India?"

Kanji actually chuckled. "Thank you for asking, dear Sylvia," he said, with a nod of his head. "Yes, all animals are sacred. And where I am from, in the southern portion of India, you are either a total vegetarian or you are not."

I didn't want to make a fool of myself by admitting I did not know the exact rules concerning vegetarians, vegans, carnivores or omnivores. I'd seen Kanji eat tuna, but if all life was sacred, then did that mean he did or didn't eat beef?

Fortunately, Kanji continued before I could figure out how to phrase my question. "Here, in the United States, many Indians eat meat but not beef. Buffalo is a fine line." He smiled, and looked at Freddy, our group's token Native American. "Of course, I am only speaking for the Indians from India."

I wasn't sure if he was being funny, or even if he'd finally answered my original question, so I followed up with a more direct query. "Kanji, do you want a cheeseburger or something else?"

"A cheeseburger will be most gratefully accepted, thank you."

Freddy's expression was unreadable. There wasn't much point in arguing with the logic of me driving Kanji's car to make the burger run, but he wasn't going down without a fight. "I'll walk you out," he said.

As soon as the office door closed behind us, Freddy took my elbow and turned me toward him. "There's something I need to tell you."

The tone of his voice further tightened the knot that had been residing in my stomach for hours. "I'm not sure anything you 'need to tell me' can make me feel any worse than I do right now," I said wearily, "but feel free to try."

Freddy minced no words. "Kanji Kumera is not who you think he is."

"*What?* Where did this come from? What in the world are you talking about?"

Freddy took a deep breath. "I ran a background check on him and—"

"You did *what?!*" I yanked my elbow away. "How dare you! Of all the underhanded, sneaky, deceitful things you could do to undermine my friendship with Kanji, you had to go and use your police clearance to run a background check on him?"

Freddy shook his head. "It's not like that, Syl. I

promise. I run a background check on all the employment applicants."

Okay, that suddenly made a high degree of sense, and took the wind right out of my self-righteous sails. I glanced over at Unit 5 where the crime lab guys were still busy processing the room and shuddered from head to toe. "Walter..."

"Walter is gone, Sylvia. I need you to focus."

"Okay. Right. Focus. So if Kanjirappally Kumera is an alias, what's his real name?"

"Kanjirappally Kumera *is* his real name, and he's really from Chicago, but he's not a retired accountant."

"So? What difference does it make what occupation he's retired from?"

Freddy hesitated before answering. "He's not retired from anything, Syl. He's working undercover for the insurance fraud division of the company that has paid life insurance benefits to Merri, Goodie, Nadine, and is now considering Nova's claim."

"Oh." I leaned heavily against Freddy's shoulder as the implications hit me. "*Oh!*"

"I've already informed the sheriff," said Freddy, "but what Kanji's doing is not illegal. And with him working at Spartina Point, I've a good chance to keep an eye on him."

"Well, he was certainly getting an earful from the ladies in the bar this afternoon."

Freddy nodded. "Bartenders, beauticians, and lounge singers hear it all."

"Now you're sounding like Mercedes."

I got into Kanji's Scion and slowly started down the driveway. Freddy had sure given me a lot to think about, starting with the fact that I had spilled my guts to Kanji about Nadine and Goodie during our tour of the south end of the peninsula Monday morning.

But as soon as I pulled out onto the highway, I had other things to worry about. Instantly, I could tell that something was wrong with Kanji's car. Whump-whump-whump-whump. The more I picked up speed, the faster the whumping noise. "Holy Criminitly! Flat tire!" I said aloud, then pulled a U-turn right in the middle of the road and slowly limped back to to the Clamshell Motel.

Kanji and Freddy had seen the vehicle pull back into the driveway and they both met me in the parking lot. "That was either the world's fastest burger run," said Freddy, "or you forgot something."

"Or perhaps there is something wrong with the vehicle?" asked Kanji, concerned.

I nodded. "I think there's a flat tire." The three of us walked around the vehicle, checking out each tire, but we were unable to locate any problem.

"What made you think it was a flat tire?" asked Kanji.

"The whole car shook. I heard and felt a definite 'whump, whump, whump' that went faster as I went faster."

"Was the steering effected?" asked Freddy.

"Um... No, I don't think so, why?"

Freddy and Kanji exchanged a look, then Kanji instructed me to get back into the car and start it up.

I did as I was told, leaving my driver's door open, and the men walked around to the passenger side. Kanji opened the back door and pressed his finger on the button to put the window up.

"It should be fine now," said Freddy, as they returned to my side of the car.

"What do you mean, 'it should be fine now'?"

Kanji looked a little embarrassed. "I left the back window down a little for the pup to put his nose out," he explained.

"It's called the helicopter effect," added Freddy.

"The helicopter effect?" I looked from one guy to the other. "I don't understand."

"It's also called side window buffeting," said Kanji. "Particularly at highway speeds, a wave of pressure pushes the air in and out of the back window of the car, making a helicopter-rotor-like din."

"So—" I tried to wrestle the thoughts around into something I could understand. "So I almost called a tow truck because a window was left down?"

Neither Freddy nor Kanji said a word, but I could tell by the way their faces puckered that they were both trying hard not to smile.

"Hey! It's not my fault! I've never had a car with four doors, or a back window you could roll down! How was I supposed to know?" I stopped myself just short of playing the 'girl card,' but it still irked me that females had not been able to take auto basics back when I was in high school.

I turned to Kanji. "It rains a lot around here." I nearly spit the words out. "You might want to keep all your windows rolled up when you're not driving your no-name dog around town."

He nodded his head in his adorable semi-bow way. "Thank you, my dear Sylvia, for your concern. I will certainly do that."

My face still flaming hot, I left for a second time to pick up our dinner, which by now was surely ready and waiting for me.

What I didn't know would be waiting for me at the High Tide was Raven, the newest ace reporter for the North Beach Tribune.

"Raven? Are you working here now?" I asked

unnecessarily. Well, duh. She was obviously working there—she was standing behind the take-out counter with an apron tied around her waist.

"I'm just an intern at the newspaper," she said, "so I still have to work for a paycheck somewhere."

"Of course. Well, good for you for being so ambitious!"

"Your order is ready, Ms. Avery: Seven tsunami cheeseburger baskets and seven shakes. Four chocolate mint and three fresh strawberry. Will that be all?"

"That should be plenty," I replied, reaching for my credit card in my back pocket, and suddenly wondering if anyone was going to reimburse me for all this food.

Raven waved off my card. "Oh no, Ms. Avery, it's already been taken care of. We got a credit card number from Deputy Morgan when he called in the order."

I was certainly grateful to hear that bit of information, but now something else was niggling the back of my brain. "How did you know I was picking up this particular order?" I asked. "I could have just been coming in to get something for myself. Did Deputy Morgan mention my name?"

Raven smiled, and by her self-satisfied smirk I knew that she knew something was up, and I braced myself for what was coming next.

Bless her heart, Raven cut straight to the point. "No, he didn't mention who was coming in to get the order," she said. "I just put two and two together."

"You put two and two together and came up with me picking up an order for seven?"

Raven shook her head. "Between customers, we listen to the police scanner back in the kitchen," she continued. "So we know a Caucasian male in his middle 70s died at the Clamshell Motel a few hours ago, and I figured both Sheriff Donaldson and Deputy Morgan would be called out on this one."

Impressed, I nodded, but didn't say anything, cringing inside for the question I knew she was about to ask.

"But we don't know who died. Can you share the man's name with me?"

"I'm sorry, Raven. I don't believe the man's family has been notified yet."

"Was he alone when he died?"

I muttered the words, "I wish" before I realized I'd spoken aloud.

Raven's eyes lit up, and the next volley of questions came at me rapid-fire. Who was with him? Was it a local? Was he murdered? Are there any suspects? Who else is at the Clamshell right now with you and Deputy Morgan? Did the motel manager see anything? What's the motel manager's name? Isn't it Jimmy something? Do you think I could interview him after I get off work?"

"Raven! Stop!"

Thankfully, she did stop talking, but I think it was because she had temporarily run out of air.

I took a deep breath. "Raven..." I knew I had to choose my words very carefully. "I appreciate that you're a very ambitious young woman, and that you are very interested in making a name for yourself while you're interning at the Tribune. But Raven, there are responsibilities that come with being a journalist. People can get unnecessarily hurt when they are falsely accused. Please be careful about damaging a person's reputation. It's a very small community."

She nodded, but I couldn't tell if she'd taken to heart anything I'd said.

I got my answer to that when she asked if there was going to be an official investigation. Apparently my well-intentioned speech had fallen on deaf ears.

Raven helped me carry the food to the car, and asked that I keep her in the loop. I couldn't do anything but nod, and despite the delicious smell of burgers accompanying me on the return trip, I drove off with the same sick feeling in my stomach I'd had pretty much all week.

Back at the Clamshell, the crime lab guys were just leaving, and Sheriff D was already out in the parking lot, so he helped me carry the food inside.

I didn't have to ask them what they'd been talking about in my absence. I was greeted with cheering and clapping as I walked through the door, and I knew it wasn't just because I'd picked up the food.

"You made it!" exclaimed Merri.

"My hero!" Nova chimed in.

"No more flat tires?" asked Freddy.

"I am happy to see you have returned without further incident," said Kanji.

And of course, Jimmy put in his two cents with, "The helicopter effect is also known as wind throb, but the technical term is Helmholtz resonance."

Only Sheriff Donaldson wisely kept his mouth shut.

I set the box of burger baskets and shakes on the table and glared at Freddy.

"Hey!" he said, "What's with the stink eye? It could just as well have been Kanji who told them."

"But it wasn't, was it?"

The question was rhetorical. And although Kanji might not have told anyone about my ignorance concerning the Scion's window function, that didn't make him any kind of Boy Scout. After all, he had been playing me since the day we'd first met.

I guessed correctly that three strawberry shakes

belonged to Jimmy, Meredith, and Kanji, and the rest of the order was all the same, so it was easy to pass out the food, and a copious amount of napkins.

Meredith and Nova remained on the couch on the living room side of the open space using the coffee table to set their food on, and Jimmy was in his command chair. The sheriff, Freddy, Kanji and I ate at the table in the kitchen. Kanji's pup was camped under the table, hoping, I presumed, for a bite of burger, while Priscilla seemed quite content to have Jimmy's lap all to herself for once.

Conversation during dinner shifted to the Mariners' new manager and the possibility of a run at the pennant this year. Nice, polite, safe conversation. Normally, I would have had a few things to contribute, as baseball is my favorite spectator sport, but today I was busy brooding. And occasionally glaring at Kanji.

As we finished eating, Freddy walked around the combined living and dining rooms gathering the paper trash while Sheriff D set up his laptop at one end of the kitchen table.

Kanji approached me and quietly asked if he'd done something wrong.

"You tell me," I said, barely keeping a snarl out of my voice.

He gave me a long, thoughtful look, and there was an unexpected sadness in his deep brown eyes. He nodded, just once. "I am truly sorry, Sylvia." Then he moved to stand between the two areas and called for the group's attention.

"Excuse me, everyone." Kanji said loudly. "But I have something of major importance to say to you all."

Sheriff D, Freddy and I already knew what he was about to say, but Merri, Nova and Jimmy had no idea what was coming.

"I must now inform you that I am not who you think I am," he began.

"You're not Kanjirappally Kumera?" asked Meredith.

"Did you know," said Jimmy, "that Kumera is another name for sweet potato? It originated in—"

"Not now, Jim," I said in the voice I usually reserve for telemarketers.

"No," continued Kanji, "my name is correct, which is most likely why my true purpose on the North Beach Peninsula has been discovered." He looked at Freddy. "I never expected to be offered a job here, and I certainly never expected my employer to be a man who also worked for the Sheriff's Department."

Jimmy perked right up. "Are you in the witness protection program?"

"No, it is nothing like that," said Kanji, shaking his head. Then he spoke directly to Freddy. "You ran a background check on me, did you not?"

Freddy nodded. "I run them on all my job applicants."

"If I'd had any idea that would be the case, I would have turned down the offer immediately," said Kanji. "But working at Spartina Point would have given me a wonderful opportunity to learn inside information about many of the local residents."

"You mean information to learn about the members of The Veiled Rainbow, do you not?" asked Sheriff Donaldson.

Meredith and Nova both gasped.

"It is true," said Kanji. "I came here specifically to investigate four of the five women who participate in that group."

Meredith caught on quickly. "Nova, Goodie, Nadine,

and me."

"But why?" asked Nova. "What have we done?"

"You're not a retired accountant?" asked Jimmy.

"No, my friend, I am not," said Kanji, bowing his head toward Jimmy, "and I am deeply sorry for the deception. I am still working. I was sent here by my employer, and I am actually an insurance fraud investigator."

"Insurance fraud?" said Nova.

Meredith patted Nova's hand and spoke directly to her. "It's okay, Hon, none of us have done anything illegal."

"When Nova's preliminary claim arrived, pending the official declaration of death, it set off a chain of events that resulted in me being sent here undercover," said Kanji. "Four women, with five major claims, all from such a small area, all under highly suspicious circumstances and inside a relatively short period of time— Well, the company felt it warranted another look into all five of the claims."

"The first two belong to Meredith, then Goodie, Nadine, and now Nova," said Jimmy to no one in particular. "Wow."

Wow, indeed. The room fell quiet, each of us silently considering the possible fallout and consequences of such an investigation.

It was Meredith who spoke up first. "You might as well know this now," she began warily. "There will soon be one more claim filed."

Every head snapped in her direction, and I, for one, was holding my breath, scared clear to the tips of my toes for what I feared was coming next.

"Walter had me help him fill out a new online life insurance policy with your company last Sunday evening," she said. Then pointedly looking at me, she added, "After we went to see a movie."

"Mother!" I exclaimed, leaping to my feet. "Please tell me you're *not* the beneficiary!"

Kanji waved both his hands in front of him to shush the group. "Meredith is not the beneficiary," he said. "I took the liberty of checking that fact after Sheriff Donaldson was kind enough to tell me the name of the deceased in Unit 5."

"I only told him Walter's name because he's the one who called the police, and because I already knew who he really was and why he was here," said Sheriff D, trying to tap dance around the fact that he'd violated his standard, "I cannot comment on an ongoing investigation" reply to any and all inquiries.

"None of the women of The Veiled Rainbow will profit from Walter's death," said Kanji.

"Does his wife Nancy get the money?" I asked.

"Ex-wife," interjected Merri. "His divorce has been final for some time. That's why he wanted to make an insurance change—so she wouldn't get any more money out of him."

"Then who?" My curiosity was getting the best of me.

Kanji looked at Meredith. "It is not my place to say."

Meredith looked at me.

"Oh no, no, no!" My heart leaped up into my throat. "Mom! Please tell me it's not me!"

"Chill, Syl, it's not you," said Merri with a shrug. "Walter's sole beneficiary is Felicity."

CHAPTER 15

Felicity. Holy Criminitly! Someone was going to have to break the news of Walter's passing to Felicity, and I hoped to hell and high water it wasn't going to be me. Felix and Walter been good friends for years, lived in the same apartment building by the high school down in Unity, and he was her unofficial teaching mentor.

Sheriff D must have read my mind. He caught my eye and shook his head. "I'll have Bill and Bob take care of all the pertinent notifications."

Still in a daze, I nodded, but mentally wrestled with the thought that I should be there when she was given the sad news. Felicity would be devastated. I looked at Sheriff D and mouthed. "When?"

He looked at his watch. "Felicity won't be notified until morning."

I weakly nodded again. "Okay. Good." Waiting till morning bought me a little time to brace myself for Felicity's grief—and shock—when she learned she was named on Walter's life insurance policy.

When I tuned back in to the general conversation, Kanji was talking. "So unless there's been foul play, or fears of a conspiracy, or some other irregularity in Walter's death when the medical examiner completes his report, Felicity will not be under investigation," he said. "My company sent me here to review the payments already made to Meredith, Goodie, and Nadine, while Nova's claim is on an indefinite hold."

"But what about the Estrella Nueva?" asked Meredith. "With the boat impounded and no money coming in, how will Nova make her payments on time without the insurance money? Mateo would not have wanted to die in vain."

"Mateo would not have wanted to die in vain," echoed Kanji. "Interesting choice of words."

Another deep silence engulfed the entire room.

"Do I need a lawyer?" Nova finally asked in a soft voice.

"Have you done anything wrong?" asked Sheriff Donaldson.

"No, she has most certainly not," Meredith answered for her. "And neither have I."

"Jimmy, do you have anything stronger than this milkshake to drink?" asked Nova, waving her paper cup in the air.

"I could make coffee," said Jimmy, missing Nova's intention.

"I have an idea." Sheriff D put the finger and thumb of his right hand under his nose and drew them apart along his salt-and-pepper mustache. "It's a little outside of the box, but we all want to see justice served, right?"

Most of us nodded or murmured our agreement, while Meredith just glared at Sheriff D suspiciously.

"Excuse me," said Kanji, looking bewildered, "but if anyone responding to your question said no, then wouldn't you think they were guilty of something?"

"It's called a rhetorical question," I explained. "It didn't really need an answer."

"So in the name of justice," continued the sheriff, "why don't we all put our heads together and see if we can't help

Mr. Kumera get the answers he needs so he can determine that no one has done anything wrong here and be on his way?"

"I'm all for that," said Freddy, far too quickly.

Much to Kanji's surprise, everyone seemed to be on board with that idea.

"It is most generous of you not to be angry with me for my initial deception," he said, "but your offer to assist me in my investigation is beyond belief."

"We've got nothing to hide," said Meredith. "Not a damn thing." She reached over and gave Nova's hand a squeeze.

"Then if I may," Kanji said to Sheriff Donaldson, "I'd like to go get my own laptop from my apartment unit. I have begun a spreadsheet on it that I believe will be of much assistance in our organization of the facts."

"By all means," said Sheriff D, as Kanji got up to leave. "Meanwhile, Jimmy, can you start us a pot of coffee?"

Kanji bowed slightly, a trait I still found quite endearing, and excused himself from the room. His pup, not having satisfied himself with the floor crumbs, helped himself to Priscilla's food dish, and Priscilla, dislodged when Jimmy got up to tend to the coffee, came over and had a bite herself.

"It's uncanny how they get along so well," said Meredith, "it's almost like they knew each other in a past life."

"Do dogs have past lives?" asked Nova. "I know cats have nine, but..."

"It's just a figure of speech, dear," said Merri.

They had left their places on the couch in the living room, and we now all squeezed in around the kitchen table, thanks to the addition of Jimmy's office chair.

Kanji returned with his laptop and we waited rather impatiently while he lifted the lid and booted it up.

"I have organized these in chronological order," he began. "So we shall start with the death of... Charles Schultz," he said, consulting his computer screen.

"No relation to the Peanuts cartoonist," said Merri, nodding.

"Charles was your second husband?" asked Kanji.

"Yes, he was. Harlan Gray was the first. He died of a heart attack, and I wasn't all that sorry to see him go. He was a bad gambler and a heavy drinker, and he got mean when he drank."

This was a portion of the story I had never heard, and my eyebrows involuntarily headed for my hairline.

Merri saw my surprise, and said, "But I didn't kill him, Syl. I had no reason to kill him. All I got out of his death was a stack of bills a mile high."

"Let's get back to Charles," said Sheriff D.

"Yes, please," said Kanji. "Harlan is of no concern to me; his life was not insured with my company."

"He wasn't insured with anybody," said Merri. "That was the problem."

"So you took out life insurance on Charles Schultz," said Freddy, trying to gently guide us back in the right direction.

"Yes," said Meredith. "I met Charles when I was working at the clinic in Unity. I knew he had health problems, but he was such a charmer that we were married before I knew just how sick he really was."

"And he died of a medication overdose?" asked Kanji, wishing to confirm the information in front of him.

"Correct," said Merri.

"And were you not in charge of dispensing his

medications?" asked Kanji.

There was a sudden intake of breath from nearly everyone in the room.

"Yes," said Merri, without flinching. "And I had given Charles his medication that morning before I left for work. It was a Tuesday, and I gave him the Tuesday pills. On Sunday I had counted out pills for the entire week and put them in the daily pill planner, all ready to go. Charles must have gotten confused, because before I got home, he'd taken all the pills for the rest of the week, plus finishing off the bottle of his tricyclic antidepressants."

"And his death was not ruled a suicide," said Kanji.

It was a statement, not a question, but Meredith nodded confirmation. "The ME determined it was an accidental overdose. Apparently, Charles took another dose about an hour after I went to work. Then, I suppose because he didn't feel well, he took another dose an hour later, and another after that. He was dead when I got home from work."

"And his death was not ruled a suicide," Kanji said again.

"No. It was not a suicide! He was only part way through his daily crossword puzzle, and he prided himself on finishing it every day. If he were going to commit suicide, the jackass would have finished his damn puzzle first!"

Kanji's eyes widened as he listened to Meredith's passionate explanation. Then he looked down at the computer screen in front of him. "His life insurance was only for one hundred thousand dollars."

Only? Had he said "only?" I thought $100,000 sounded like an awful lot of money. "Mom— where did that money go?"

Meredith rolled her eyes. "I didn't make enough at the clinic to pay the premiums on a larger policy," she said. "I just wanted enough money to pay for his funeral and maybe pay off the house, but you came along soon after that, and I needed the money to live on while I took a leave of absence at the clinic."

Oh, so it was my fault she still had a mortgage when Robert entered the picture? I had kind of liked Robert, the only father I'd ever known, and hoped Meredith had nothing bad to say about him.

"Okay," said Kanji, "those circumstances are satisfactory and have been documented. Next is Robert Allen."

"This is like listening to a radio soap opera," said Jimmy, pouring coffee for everybody but himself and me. "I'll make us some decaf next," he promised as he walked by my chair.

"Robert had a fatal car accident," said Merri. She shrugged. "End of story."

"And you had him insured for a million dollars," said Kanji.

"Women my age have every right to hedge their bets," said Meredith, becoming defensive. "He died, his income went away, and—"

"You don't have to explain yourself," said Nova.

"No, I don't," said Merri. "It was an accident, plain and simple. He never took his car in for service, even when he knew the brakes were going out. One day they failed completely, and his car left the road and hit a tree."

Freddy sputtered into his coffee cup. "His brakes failed?" he echoed.

Sheriff Donaldson disrupted the possible sidetracking of the conversation by telling Freddy that the accident had been fully investigated, and there was absolutely no evidence to suspect tampering of any kind.

"It is not the intention of my insurance company to challenge the investigations of the police," said Kanji. "Unless, of course, no investigation had been done."

That sound reasonable to us all, and Kanji went on to the next deceased husband, Lawrence Godwin.

"I filled in most of the information about Lawrence's unfortunate abrin poisoning after the conversation at the party Saturday night," said Kanji.

"But we still don't know if it was by ingestion or injection," said Sheriff D.

"Or whether it was accidental or intentional," offered Jimmy.

"Jimmy! Whose side are you on?" I asked.

"Chill, Syl," said Freddy, momentarily placing his reassuring hand on my lower arm. "There is only the side of justice here.

"And our purpose—at least my purpose—" continued Freddy, "in helping Kanji tonight is so that he can get all his questions answered without any more sneaking around."

I'd certainly vote for that. I was still wrestling with my emotions, not sure which of my budding feelings for Kanji were real, and which were just a product of the charming part he'd been playing so well. And since at least part of the time he'd been playing me, did that mean *everything* he'd said or done had been a lie?

"Of some importance, I believe," began Kanji, "is the fact that Goodie ordered the rosary seeds online herself."

"Yes," said Sheriff D, "these women are all fairly computer literate."

It was just a statement, but Meredith glowered at the sheriff. "Adapt or become extinct," she said. "These days, you'd be hard-pressed to find anyone under 80 who does not have email, or access to the Internet."

Sheriff Donaldson nodded. "We're just gathering facts, Meredith."

"Let's move on to Nadine's husband, Claude Larsen," said Kanji.

"Alzheimer's," said Meredith. "He drowned out on the tide flats between the bay road and Elk Island."

"But his body was never recovered?" asked Kanji.

"Claude's car was found parked at the turnout straight across from the island," said Merri. "He had taken off his shoes and left them at the edge of the mud flats when the tide was full out. His hat was found about 12 hours later—after the tide had come in and back out again. You do the math."

"An alert was put out the moment Nadine realized Claude was missing," said Sheriff Donaldson.

Jimmy was right on top of a specific factoid we could actually use. "You do not have to wait 24 hours to report someone as missing. If you have serious concerns for the safety and welfare of a person, and their whereabouts are unknown, then you may immediately report them missing to your local police."

"Jiminy Cricket strikes again," Meredith said, under her breath.

"He's right," said Freddy, "Claude's medical situation made him a special case."

"Approximately how long was it until his car was located?" asked Kanji.

"Not long," said Sheriff D. "We put out a Silver Alert."

"Oooo! Oooo!" Jimmy raised his hand and wagged it in the air, then without being acknowledged, he blurted out, "Activation of a Silver Alert is for persons over the age of 65 who have been medically diagnosed with Alzheimer's disease, dementia or a mental disability."

"Is there anything he doesn't know?" asked Merri.

"He reads a lot," I said, dismissing the judgmental tone of her voice as a result of all the stress she'd been under the past week.

"But the abandoned car might have been reported sooner if there had been reliable cell service in that area," said Freddy. "As it was, the tide was almost fully back in before we were dispatched."

"And the car, shoes, and hat were the only evidence found?" asked Kanji.

"Yes," said the sheriff. "A pity, really. Nadine could have used some closure." He looked at Nova with compassion.

"So..., and I'm just playing the devil's advocate here," Kanji began. "Claude's disappearance could have been staged at an area notorious for poor communications while he was actually murdered and disposed of somewhere else."

The room erupted with protests, but my voice outshouted them all.

"How dare you, Kanji!" I could almost picture actual fire coming from my nose and steam from my ears. "To imply that Nadine had anything to do with Claude's disappearance is purely conjecture on your part! In the first place, Claude outweighed Nadine by close to one hundred pounds. And in the second place—"

This time it was Meredith's gentle but firm hand on my arm that stilled my rising voice, and I clamped my indignant mouth shut.

"If you're going to play the part of Staunch Defender," said Freddy, not unkindly, "you're going to need a red cape."

"If I may continue with my theory..." said Kanji.

Nobody said a word.

"What if..." Kanji continued, "...what if the Merri's Widows were all in this together? What if Mateo was not the first of the husbands to go missing while out on the Estrella Nueva?"

I was too shocked to protest, but Meredith, her fingernails now suddenly digging hard into my arm, instantly took up the banner.

"You, sir, are a stranger here. You do not know us, or our morals. You are way out of line to imply that any of my friends would have been complicit in either Claude's or Mateo's disappearance. You are way out of line, and you, sir, are about to end up owing all of us much more than a lame-ass apology."

It was a borderline threat, and we all knew it, from Sheriff Donaldson on down, but Kanji continued unfazed.

"It is only a theory," said Kanji, "but since neither man has been found, there is a link here that I believe must be explored." His eyes met Sheriff D's. "Don't you agree, Sheriff?"

Sheriff Donaldson's ruddy face looked more ruddy than usual. "It is certainly a theory worth our consideration."

"Carter!" I slammed both hands down on the kitchen table. If I'd been closer, I might have committed assault. "You know these women!"

"Money is a strong motive, Syl." He looked sorry to say such a thing, and I mentally tried to cut him some slack.

"Let's everyone just take a breath," said Freddy. "At this time, no one is being accused of anything."

Priscilla momentarily broke the tension in the room, drawing our attention outside by incessantly chattering at the large living room window, which was really an unused sliding glass door. The pup roused himself from a nap on the couch and joined her, bouncing and whimpering at the glass pane.

Two large black birds were hopping about on the small lawn, illuminated by the motel floodlights. I was surprised to see them out there, poking around the shrubs, since it was well after dark, but Jimmy took their appearance in stride.

"That's just Heckle and Jeckle," said Jimmy matter-of-factly. "I guess all the noise and activity around here this evening must have disturbed them. Normally, they'd be nesting by this time of night."

"A murder of crows," said Freddy under his breath.

"Actually those are ravens," piped up Jimmy, "and although ravens usually travel in pairs, a group of them is called either an unkindness or a conspiracy."

The silence deepened, if that were possible, and in those brief seconds, the thought crossed my mind that Raven Coldwater was certainly an interesting name for someone eagerly embracing the challenge of investigative reporting.

Jimmy, suddenly realizing, for once, that his little spontaneous factoid might have made things worse, quickly brought around the coffee pot, now filled with decaf, and almost everyone accepted a refill.

Priscilla and the pup, since there was no way they were going to be let outside to chase the birds, returned to the couch and quietly curled up together.

"So Nova," said Kanji, blowing out a breath after Jimmy returned to his seat, "I believe that brings us to you."

"I didn't kill anybody," said Nova, fairly spitting out the words, "and that's all you need to know."

But Kanji was not to be dissuaded. "It has already been established how close you ladies all are—how fiercely loyal and supportive of each other. So perhaps Claude was just a practice run for the disposition of Mateo."

Kanji had taken a little liberty with the English language, but none of us missed his intention.

"Disposition?" asked Nova. "You mean like disposing of him?"

"Two missing husbands with extreme, in fact eventually fatal, medical issues," Kanji began his summation. "The men were spouses of women friends who have seen two other women friends of theirs recently inherit a sizeable insurance benefit. It is not outside my thinking that the Estrella Nueva may have been the scene for two very similar, if not identical crimes. The car, shoes, and the hat could have been set in place by anyone."

"Carter—tell him he's wrong," I begged.

"I can't do that, Sylvia," said the sheriff. "It is certainly something to consider, and it will be duly investigated. My department may never have seen the connection without Mr. Kumera's presence here, and we owe him our gratitude for pointing it out."

I don't think I was the only woman at the table who was suddenly sick to her stomach. And to think, I had actually been sweet on this guy!

The sheriff's collar radio buzzed, and we all heard the dispatcher asking him if there was a landline he could use to call her back.

Jimmy nodded, and pointed to the outer office. "Help yourself."

There was palpable hostility aimed at Kanji from all around the table, and I almost felt sorry for the guy. Almost is the operative term. I realized he was only doing his job, but I couldn't help feeling a deep sense of betrayal.

Thankfully, Sheriff Donaldson wasn't gone for more than a few minutes, and we'd filled the time talking about—what else?—the likelihood of the Mariners ever being in the World Series. Baseball always seemed to be our go-to topic in difficult times.

"There were fish spotters out today looking for a gray whale reported to be tangled in crab pot lines a little north of the peninsula," Sheriff D began.

Jimmy piped right up. "Last year, California had 66 whale entanglement incidents, while Washington and Oregon combined only had 5 such cases."

Sheriff Donaldson sighed deeply, and it fell to me to say, in my sternest voice, "Not now, Jim. The sheriff has something to tell us."

"After an inconclusive sighting by air, a Coast Guard Zodiac boat out of Westport was dispatched to investigate." He paused, running his finger and thumb out along his mustache, apparently thinking about how or what he was going to say next.

"Excuse me," said Kanji, "but I do not know of a town called Westport." He looked at the sheriff for help, but it was Freddy who answered.

"It's another small, coastal fishing community north of here," said Freddy. "By land, it's about 80 miles, but by sea, it's more like 40.

"And the prevailing currents this time of year..." Kanji let his question trail off.

"Run north," said Sheriff D.

"And?" asked Nova.

I'm sure everyone in the room was holding his or her breath as we all anticipated, with varying degrees of dread, the sheriff's next words.

"And..." Sheriff D put his hand gently on Nova's shoulder, "a body has been recovered and positively identified as Mateo Rodriguez."

CHAPTER 16

I'm either going to have to get my cell phone number changed, or start remembering to turn the darn thing off at night.

Well before I was ready to crawl out of bed Wednesday morning, it rang with the twangy country-western ringtone I'd designated specifically for Meredith: "Your Mama's calling you... Wants to see what you're up to... If you wait till the song is through... You just might miss her."

Right at that particular moment, I almost wished I could miss her all day today and ignore the song that was sure to become my morning earworm.

But no, at my age I already had far too many friends whose mothers weren't around to pester them like mine was, and I picked up the phone during the second verse.

"Mom, don't you ever sleep?"

"Good morning, Sunshine!" said Merri, sounding far too perky for my break-of-dawn tastes. "I hope you slept well."

I wasn't sure how she defined "well," considering we'd both been up much later than usual the night before. It was bad enough that we'd all been dragged through the wringer answering Kanji's questions, but then trying to console Nova, whose grief had suddenly doubled and redoubled with the news about Mateo's body being recovered, had to have taken a hard emotional toll on everyone present.

Meredith was apparently waiting for some kind of

response, so I muttered, "Well enough, I guess," and hoped she would be satisfied with that reply and cut the conversation short. I knew it was too much to hope for, but I really, really wanted to snuggle back down and get another hour or two of sleep.

"Glad to hear it, Honey," she said, still in contention for the Perky-Mother-of-the Year award. "Good sleep is important. You never know what the next day will bring, so you must catch it when you can."

I don't know what it was about the way she said those words that made the hair on my arms stand up, but there was something in her voice that suddenly put all my senses on red alert. I threw the covers back and sat up on the side of the bed.

"Mom?" I didn't want to know, but I didn't want to be the last to know, either. "What's wrong?"

"Nothing's wrong, per se..."

"Per se?" I echoed, feeling my heart begin to race. "Latin for 'in and of itself'? Merri, you're starting to scare me. What's up?"

"I take it you haven't seen the Tribune yet this morning?"

"I'm not out of bed yet, so no, I haven't seen the newspaper." I took a deep breath and mentally braced myself. "Why don't you just fill me in?"

"There's another front page story by Raven Coldwater," Meredith began. "No photos this time, and it's below the fold, but I found the headline quite..." She paused, then finished her sentence with "upsetting."

"Come on, Mom! Just spill it! What's the headline say?"

"Well, okay, but I don't want you to go working yourself all up into a tizzy about it," said Merri. "Promise me you won't freak out or anything."

I said nothing. Sometimes I just can't figure her out. Was Meredith intentionally putting me through hell for the sheer satisfaction of her control freak issues, or was she oblivious to the amount of stress she created by dangling just a tidbit of the news in front of me and then saying not to freak out? I felt like I was the rodent in some weird game of cat and mouse.

"Well, okay, Honey," she said in her funny, but not ha-ha funny, voice. "The headline reads, 'Veiled Widow Strikes Again'."

"Holy Criminitly!" I stood up and started for the bathroom. "Meet me at Jimmy's as soon as you can! We have to start planning some damage control!"

I pressed the red button at the bottom of the cell phone screen before she could say another word, decided to skip my shower, pulled on some clothes from the clean laundry pile that was strewn across the unused side of my bed, and was out in the garage climbing into the Mustang in less time than it takes to say, "Here's another fine mess you've gotten us into, Ollie!"

Good grief and gravy! Somehow Raven must have found out about Meredith being with Walter when he died. How could this be? Had she been lurking in the rhododendrons outside the motel office after she got off work at the High Tide? Soon the whole town would be buzzing, and I had no idea how we were going to be able to fix this.

But as I wheeled into the Clamshell parking lot, all the events of the last evening suddenly rushed in—all of them—not just the circumstances of Walter's death, but the betrayal of Kanji, as I chose to call it, and the "fact-gathering" spreadsheet he created, and the news that

Mateo's body had been recovered.

It was almost too much for me, and despite my earlier haste, I couldn't make myself get out of the car. I just sat and leaned my head against the steering wheel, fought against the rush of tears, and struggled to breathe deeply enough to calm myself.

A tapping on the car window pulled me back from my dark thoughts of mortality, as well as all the victims and potential perpetrators of both known and unknown crimes.

"Syl?" asked Jimmy, standing next to my car. "Syl? Are you alright?"

I looked up at him and nodded. Then I opened the door, stepped out, and felt my knees threaten to go all woozy on me. "I just needed a moment, thank you." I took a few tentative steps toward the motel office and drew in another deep breath. "May I see your newspaper?"

"My newspaper? Is that why you're here?" Jimmy looked confused.

"It's deja vu all over again," I said, noting that my voice sounded surprisingly strong. We mounted the office steps and went on into the kitchen.

"Sorry, I'm not following you," said Jimmy.

"Mom's on her way. We've got to put our heads together to figure out what kind of a spin we can put on today's news."

"*Still* not following you," said Jimmy, handing me his neatly folded newspaper.

I flipped the paper over and pointed to the headline, which read just exactly as Meredith had told me: 'Veiled Widow Strikes Again'.

"Have you read this?" I asked Jimmy.

"Well, yeah," said Jimmy, taking a seat at the kitchen table. "But it's got nothing to do with Meredith, or even with Walter's passing, if that's what you're thinking."

"Wait." I scowled, tilted my head as if that would help me hear more clearly, and peered at him. "It doesn't?"

"You need some full-strength coffee, Syl." He got back up to pour me a cup. "You need to stop and think this through a minute."

"Think what through?"

"The Tribune goes to press at 6 p.m. on Sundays, Tuesdays and Thursdays," said Jimmy, placing a steaming mug of joe in front of me. "You didn't go to the High Tide for the burgers until after everyone's normal dinnertime—"

"—and Raven was trying to get me to tell her who had died when I went in!" I smacked my hand against my forehead. "So this isn't about Merri being with Walter when he died."

Jimmy looked at me like I had straw sticking from my ears. "That's what I said."

"Oh! Thank heavens!"

I took a big swig of coffee and glanced down at the paper. My brow furrowed. "But this headline..."

Jimmy smiled. "Nothing more than a swing and a miss at yellow journalism."

"Huh?" I looked up at him. I really did need to get more coffee into my system. "What kind of a screwy mixed-up baseball metaphor is that?"

"Yellow journalism and the yellow press are American terms for journalism and associated newspapers that present little or no legitimate well-researched news while instead using eye-catching headlines for increased sales. Techniques may include exaggerations of news events, scandal-mongering or sensationalism," recited Jimmy.

I said nothing, but I couldn't keep from rolling my eyes. Then I picked up the paper and started reading aloud:

"Nadine Larsen, 80-year-old member of The Veiled Rainbow geriatric belly dancing troupe, was arrested late Tuesday afternoon for violation of a court injunction to stop feeding the bears in her neighborhood."

I looked up at Jimmy. "Nadine was with the gals up at the casino yesterday afternoon."

"Yes, but apparently the party broke up just as soon as you and Nova hightailed out of there," said Jimmy.

I continued to read:

"Larsen called the police herself after letting her toy poodle outside for a few minutes and hearing a ruckus on her back porch. When she opened the door, she discovered two large bears on her deck, and her dog lying dead out in the yard."

My mouth dropped open. "Oh my gosh! Poor Claudette! She was a yippy little creature, and no one, not even Nadine, liked her all that much, but what a terrible thing to have happen to her!"

"I guess the bears thought Nadine had put more dog food out for them when she got home, and were mad when they didn't find the handout they thought would be there," said Jimmy.

"But why was Nadine arrested?"

"Keep reading," said Jimmy.

"Larsen confessed that she often fed her own dog out on the deck, and the investigating deputy found over 150 pounds of dog food stored in her utility room just inside the back door."

I nodded. "That's an awful lot of dog food for an awfully small dog, alright. So Deputy Bill, or Bob, it doesn't say which, jumped to the conclusion that Nadine was still feeding the bears and arrested her."

"That about sums it up," said Freddy.

Meredith's red Saturn pulled in between my Mustang and Kanji's Scion, and I met her at the door.

"Shame on you, Mother! Shame on you! You got me here under false pretenses."

"My, my," said Meredith, not even pretending to be ashamed of herself, "aren't you just loaded for bear."

"Not funny, Mom."

Meredith stopped and gave me a long hug, which was rather uncharacteristic of her. "I just needed to spend time with my daughter today," she said quietly into my hair. "Nova is going to meet me here while we wait for the preliminary autopsy report."

Jimmy ruined the moment by asking if he could get a bear hug too, and Meredith released me and hugged him just as tightly.

"Thank you for all your help yesterday," she said to him before ending their hug.

"I don't know how much help I was," said Jimmy as we entered his apartment. "After all our planning, we got caught red-handed."

Meredith waved him off. "It's water under the bridge now." She turned to me, "I only knew Walter a short time, but I really liked him, Syl. I really did. It's a shame about what happened, but..."

"But what?" I prompted her.

"Well.... Are you going to get all pissy with me if I say that at least he died with a smile on his face?"

"Yes!" I said without hesitation. "Yes, I am!"

Meredith picked the newspaper up off the table, and grimaced. "Raven just had to throw the word 'geriatric' in there, didn't she?"

Jimmy set a cup of coffee in front of her. "I knew you weren't going to like her referring to your troupe, spelled with an 'e'," he said pointedly looking at me, "as geriatric belly dancers, but just imagine how would you feel if she'd written 'bariatric jelly dancers' instead?!"

Meredith had her coffee cup half way to her lips, and she set it so hard back on the table that some of it sloshed out of the cup. "Jimmy! I'll have you know, young man, that not a single one of us has had bariatric surgery, and there is no more 'jelly' on our bellies than you'd find on other women our—" Merri abruptly stopped talking when she saw Jimmy's smirk.

"How long did it take you to come up with that this morning?" she asked.

Jimmy shrugged. "I just thought it was funny," he said, pushing his glasses up with his middle finger, "and we all could use a laugh about now." He handed her a paper towel to clean up the spilled coffee.

"On the point of needing some levity, I totally agree," I said.

Meredith finally got her first sip of coffee and looked again at the newspaper. "On the bright side, yappy little Claudette didn't suffer," she said. "It was a clean neck snap. That bear took her out with just one massive swipe of his paw. Knocked her clear out into the backyard. She never knew what hit her."

"You've talked to Nadine?" I asked.

"Of course," said Merri. "They couldn't hold her at the jail last night; the alleged 'evidence' that she was feeding the bears was all circumstantial."

"Which Raven couldn't have known, since she must have gotten most of her information off the police scanner at the High Tide," I said.

"And the paper goes to bed at six," Jimmy reminded us.

Meredith nodded reflectively. "So now we have three funerals to attend." She sighed.

"Three?"

Merri ticked them off on her fingers, "Mateo, Walter, and Claudette."

I rolled my eyes. "I am most certainly not attending a funeral for that dog!"

"Why not?" asked Merri. "It'll be fun. The whole belly dancing troupe will be there, and we'll all be struggling to say something nice about that little bitch, and—"

"Mother! Your language!"

"Technically, she's correct in her terminology," said Jimmy. "A female dog is—"

"I *know* what a female dog is called! I just don't think it's appropriate for us to compare burying two wonderful human beings with Nadine's ankle-biting poodle!"

Meredith shrugged. "Suit yourself, but you'll miss out on a lot of good food. Nadine said she was planning on having the reception catered."

Before I could say anything more about the insanity of the situation, a timid rap came at Jimmy's inner door, and Nova stepped inside, followed by Goodie, who carried a familiar-looking pastry box from the Buoy 10 Bakery.

Merri jumped up to give them both a quick hug, and Jimmy left the doors open so Priscilla could go out and make her morning rounds in the dune grass while he started up another pot of coffee.

"I hope you don't mind me tagging along," said Goodie, setting the bakery box down in the middle of the table and taking a seat at the far end. "We stopped in Tinkerstown to pick up donuts in case anyone was hungry."

Jimmy wisely took down the roll of paper towels from by the sink and placed them next to the box on the table.

"Donuts are always welcome," said Merri, lifting the lid off the box and taking a big whiff of the delicious aroma, "and so are you. But I'm kind of surprised you're not with Nadine today in her time of need."

"Nadine." Goodie looked at the ceiling and sighed. "When she called to tell me about Claudette this morning, she said she'd been praying all night to Saint Dymphna that I would find it in my heart to forgive her for not taking better care of her poodle."

"Saint Dymphna?" I asked.

Goodie managed a small smile. "It's a Catholic thing."

"But Nadine's not Catholic—is she?" asked Nova.

"No," said Goodie, "but when Claude was suffering with dementia, Nadine was at wit's end, and she asked me which of the saints to pray to for comfort, and I told her Saint Dymphna was the patron saint of dementia and mental illness."

"And so...?" Merri prompted, between bites of glazed donut.

"And so it's the only saint Nadine thinks she knows well enough to pray to," said Goodie. "And for some reason she thinks praying to a Catholic saint will patch it all up between us, since I'm Catholic."

"But you two are best friends," I said, succumbing to the urge to take one of the donuts myself.

"We were," said Goodie, "but right now I'm so upset with her I don't even want to see her face."

Jimmy asked for both of us, "What happened?"

"Well, I suppose when you come right down to it, the whole thing is my fault," Goodie began.

"I don't see how that's possible," said Nova. She, too, took a donut from the box.

"Well, I'm the one who picked up the dog food for her

from Costco, since her smart car is too small to carry the giant size bags."

"That doesn't make you responsible for what happened," I said, patting her arm. "Nadine loves all living things, so of course she wanted to make sure the bears had food to eat after their homes and hunting grounds were bulldozed. I'm sure her DNA is made up of a high percentage of Greenpeace genes."

"Don't I know it," agreed Nova. "She even took me to task for making a living crab fishing—until I assured her that all the crabs we caught were strictly free-range."

This time it was me who snorted coffee out my nose, and Jimmy quickly pushed the whole roll of paper towels in my direction.

Goodie looked skeptical. "But I'm also the one who convinced her to adopt poor Claudette," she said sadly. "I convinced her that toy poodles make good watchdogs because they bark incessantly."

"And Claudette sure did," interrupted Nova. "Yip-yip-yip-yip, all day long."

"Nobody else ever gave that yappy little dog a second look," continued Goodie, "and I felt sorry for it, with its matted hair and sour disposition." She sighed. "In hindsight, I should have thought the whole thing through a little better."

"Well, now that Nadine has sworn off bear feeding for good, she can always adopt another dog," said Jimmy.

"Oh, no she can't!" said Goodie, sudden anger flashing in her eyes. "Nadine willingly endangered Claudette, whose name at the shelter was Itsy-Bitsy, by the way, and now she's banned from adopting an animal from the Humane Society for the next 10 years!"

As if on cue, Kanji's pup bounded into the room,

wagging and wiggling every part of his body, happy for every ounce of attention we lavished upon him.

But wherever the pup went, Kanji was sure to follow, and I braced myself for the appearance of a tall, dark, and definitely handsome undercover insurance fraud investigator to be the next one through the door.

"Excuse me," said Kanji, standing in the doorway not 30 seconds later. "I do not wish to interrupt, but if I may, I'd like to just collect my pup and leave."

The words 'chicken shit' flitted through my head faster than the pup was cleaning up the kibbles in the bottom of Priscilla's bowl.

"Come on in," said Jimmy. "Thanks to Goodie, there's donuts." He motioned to the box on the table. "I don't have any Chai tea, but I just made a fresh pot of coffee."

"I have a feeling," said Kanji, with just a bare hint of a smile, "that with all the comings and goings of people through your residence, your coffee doesn't have much time to be anything but fresh."

Meredith pointed to the last empty chair remaining at Jimmy's table for six. "Have a seat," she said. "No one is angry with you."

"That's not entirely true, *Mother*," I said with emphasis.

"I stand corrected," said Meredith. "Sylvia is still angry, but she's outnumbered four to one, so won't you please join us?"

Jimmy nodded. "Democracy in action."

Kanji maintained his position at the door, looking exceedingly uncomfortable. Good, I thought. Let him squirm.

A long moment passed, then I shrugged. "As Meredith so deftly pointed out, I've been outvoted. Come on in." I nodded toward the open chair with my head. "You're welcome to join us."

But Kanji did not immediately sit down. Instead, he walked around the table to where I sat, and did his semi-bow. "Sylvia," he said, in front of everyone there, "I want you to know that my attraction to you was genuine. I know you must think otherwise, but I am quite sincere when I tell you that I was not using you to get close to your mother and her friends for investigative purposes."

I'd never heard my mother so silent. The last thing I'd expected today was a public apology from Kanji, and tears sprung to my eyes.

"Thank you," I choked out. "I appreciate you saying that."

But Kanji was not quite finished. "I realize that I have destroyed the trust that had just started to grow between us, and I hope you will allow me the honor of working to earn it back." Kanji cleared his throat. "Sylvia, will you allow me that honor?"

I could have heard a pin drop in that room, but thankfully the spell was broken before I had to give Kanji an official answer.

Priscilla had come back from her morning dune constitutional to find the pup had cleaned out her food bowl. She began meowing loudly for Jimmy to refill it, and at the same time my cell phone started ringing like a police siren.

I didn't need to look at the display screen. Instead, I made eye contact with each one gathered around the table before I spoke. "That's my ringtone for Sheriff Donaldson."

CHAPTER 17

"Yes... Yes... Yes... Absolutely..." I pressed the disconnect button on the phone and was bombarded with questions from each of the five sitting at the table with me.

"What did he say?"

"Is there any good news?"

"Has the preliminary report come in?"

"Can you tell us anything?"

"Spill it, Syl."

I held up my hands for silence. Meredith, Nova, Goodie, Jimmy, and Kanji had all spoken at once, and I wasn't exactly sure who had said what, other than it was most likely my mother who had admonished me to "Spill it, Syl."

And it didn't really matter what any individual had said anyway, because they were all going to get the same answers at the same time.

"The sheriff is on his way," I began. "He wanted to know if I was at the Clamshell. He wanted to know if Nova and Meredith were also here. He wanted to know if I would have you all just sit tight until he arrives. And—" I shot a look at Jimmy, "he wanted to know if the coffee was on."

"Yes, yes, yes, and absolutely," said Jimmy, nodding. "That about sums it up."

"So there's nothing more to tell you until he arrives," I said, "because he didn't tell me anything else."

"Thank you," said Meredith, speaking for the group.

They all nodded, and continued picking at their donuts in the thoughtful silence that followed. The sheriff's phone call had certainly curtailed most of our appetites.

Fortunately, it isn't far from the police station in downtown Tinkerstown to the Clamshell on the northern city limits, and it didn't take long at all for Sheriff D to appear at the inner office door. I suspected he'd turned on his flashing blue lights to clear the way, but it was only a hunch.

We hadn't thought to pull up another chair for him, so Sheriff Donaldson stood at the end of the table closest to the door and launched into a dispassionate preliminary speech the moment he arrived.

"Normally, it would take at least a week before I'd have anything to share with you," said Sheriff D, addressing the six of us together. But even though he spoke to us all, his eyes were focused on Nova, and his face looked as weary as I'd ever seen it.

"You can thank the medical examiner for putting a rush on this. Instead of sending—the remains—directly to Olympia for processing, John Stark went above and beyond the call of duty. He stayed up all night, collecting and processing samples, just to be able to give us some kind of preliminary report this morning."

I tried silently willing him to cut the lengthy explanations and get on with it, already, but Sheriff D, bless his little pea-picking heart, all too often enjoys his brief moments at the center of attention. Today, however, I suspected he was stalling for a little time, letting us brace ourselves for difficult news.

He cleared his throat, and rocked back and forth on his heels. Then he politely took his Stetson off and held it with both hands in front of him. It was a genuine gesture of respect for Nova's situation, and it so warmed my heart that I instantly forgave him for taking so long to get to the point.

"As you all know, Mateo's body had been in the ocean a full week before recovery, and—"

There are times—too many times, and this was one of the worst—that Jimmy's encyclopedic brain simply cannot, or will not, be restrained.

"On the open ocean, flies and other insects are largely absent," said Jimmy. "But if the body is floating in water less than 70 degrees Fahrenheit, and our area hovers around 50 degrees this time of year, the tissues turn into a soapy, fatty acid known as 'grave wax' which halts bacterial growth. The skin will still blister and turn greenish black, though, and crabs and small fish may feed on the soft parts of the face like the eyes and lips—"

"Jimmy! *STOP!*" I don't know who else besides me shouted for him to clamp his damn mouth shut—maybe we all did. I just know our emphatic cacophony got through to him and his hand abruptly flew to his mouth as he sucked air in.

"Nova! Oh my gawd! I'm so sorry! Please forgive me! I didn't think before I—"

"I know," said Nova, sadly, letting go of Meredith's hand and reaching out to touch Jimmy's arm. "And it's okay. Really, Jimmy, it's okay. It's not like all of us crabbers out there don't think about those kinds of things from time to time.

"It's a tough life, but crab fishers are a tough bunch. We all know that every wave has the potential to overturn our boats, even in good weather. And we all know accidents happen every day. It's one of the most dangerous professions in the world, but not too many of us out there would ever think of giving it up."

She swallowed hard, blinked back tears, and refocused on Sheriff Donaldson. "I pretty much cried myself out last night, Sheriff. I think I can handle whatever it is you have to say, so please continue."

With some of his thunder stolen by Jimmy's interjection of decidedly gruesome details, Sheriff Donaldson got quickly down to the specific facts at hand.

"John has been able to determine, with some confidence, that there is no evidence of foul play. There were no sleeping pills in Mateo's system, no defensive wounds, no skull trauma, and no ligature marks indicating his hands or feet had been bound before he went overboard."

"I told you so," Meredith said pointedly to the sheriff. "It was nothing more than a horrible, tragic accident, plain and simple."

"Not necessarily," said Kanji.

Six heads snapped in his direction, and I swear I could feel the blood in my veins chill a few degrees. What did Kanji know that the rest of us did not know?

Sheriff D was the first to speak. "Alright, Kanji." He nodded thoughtfully. "You have my attention, and I'm listening."

So were the rest of us, also with rapt attention, but no one else dared utter a word. I think I might even have been holding my breath as I waited for Kanji to propose his newest theory concerning the deceased.

"Mr. Matthew Rodriguez was depressed about his advancing illness, was he not?" Kanji asked Nova.

"Yes, of course," said Nova, scowling. "Wouldn't you be?"

Kanji ignored the rhetorical question and continued, "And it was his idea to modify the boat, was it not?"

No one answered. It was common knowledge on the docks, and in the community, that Mateo had been the one to fervently suggest the modifications. For several months he'd been pushing hard to get the Estrella Nueva wheelchair accessible as quickly as possible.

I briefly considered, for just a heartbeat or two, where Kanji was going with his line of questioning, and although I didn't like it one bit, I had to admit that his theory had some possible merit.

"And Mr. Matthew Rodriguez—"

"Please," interrupted Nova. "Call him Mateo."

Kanji nodded. "And Mateo was in some hurry for you to finish the boat modifications, is this correct?"

Again, not a word from any of us.

"So is it not possible that—*Mateo*—had decided he would choose when and where to end his life, and that he would do it as soon as he was able to get back out on the ocean?" asked Kanji, looking around the group for possible confirmation. "In which case, time was of the essence, before his condition further worsened."

The sheriff, rocked back and forth on his heels several times while he carefully chose his words. Finally he said, "Washington's Death with Dignity Act permits a doctor to prescribe a lethal drug if the patient has less than six months to live. There were no such drugs apparent in Mateo's body, although, to be honest, we still cannot rule out suicide."

"There were no such drugs apparent in his body," said Kanji, "and I apologize for saying this, but taking someone out on the ocean, knowing that he is despondent and suicidal, may yet qualify for 'assisted suicide'."

"Oh no you don't!" shouted Nova, jumping to her feet. "It wasn't suicide, assisted or otherwise, and I deeply resent your implication that it was anything but an accident!"

Meredith reached out to quiet her, but Nova pulled her arm away and would not be consoled. "My husband most certainly did not commit suicide, no way in hell, and I think I know how I can prove it."

"Now *I* am listening," said Kanji. He sat back in his chair and folded his hands in his lap, his stoic face unreadable.

"My husband—Mateo—was notoriously cheap," said Nova, breathlessly.

Sheriff D narrowed his eyes in concentration. "As far as I know, there's no law against being frugal," he said.

Nova continued without missing a beat. "And he insisted—he absolutely *insisted*—right after he became dependent on the wheelchair, that we buy him a casket when he saw that they were on sale in Costco's online coupon book." She looked around victoriously.

"And so?" said Goodie, who hadn't had much to contribute until now, and still didn't.

"And so," said Nova, "we bought a casket." She looked around the group for signs of support. "We bought a casket! Don't you get it? We. Bought. A. Casket!"

"Technically," said Jimmy, "unless it has six sides and is tapered from top to bottom, you bought a coffin and not a casket."

I glared at him, but he just shrugged. "A coffin has only four sides. A lot of people confuse them."

"Oh!" said Merri, bringing us back from another of Jimmy's untimely factoids to the issue at hand. "I think I see where Nova's going with this! Coffins are one of the only things that Costco does not take back!"

Nova nodded. "Yes. Exactly. And Mateo was totally aware of that policy. We talked about it before we made our purchase."

"Although they say you can return anything," said Jimmy, "Costco only sells coffins for customer convenience. The guarantees are all from the Universal Casket Company, and they insist that only those seriously damaged in shipping are returnable."

"Don't you mean Universal *Coffin* Company?" I asked sarcastically.

Jimmy smiled. "These days, although it's unfortunate, most people are not well-informed and use the words interchangeably."

Goodie clapped her hands three times for attention, and we all fell silent. She beamed. "Soooo..." She drew out the word as if it contained two or three syllables. "Nova? What does any of this not-so-fascinating return policy information really mean?"

"It means," said Nova, "that Mateo would never have committed suicide. Never, ever. For one, suicide is against his religious faith, as you well know, as you are also a Catholic. And for two, since we had already bought a casket—I mean coffin—and it can't be returned, he would have considered that a huge waste of money, and as I said a few minutes ago, that otherwise wonderful man I married was notoriously cheap."

She paused briefly, the energy of her outburst expended. She took a breath, then continued softly, "I guess now it's a good thing I still have the coffin." She sighed. "We will have to have some kind of a funeral for him, of course."

We all nodded, even Kanji, who leaned forward and asked, "Mateo was what is considered a practicing Catholic, was he not?"

"Of course he was." Goodie answered for Nova. "And

very devout." She nodded. "However, since 1963, the Vatican has allowed cremation, if it is not a denial of faith about resurrection." She looked at Nova, "So it would be okay if you decide, considering the condition he's in, to have him cremated."

"No," said Nova. "He was pretty old school, and although we did not share the same faith, I will make sure he has a full Funeral Mass." She shuddered and shook her head. "We also talked about this before we bought the cask—the coffin. I suggested maybe he'd prefer to be cremated and have his ashes scattered at sea, but he would not hear of it."

"So what do you think?" Meredith asked Kanji. "Are you ready to rule out suicide as the cause of death?"

Kanji was thoughtful for a moment or two, scanning the faces of everyone in the room. Then he nodded. "This entire ordeal has been an unnecessary and extremely emotional waste of everyone's time, and I am sorry. The obvious resolution to the investigation is for me to report it as a perfect example of Occam's Razor."

"The simplest solution is often the best and right answer," Jimmy piped up.

For once, none of us were annoyed by Jimmy's interjection.

"Yes," said Kanji. "But you must understand that my company was very insistent that I personally come here to investigate. I had no choice."

"We always have a choice," said Merri, squinting her eyes at him.

Kanji nodded again. "You are correct. And I chose to keep my job." To Nova he said, "You have answered all my questions, and I offer my sincere condolences. If the official autopsy in Olympia discovers nothing to the contrary—"

"It won't," Merri snapped.

"—then your insurance check," Kanji continued to Nova, "will be issued within 10 business days after the death certificate is completed and filed with the state."

Nova nodded. "It's a small consolation," she said, "but Mateo would be happy that I will not have to worry about where the next boat payment is coming from."

Kanji stood, collected his pup, who had been curled up on the couch with Priscilla, and headed for the door. "I must now go to get ready for my shift at Spartina Point," he said to no one in particular.

"I'll walk you out," said Sheriff D to Kanji. Then he turned to the rest of us, still quietly seated around the table. "Believe it or not, there are other things in the county that require my attention today." He put his Stetson back on, touched the brim in farewell, and the two men, plus one sleepy puppy, exited.

"The sheriff never even had any coffee," said Jimmy, thoughtfully, as the outer office door closed. "He's never left here without having at least one cup."

No one else said anything. We all just sat quietly and waited for a cue from Nova. Finally she took a deep breath and blew it out. "Well— I guess it's better to know than not to know," she said. "And I'm just so grateful to have good friends around to help me through all this." She reached out and squeezed the hands nearest her on each side.

Meredith turned to Goodie. "I bet Nadine could use a good friend about now, too."

Underneath the edge of the table, Goodie had been working through the beads on her rosary. "I don't know... I just don't think I'm ready to forgive her."

Jimmy said, "I know how hard it's been for me every time I've had to bury one of the Priscillas, so I'm sure

Nadine doesn't want to be alone right now."

"I don't know if she's buried Claudette yet." Goodie shrugged.

"I doubt it," said Meredith. "I know I talked to her before you did, so you probably have more current information, but she was planning to cater a funeral when we spoke."

"Oh, she'd given up on that idea by the time she talked to me," said Goodie. "But I was so upset that I hung up on her when she said she still wanted to put a little beret on the poodle and have a wake."

There was nothing I could think of to say in polite company right then. All I knew for sure was that I dared not make eye contact with anyone at the table for fear I'd spew coffee all over the place. A wake? For a French Poodle? Wearing a beret? No doubt about it, my mother sure had some "interesting" friends.

"Well," said Jimmy, looking in the bakery box, "we're all out of donuts. So should I make another pot of coffee, or what?"

Meredith looked tenderly at Nova, who was, I must admit, holding up remarkably well under the circumstances. "I think Nova and I have some funeral arranging to attend to," she said.

Nova nodded, wiping her tears away with one of Jimmy's ever-handy paper towels. "Thank you all again for being here for me." She sighed. "It's good to have some definite closure, and I guess I'm kind of glad they won't let me see him."

I couldn't wrap my mind around anyone *wanting* to see him, in the condition Jimmy had so colorfully described, but again, I restrained myself from comment.

"Well," said Goodie, standing up and taking her coffee

cup to the sink, "I guess you're all right. I suppose I really should go to check on Nadine. After all, that's what friends do, isn't it?" She paused, but no one had anything to contribute. "But so help me—"

We all knew what she was going to say, but politely waited for her to finish the sentence herself.

"—if she starts up with having a wake or a funeral or a memorial or anything like that, I am so out of there!"

"Fair enough," said Merri. "But you do need to go see her. She lost a pet. She's grieving. She probably will appreciate just the fact that you cared enough to stop by."

Goodie frowned. "I guess so. Friends are friends even when they disagree with you. And besides, she might need help burying Claudette."

"If you want, you can borrow my post-hole digger," said Jimmy.

We all gasped in some form; I think Nova actually hiccupped.

Jimmy shrugged. "I'm just being practical. I've used a post-hole digger to dig a grave for all my Priscillas. It's much easier than trying to dig with a garden shovel. You can get straight down into the earth deeper and faster without wasting energy. It works great."

When he put it that way, it made total sense. So as we all walked out, Goodie followed Jimmy to his barn-shaped tool shed.

Merri and Nova got into their respective cars and headed for the funeral home, and I had a sudden desire to drive up to the north end of the peninsula and personally fill Mercedes in on the preliminary autopsy report.

But before I could depart, Kanji appeared in his doorway. He held both hands up in front of him and motioned for me to stop. I couldn't just pretend I didn't see him, so I waited beside my car for him to approach.

"Sylvia," he said quietly when he stood next to me. "I know how you must feel."

"No, I don't think you do!" It came out more harshly than I anticipated.

"Okay, then I don't know how you must feel, but I know how I would feel if I were in your circumstances."

"You already apologized." I looked away from his penetrating brown eyes, glad for the distraction of watching Jimmy load the post-hole digger into Goodie's Corolla.

Goodie started her car, backed around, and waved as she left the parking lot. Then Jimmy wisely went inside without joining us, giving Kanji and me our moment alone.

"But Sylvia," said Kanji, returning to our exact point of interruption, "you did not then indicate that you accepted my apology."

I took a breath, and looked back into his face. Either he was in honest emotional pain, or he should have been nominated for an Oscar. "Kanji..." I began softly. "Kanjirappally Kumera..."

He tenderly took both my hands in his warm ones and pressed them to his chest. "Please say you forgive my deception, Syl. Please tell me you forgive me for doing my job. It was wrong of me to toy with any affection you might have been developing for me."

I wanted to continue being mad, but there were tears in both our eyes, and deep in my heart I believed that his tears, like mine, were genuine.

"I forgive you, Kanji."

When he pulled me into his arms, I did not resist. It felt good to have our differences resolved, and I knew I would not hesitate to give him another chance to earn my trust—if only he weren't going to be leaving so soon.

CHAPTER 18

Mateo, a.k.a. Matthew Rodriguez, was finally laid to rest the following week. I'd never been to a Mass before, much less a full Funeral Mass given in both Spanish and English. I wondered if the fact that it was bilingual had anything to do with the length of it. An hour and a half inside a church kept making my eyelids want to close.

I hate to say it, but all that Catholic standing, kneeling, standing, kneeling, is the only thing that kept me awake. What with the Greeting, Gathering Hymn, Invitation to Prayer, Opening Prayer, First Reading, Responsorial Psalm, Second Reading, Gospel, Homily, General Intercessions, Prayers of the Faithful, Presentation of the Gifts, Lord's Prayer, Communion, Song of Farewell, Prayer of Commendation, and Recessional Hymn, I was totally worn out and ready for a long nap by the time the service concluded.

"Wasn't that lovely?" asked Goodie, smiling and looking oddly angelic as we stepped outside the darkened church and into the bright midday sunlight. She'd worn a yellow tailored linen suit with a matching pillbox hat and white gloves for the occasion.

"Of course you would think so," said Nadine. "You were raised with all this silly rhetoric and redundant tradition." Nadine was wearing a poodle skirt and peasant blouse, as she often did, only today it was like she was daring anyone to mention it.

"You have to admit, Nadine, that it was a lovely service, no matter how you were raised, or what faith you are. Even if you're a heathen," said Goodie, just as sweetly as if she hadn't been aching for days to smack Nadine a good one on the nose.

"I don't have to admit any such thing," said Nadine. "The service was too darn long for my tastes. Maybe it was all that Spanish they added in."

I smiled. It was actually a comfort to hear the two old friends bickering again. I sneaked a quick peek at Goodie's feet and saw that she'd worn a modified strappy yellow sandal-type shoe with a heel. Nadine was sure to mention Goodie's shoes if they continued taking pot-shots at each other, and I actually looked forward to their routine. It somehow gave me comfort, and made things seem more normal again.

Felicity joined us out front, wiping her tears on an intricately embroidered hanky. There was a small red cardinal in each corner, and delicate flowers dancing all along the lacy border. I must have been staring at the hanky too long, for when I looked her in the eye she said, almost apologetically, "It's my funeral hanky. The only one I own."

Changing the subject, Felix added, "I just loved the way they interjected so much Spanish into the service."

"You know that you're the only one of us who's fluent in Spanish, don't you?"

Felicity chuckled. "You mean to tell me you weren't as engaged as I was during the service?" she asked, playfully raising her eyebrows. "If you're interested, I'm teaching a community college Spanish class next quarter."

I smiled. In another 20 years or so, I could hear us bickering and sniping at each other just like Nadine and Goodie were doing now.

Four-foot-ten-inch Orpha elbowed her way to the front of the crowd. "Well, wasn't that something?" she said. "I had no idea we had so many Mexicans living around here."

"We had a lot more before ICE started sneaking in and hauling them all away," said Felicity through tight lips. "It's certainly a shame what's been happening all over our country. There's just got to be another way to treat immigrants. We need to provide them a route to citizenship."

It was unusual, but somehow quite refreshing, to hear Felix being so political.

Nova joined us under the awning. She was wearing the traditional black dress and sensible black shoes, and I could tell she felt like a fish out of water. She sighed heavily. "Ladies, I'm exhausted. What do you say we all go rogue and bug out on the reception they're setting up in the fellowship hall?"

"What?" I asked incredulously. "Aren't you supposed to go and stand in some sort of receiving line or something?"

Nova gave me a weak little smile. "I've already 'received' all the condolences I can handle. For nearly two weeks, it's all I've been doing. Enough is enough."

"But what about all that good food?" said Orpha. "We can't let it go to waste."

"It won't go to waste," replied Nova. "The church ladies will divvy up the leftovers and send it home with anyone who wants to take some."

"It's important that we all eat something pretty darn soon," Orpha insisted. "At our ages we have to keep our bodies fueled, you know. We wouldn't want to collapse on the church steps for lack of something to eat while the fellowship hall is brimming with sandwiches."

"Nova wants to leave," said Merri quietly, placing her hand on Orpha's shoulder. "Let's honor her request. It's the least The Veiled Rainbow can do to support her."

"How about we head over to the Cinco Amigos Chinese Cuisine?" I asked, looking for a good compromise.

"Great idea!" said Orpha happily. "All that kneeling and standing has worked up a powerful appetite."

"But... But I don't like Chinese food," said Goodie. She squinted her eyes at Orpha. "And I think you know that."

"Then you can just have a bowl of egg flower soup," Orpha replied, bobbing her head up and down enthusiastically. "Egg flower soup is just chicken noodle soup, only it's made with very young chickens."

I could tell Goodie wasn't quite buying it, but she didn't want to be left out, and all the other gals were in agreement.

Cinco Amigos had been closed during the late morning funeral service so that the five Mexican friends who owned the place could bid farewell to their amigo Mateo. It was just now opening for the day when we arrived, en masse, and I think they were a bit overwhelmed as we suddenly descended upon them.

Nova had pulled a blue, plaid. flannel shirt on over her funeral dress like a jacket, so she looked a little more like herself, but the Cinco Amigos all knew her, of course, so she had to receive all five of them showering her with more condolences after all.

"Mesa para..." Juan started counting. "Uno, dos, tres, cuatro, cinco, seis, siete?"

"Sí," said Felicity.

"Hey, I understood that!" Orpha said happily. "Meredith, Goodie, Nadine, Nova, Sylvia, Felicity and me makes seven!"

Juan gathered siete menus and led us to the banquet table in the back alcove. I suspected he wanted to give us some privacy, but perhaps he just remembered how loud we'd gotten the last time so many of us ate here together.

Fortunately, it was early enough in the day that I didn't think there'd be as much wine flowing this time. But as it turned out, I thought wrong.

Just as soon as Juan brought us hot oolong tea, and set seven small porcelain cups in front of us, someone—I think it was Meredith—asked about the possibility of getting something "a little stronger."

Juan nodded slightly, a motion reminiscent of Kanji, and left without a word. He returned almost immediately with a bottle that looked more like an urn for ashes than a bottle of alcohol. He held the bottle for Merri's inspection.

Merri exploded into laughter. "Juan, darling, I do not speak Chinese!"

Juan bowed again. "It is baijiu."

It sounded to me like he said "bye-joe," but maybe that was because his ancestry traces back to a farming area outside Patzcuaro and not Beijing.

Meredith hesitated, all eyes upon her. "What's it made of, Juan? Rice? Like Sake?"

Juan nodded. "Rice. Yes. And sometimes other grains."

Right about then, I was missing Jimmy's bottomless knowledge. I selfishly needed to know what these—dare I say elderly?—women were getting themselves into. If they weren't careful, Felicity and I, the only two non-drinkers among us, would be the designated drivers for this whole motley crew.

"What's it taste like?" asked Goodie.

"What's it matter?" asked Nadine.

Goodie looked around the table and shrugged. "I just wanted to be sure it mixed well with communion wine."

"It is called Chinese vodka," said Felicity. "It's the most popular drink in the world, but I think that's because there are so many Chinese." She smiled and looked at Juan. "Do you have any Sinkiang black beer? Maybe something with a little less proof?"

Six pairs of eyes stared at her—seven if you count Juan's.

Felicity smiled. "I went to China for a teaching exchange last summer, remember? I lived with a Chinese family for over a month and immersed myself in the culture."

"I thought you didn't drink!" I said. "I've known you for more than a decade and I've never once seen you drink!"

Felix smiled apologetically. "I don't drink often, but I was interested in learning everything I could about the people of China while I was there, so I broke my own rule." She looked around the group. "I didn't care for it much."

Juan looked mildly disappointed, but said nothing.

I could tell the ladies were all teetering with indecision, looking at each other, but not wanting to be the first to commit to trying Juan's "Chinese vodka."

Then Orpha held up her teacup. "I'm not getting any younger over here, and I'm for sure not going to be able to go to China to taste it over there, so fill 'er up, Juan."

With a general sigh of relief, the ladies of The Veiled Rainbow all agreed to "just a taste."

"Please excuse me while I go get five shot glasses," said Juan, bowing again.

"What's the matter with our teacups?" asked Nadine.

"It's a sipping drink," said Felicity.

"I can sip from a teacup just as well as from a shot glass," said Merri.

"Or a communion cup," Goodie chimed in.

"While you guys are busy debating the appropriate glassware, I'm dying of thirst over here," said Nova.

We all laughed, and Juan poured a small amount of baijiu into each of their teacups while Felix and I filled ours with oolong tea.

"Leave the bottle!" said Orpha. "Some of us might want a second taste."

Juan set the bottle on the table, and asked if we were ready to order.

"Deluxe Dinner A. Family style for seven," said Meredith, without bothering to consult the others.

It was a good choice, and nobody objected, so Juan, delighted in the simplicity of the order, trotted off to the kitchen. Had we each ordered separately, he would have had to write down a list of substitutions and special requests. And this way, there would only be one check, and the ladies could divide it all up themselves.

Nova raised her teacup. "To Mateo," she said softly.

"To Mateo," we all echoed, and sipped at our drinks.

Only Felicity and I did not make a face after that first sip.

"Maybe it's an acquired taste," said Goodie.

Everyone nodded.

"To Walter," said Merri.

"To Walter," we echoed, and took another sip.

"Yes," said Orpha. "I think that second swig was a lot easier to swallow."

Nadine lifted her cup a third time. "To Claudette," she said.

There was a momentary pause, not much more than

the blink of an eye, while Goodie considered whether to toast or not to toast. Then she lifted her cup and said, "To Claudette."

We all took a third sip, and Orpha reached for the bottle of baijiu. "This bye-joe stuff isn't so bad once you get used to it."

Goodie agreed. "It does kind of grow on you."

Orpha generously restocked her teacup, then passed the bottle along to Nadine, who followed suit, passing it on to Goodie, who passed it on Nova, who passed it on to Merri, who looked at Felicity and me, then sent the bottle back around the other direction.

I bit my tongue. It was only one bottle, and there were five drinking from it, so I hoped everyone had had a hearty breakfast this morning to keep the alcohol from affecting any of them too much.

Deluxe Dinner A begins with egg flower soup, so thankfully, there wasn't time for any more toasts before something to eat was set before us and the baijiu was temporarily forgotten.

"What's that stuff floating in it?" asked Goodie, the only one who hesitated before picking up her spoon.

"That's the egg in egg flower," said Orpha.

"But you said it was like chicken noodle soup," said Goodie, and there aren't any eggs in chicken noodle soup."

Orpha sighed. "Well what do you think egg noodles are made out of?"

"Just give it a small taste," said Nadine, trying her hand at diplomacy. "If you don't like it, you don't have to eat it."

Goodie took a small sip from her soup spoon, and her eyes lit up with pleasure. "Why, that does taste a lot like chicken noodle!" she said with surprise.

"Told you so," murmured everyone at the table whose

mouth was not full.

We slurped in silence for a few minutes, and well before most of us had time to finish with our soup, the rest of our food began arriving. Juan, José, and Fernando all carried a tray of platters to our table, and something told me there was a lot more food there than what we'd ordered. Perhaps it was their way of honoring Mateo. My still-growling stomach embraced the abundance.

"Family style" creates an assembly line of passing food, and with the amount moving around the table, our plates began to fill up much too quickly. All but Goodie's.

Goodie was warily looking at each dish as it passed, sniffing one and then the other, but her plate remained bare. Nadine, like a mother serving a petulant child, began putting a spoonful of each dish on her own plate, then a smaller spoonful on Goodie's plate.

"You didn't hesitate to try the baijiu," said Nadine to Goodie, "so you can either suck it up, Buttercup, and try a bite of each dish, or you can ask to finish off everyone's soup. Your choice."

Goodie nodded. "Okay. I'll give the food a try."

I wasn't sure if it was the alcohol making her more receptive to trying the food, or if it was her way of letting Nadine know that things between them were going to be alright.

"Company halt!" said Orpha before all the platters had gone around. "Let's eat what we've got before us, then pick it up where we left off."

It sounded like a great idea, and silence fell as we all attacked our food with gusto. A few bites in, I noticed that Felix and I were the only ones using chopsticks, but I wasn't worried about getting enough to eat. There was food everywhere!

"Have you been to see Mrs. Winston?" I quietly asked Felicity.

She nodded, swallowed her mouthful of food, and demurely wiped her mouth with her napkin before replying. "She's actually taking it really well."

"Which part?"

"I'm afraid I don't know what you mean." Felicity looked at me pointedly over the top of her glasses.

I suppose in a classroom, that teacher look could be quite intimidating, but I chose to ignore the signal to stop talking. "The part about him dying, or the part about you being the beneficiary on his life insurance?"

"Oh, that." Felicity took another piece of sweet and sour chicken and popped it whole into her mouth. I wondered if she did that to keep from having to answer me right away, but I wasn't going to be deterred. When I really want to know something, I can be uncommonly patient.

At the mention of 'life insurance,' I'm sure I saw my mother's ears perk up. Then I noticed that no one else at the table was talking right at the moment.

Felicity finished chewing and swallowed. "They've been divorced over a year. I know she was disappointed that he'd changed his will and insurance policies already, but what could she say?" Felix shrugged.

From the other side of me, Orpha piped up. "So what are you going to do with all your money, Honey?"

Often her social gaffes are attributed to her age, and Orpha gets away with saying inappropriate things all the time. Occasionally, and only for that reason, I can't wait to be her age, whatever that is. She admits to 85, but I'm thinking she's been claiming that number for several years now.

Although everyone kept steadily eating, all eyes were

on Felicity.

"Okay." She set down her chopsticks. "First," and she held up one finger, "I'm going to set up two modest Walter Winston college scholarships—one in science, which he taught at the high school for almost 40 years, and the other in drama, which was an after school activity he coached for nearly as long."

We all nodded.

"And secondly," and she raised another finger, "I'm donating another modest amount to a number of local charities—the North Beach Peninsula's Boys and Girls club, the Swiftstone Lighthouse restoration committee, and the Unity Historical Museum, to name three."

"What about the Humane Society?" asked Goodie. "The animals just keep coming, and we can always use more dog and cat food, litter and cleaning supplies."

"Yes, Goodie, rest assured there will be some money coming to the Tinkerstown Humane Society as well." Felix smiled, abruptly stopped explaining the intended dispersion of her unexpected windfall, and picked her chopsticks back up.

Meredith asked the obvious question. "Will there be any money left for you, dear?"

I would swear Felix blushed. "I didn't do anything to earn it, Merri, and I think Walter had you put me down as the beneficiary to do good with it, in his name." She took another bite of moo shu pork, hoping to put an end to further discussion.

"But that doesn't answer the question," Meredith persisted.

I purposefully glowered at her, but her question was already hanging in the air.

Felix swallowed again, wiped her mouth on her napkin

again, and nodded. "Yes, Meredith, there will be some money left for me. There's another teacher exchange I'm interested in participating in, and you have to pay your own way. This one is to Brazil with an emphasis on protecting the Amazon rainforest."

"Oh!" said Goodie. "I guess your Spanish will come in handy there."

"Wrong!" said Nadine before Felix could reply. "Portuguese is the national language of Brazil, because they were a Portuguese colony." She scowled. "But I don't think that's the language they speak along the Amazon, is it? They're pretty isolated out there."

"I'm sure our guide will be fluent in whatever languages are necessary," said Felix.

"Then here's to safe travels!" said Orpha, hoisting her teacup again.

All the ladies drank to Felicity's safe travels, and when Juan came to ask us how we were doing, Nova asked if he had another bottle of "the Chinese good stuff" in his back room.

I resigned myself to being one of the designated drivers, and leaned closer to Felix to whisper, "Nova, Goodie and Orpha all live on the south end, Meredith lives on the north end, and Nadine's in the middle, so I'll take her with me."

"Deal," Felicity whispered back.

"I heard that," said Meredith.

"Ears like a bat," I chided her.

Juan returned with another bottle of baijiu and poured a small amount in all their cups again while I was silently praying that there were no more bottles of "the good stuff" back in his storeroom.

Meredith immediately raised her cup. "And here's to

thoughtful, kind, and most generous teachers everywhere!"

They all sipped, and Felix surprised me by keeping her own teacup, filled with actual tea, high in the air. "And here's to there being no public service for Walter," she said matter-of-factly. "My students have been through enough this spring, and the grief counselors are working overtime."

Under normal circumstances, Felicity's comments would have put a somber lid on the boisterous nature of the group, but the affects of the "bye-joe," despite the amount of food eaten, had taken over.

"And here's to Nova and Meredith, for being cleared of all charges!" said Nadine, and another round of sips were taken.

"How about we pass around a little more food?" I offered, hoping to slow down their drinking a little.

"Is anybody still hungry?" asked Merri.

I glowered at her a second time, with much the same non-effect.

Merri, being Merri, refused to take the hint and continued to push the envelope. "Then here's to none of us being charged with any wrong doing in the deaths of any of our husbands, and to nobody having to return any of the money!"

Everyone cheered.

Then Orpha, apparently carried away with the baijiu, or maybe just by the rambunctious energy of the joyful, albeit slightly tipsy women, exclaimed, "Ain't it a pip? Ain't it just a doggone *pip?!* I was the only one of us not under investigation, and I'm the only one of us who actually offed her husband!"

CHAPTER 19

It was as if we were all co-starring in another bad remake of "The Day the Earth Stood Still," and it flitted through my mind that both Jimmy and Freddy would be so proud of me for referencing a classic science-fiction film.

Nobody moved. Nobody said a word. And time really did seem to stop.

"That's right," said Orpha. She bobbed her head so rapidly the curls on her Brillo-pad perm bounced all over her head. She appeared to enjoy having our full attention focused on her, pleased as punch to be the sole senior in the spotlight. "I killed Bill."

"Orpha, Honey," said Felicity, reaching across me to push Orpha's teacup away from her. "I think you've had a little too much to drink."

"The only problem is," Orpha continued, "that I wasn't as smart as the rest of you—I didn't get any money for it." She frowned, then brightened. "But I was so sick and tired of waiting on him hand and foot for decades that it was still well worth it."

I looked around the table at the gaping mouths. "She's confused," I said. My voice was low and level and surprised even me. "You know how she sometimes gets details confused and forgets things."

The somber, silent faces all nodded.

"Forgets things? Not on your life, Missy!" Orpha laughed at her own morbid joke. "Let me tell you exactly how it happened. One day Bill had a bout of chest pains, which usually turned out to be nothing more than indigestion, because that man often ate too much and too fast. But this time the pains got so strong he called for me to bring him his nitroglycerin."

She waited expectantly, looking from face to face like we were supposed to ask her to continue or something, but since none of us could think of a single thing to say, she continued without our encouragement.

"I decided then and there that maybe I was in the other room when Bill called out to me, and maybe I simply couldn't hear him." She beamed, and used both index fingers to tap her hearing aids, illustrating her point.

"I didn't have to wait very long at all, and nature took its course. Bill died right there in his recliner, and I figured if he were too dumb to keep his meds within reach, then he probably deserved to die." She grinned like she'd just won the lottery. "And all I could think of was that I was free, free, free at last!"

"Orpha, you did not kill Bill," I said, rather sternly. "Bill had a heart attack, and you weren't home when it happened."

"Wanna bet?" Orpha crowed. "I was only home that afternoon until the minute I was absolutely sure he was dead, then I went to the grocery store for an alibi."

"An alibi?" asked Nadine, her eyes were large and round, and it was quite apparent she really had had too much to drink. "Do they sell alibis at the grocery store?"

"How much do alibis cost?" Goodie piped up. Her yellow pillbox hat had slid over one eye, making her look rather comical—like a lemon-drop Popeye the sailor man. "They way things have been going around here, I might need to get one of those alibis to keep on hand. One just never knows."

The members of The Veiled Rainbow all laughed hysterically.

Oh boy. It looked like five of the seven of us were now under the influence of a total snootful of Chinese booze.

"I made sure everyone saw me at the grocery store, gathering the ingredients to make Bill's favorite meatloaf." Orpha chuckled. "And why would I be planning on making Bill a meatloaf if I knew he was already dead? It was the perfect cover story!"

"Ladies! Ladies!" I implored them. "Let's all just hush up a moment."

Unbelievably, the group quieted.

"Now let's think this through," I said. "Even though Orpha didn't profit from Bill's death, it would be a terrible ordeal if she were to be criminally investigated."

The ladies all nodded, somberly.

"So I suggest it would be in everyone's best interest if we pinky swore to never, ever, ever, talk about this again, to anyone. Agreed?" I held my right pinky finger out to link with Orpha, and extended my left pinky to Felicity. "Agreed?" I asked again, but they still sat frozen, and no one moved a finger—not even a pinky finger.

"You forget," said Orpha, giggling maniacally, "I'm named after Orpheus, the charmer of brutes. According to mythology, he could charm all people, even the stones."

"Orpha," said Goodie, "You're confused again. We're all drunk, not stoned."

"Rock on!" said Nadine, and she started loudly singing. "But I would not feel so all alone! Everybody must get stoned!"

Nova lifted her teacup and found it was empty. "Any more of that bye-joe left?" she asked of no one in particular.

Goodie ignored Nova's request for baijiu and joined Nadine in singing, "They'll stone you when you're trying to be so good, They'll stone you just like they said they would, They'll stone you when you're trying to go home..."

I hated to admit it, but their singing wasn't half bad.

"Oh, I just love Bob Dylan!" said Merri, happily clapping her hands.

"Hey! I wasn't done talking!" said Orpha, shouting to be heard above the singing.

"Yes, I think you were," said Nova. "You're done talking, and I'm out of bye-bye-joe. We might as well go home." She paused, then belted out, "Home, home on the range..."

Apparently Nova did not know the words to the song Nadine and Goodie were singing, but I guess she didn't want to feel like she had nothing to contribute.

I shot a look at Felicity, who was working overtime to keep a straight face, so I quickly looked away, knowing that if we actually made eye contact, we'd both start giggling like we had good sense.

But Orpha was not to be deterred, and pulled us all back to the point of her story. "Listen up, all you aging hippy chicks! I'm telling you that with age comes privilege!"

"What's that supposed to mean?" asked Merri.

"I'm old. I'm named after Orpheus. And I'm sure I'd have no trouble at all with the police if I were ever arrested. It would be a piece of cake to charm them all into believing I was just a silly old woman, who gets 'confused' easily." She looked pointedly at me. "They'd all just chalk it up to my age, call me bonkers, and let me go."

Perhaps she was not as drunk as I'd thought.

"Ladies! Please! Let's not go looking for trouble." I held out my pinky finger again. "Let's vow to never speak of this again."

On my left, Felicity held out her right hand to me, and her left hand to Meredith, and we completed linking pinkies around the table.

"Good! Much better!" I breathed a sigh of relief. "Now let's talk about something else."

"Yes," said Meredith, "let's talk about why my daughter can't choose between two very charming and eligible beaus."

"I've wondered that myself," said Goodie. "If I were a little younger, I'd be hot for that young man in uniform. He's the berries!"

"A *little* younger?" asked Nadine. "Face it, Gigi, you'd have to be half your age to get Freddy to give you a second look, and even then, he might not look your way. You'd have to stop cutting your own bangs, that's for sure."

"You're a fine one to talk," said Orpha, defending Goodie. "Do you even know what color your natural hair used to be?" She eyed Nadine warily.

"I don't know what you're talking about," said Nadine, fluffing the back of her shoulder-length, sixties-flip hairdo. "This is the color I was born with."

"Oh, pull-eeze" said Orpha. "You change your hair color so often, your driver's license should come with a color wheel."

The ladies, including Felicity and me, all chuckled. It was an ongoing debate, whether it was delusional for aging women to color their hair or let it go gray naturally, and it was a debate that nobody would ever win.

"So what about the hot cop?" asked Nova, looking at me. "He's younger, so he's likely to live longer than the insurance guy."

"But Kanji is so exotic!" exclaimed Nadine. "And

he's..."

"And he's what?" prompted Meredith.

"And he's so much closer to Sylvia's age," finished Nadine.

"And he's got that great accent," said Goodie.

"And he's not from around here, so he hasn't already dated the entire peninsula," said Nova.

"And he's got that cute puppy," said Felicity. "How can you not love a man who has a cute puppy?"

"Felicity!" I elbowed her. "You're supposed to be on my side here!"

"Get them young, so you can raise them right!" Orpha chimed in. "I'm voting for the hot cop."

"They each have their own merits," said Meredith. "I think Sylvia might just want to have the best of both worlds, but it takes one of them off the market for anyone else, and we all know the peninsula is top-heavy with single women of all ages."

"Mother! Stop talking about me as if I'm not here!" I exclaimed.

"Everything we've said is true," Merri persisted. "You've got two men, and now that Walter's gone, none of us have any."

Orpha leaned over to whisper, "You're a greedy little piggy, Miss Syllee."

The alcohol was responsible for most of their comments, but the underlying truth in what they said made me feel uncomfortable.

"If you wanted to assassinate my character, why did you bother to invite me to join you for lunch?"

"Oh, that's easy," said Orpha. "With seven you get egg rolls, BBQ pork, and crab puffs with the family style dinner."

"And we'd be talking about you and your men whether you were here or not," said Nadine. "It's just what we do."

Felix was on the verge of totally losing it once again. "That baijiu is better than truth serum," she said, laughing. "These gals are a hoot!"

"So Nadine," I said, trying to change the subject once and for all, "are you ready to swear off any more wild animal feeding?"

My statement, as I intended, immediately toned done the wild party atmosphere.

Nadine nodded sadly. "Yes. What happened to Claudette was horrible, and I deeply regret having lured the bears to my porch with dog food. From now on, I'm only going to put out hummingbird feeders."

"That's good to hear," said Goodie.

"And maybe some birdseed feeders for the sparrows," continued Nadine.

"I totally approve," said Goodie, reaching out to squeeze Nadine's hand.

"But..." Nadine's eyes twinkled mischievously, "I hear that sometimes squirrels and even raccoons find ways to get into the suet and bird seed. And those little raccoons look just like masked bandits, don't they? And they're just so darn cute, it's pretty hard to resist feed—"

Goodie jerked her hand away. "Deenie! You're incorrigible."

The rest of us held our tongues, but I'm sure that every single one of us, other than Nadine that is, participated in a group eye roll.

"So," said Felicity, abruptly going off on what should have been another safe subject, "where are you Rainbow Gals performing next? I loved seeing you dance at Mercedes' homecoming party."

Conviviality restored, the women chatted amicably about how they designed their costumes, what online site had the best price for coin belts, the advantages of chiffon over silk veils, and whether harem pants should have elastic or draw-string waistbands.

"As for me," Nova confided quietly to no one in particular, "I don't care how they're fastened, but I'd be happier if the harem pants were made of denim. They'd be much more comfortable, and much less see-throughy, but no one else ever agrees with me." She ran her hand through her spiky hair and sighed.

"You should join us," Goodie abruptly said to Felicity. "It's great exercise."

Felicity smiled. "You forget that I still work," she said. "I wouldn't be able to come to your practices during the day at the Senior Center."

Goodie nodded. "Oh, that's right. And you're not old enough to be a member at the Center yet, are you?"

"The Senior Center doesn't discriminate," said Orpha. "It's against the law."

Nova snorted, but refrained from comment, and merely asked to have someone pass her the pork fried rice.

"We understand," said Goodie, "no belly dancing for you." Her eyes twinkled as she continued, still speaking only to Felix, "but perhaps you'd like to join us in our next exciting adventure."

Orpha winked at Felicity. "Trust me, it's going to be a hoot."

But before I could inquire as to the specifics of whatever scheme they were planning now, Goodie directed her next invitation directly to me. "So what about you, Syl?" she asked. "Have you changed your mind about joining our troupe?"

"Me? No!" I choked on a swallow of tea. "I thought we already settled this last week at the casino bar." I looked at Orpha. "You were going to invite Jimmy to join the troupe, remember?"

Orpha narrowed her eyes and glared at me. "Of course I remember. Why does everyone think I can't remember anything anymore? Is it because I choose to call my cat Cat?"

I ignored her attempt to detour the conversation and followed up with, "Did you ask Jimmy to join the troupe, or not?"

"Oh sure, we asked him," said Orpha. "And he turned us down flat. He said he didn't want to be invited just because we needed a token male so we could meet the integration standards for a non-profit."

Say what? I shook my head to clear it.

"Never mind her, dear," said Nadine with a shrug. "You're already a member of the Senior Center, so why not join us for dance classes? Just give it a try."

"And even though your mother won't admit her age, we all know you're plenty old enough to be a full-fledged member of The Veiled Rainbow," said Orpha.

Meredith wiped her mouth on a paper napkin, and pointedly looked at me. "We do need the final color of our rainbow."

"Yes." Nova nodded thoughtfully. "Violet is still missing."

There was a sudden eruption of excitement around the table, during which I felt a high-pitched buzzing in my ears as I heard my future with the troupe being discussed as if I weren't there, once again.

"Whoa there! Hold everything!" I waved my hands back and forth in front of my face to get their attention.

"I'm not nearly old enough to consider—" I bit my tongue and started over. "I mean, I'm flattered that you ladies would like me to join you for aerobic exercise, but—"

All eyes and ears were aimed at me as I struggled to find a good reason not to become the sixth member of The Veiled Rainbow.

"But I— I, uh—" I faltered, flushed, and fanned myself with my paper napkin. Then I looked desperately at Felicity for some kind of signal or support or viable excuse why I could not join them.

"You do look good in purple," Felix said, with just the slightest twitch of a smirk.

"Isn't it ironic?" said Merri, sighing. "Your father brought me a small bouquet of violets during our brief time together—it might have been the very day you were conceived—and when you were born a girl, I actually considered naming you Violet."

"You almost named me Violet?" I echoed, my voice all high and squeaky.

"Mm-hmm," said Merri. "It was a toss-up, and when it came right down to filling in your birth certificate, I decided to name you after your father Sylvester instead." She shrugged. "So it's kismet that you should now become Violet. You can't fight fate."

Maybe *she* couldn't fight fate, but I had no intention of going down without swinging.

None of the dance troupe had blinked at Meredith's mention of my father, but it had certainly caught Felicity by surprise.

"You're named after your father Sylvester?" she whispered. "I thought you didn't know who your father was."

"She's always known his name," said Orpha, "she's just

247

never met him."

Well! Between my love life and my paternity, I seemed to have no privacy control. My face flushed with embarrassment. Was nothing sacred?

"You know," said Nadine, "you could dye your hair purple. Then no one would ever guess you weren't as old as the rest of us."

"Is that what you think you're doing with all the color changes?" Orpha asked Nadine. "Trying to disguise your age?"

"Or you could use Violet as a pseudonym when you danced with us," continued Nadine without bothering to acknowledge Orpha's questions.

"I miss the sixties," said Goodie wistfully. "I miss the flower children with names like Moon Song and Wildflower and Charity and Chastity."

"If Meredith had been Chastity, she wouldn't have had Sylvia," said Orpha with a knowing smile.

"We don't know that for sure," said Nova. "From what I've heard, Sylvester was a total stud muffin."

The room erupted again into the wisdom of naming children after virtues, colors, or plants, and whether my conception was inevitable, given the decade of free love.

"Hello? I'm still here, remember?" I said, much louder than I intended. "Can we pick a topic that leaves me out of center of conversation?"

The room grew quiet until Felicity turned to Meredith. "I know it's none of my business," she said. "and I want you to know I'm not blaming you or judging you or anything in any way."

"Sounds ominous," said Meredith.

"I just want to know," continued Felicity, "if you are planning to get another cat, and if you are, are you going to name him Walter?"

The question momentarily splashed some cold water on all of us.

"No," replied Meredith, resolutely shaking her head, "No, I'm not. No more cats." She tilted her head. "But why are you asking?"

Felicity blew out a breath and looked uncomfortably at the elderly women seated around the table. "Because I'd like to adopt a cat from the Humane Society," she said, her eyes first settling on Goodie, then back to Meredith, "and I need to know if the name 'Walter' has already been spoken for."

Suddenly, we all had tears in our eyes, and Nova sounded like a foghorn blowing her nose on her paper napkin. "That's just beautiful," she said, "just beautiful. You two had a very special friendship."

Felicity looked at me. "Do you think it's alright?"

I nodded. "I've never quite understood why people might do that before, but right now I think it's a fine tribute."

Then to lighten the mood back up, I asked, "Would someone please pass me the crab puffs? They're my favorite."

I smiled as I watched Goodie put one on her own plate before she handed the platter to Orpha. Then as Orpha handed them over to me, she winked again and said, "Here you go, Violet!"

My cell phone rang before I could think of a snappy comeback, and the ringtone made it unnecessary for me to take a quick peek at the screen: "Bad boys, Bad boys, Whatcha gonna do? Whatcha gonna do when they come for you?"

Six faces beamed at me as each of them realized it was Freddy calling, and once again my face flushed scarlet. Too bad "Red" was the Veiled Rainbow color already taken by my mother!

There was no point in stepping away from the table, so I answered the call right where I sat. Unless I slipped up, I knew they'd only hear my end of the conversation, and I thought, since I was not under the influence of anything but crab puffs, that I could manage that just fine.

"Hello?... Yes... That's very generous of you." I laughed. "Yes, and I hope you added a very large tip. Yes... I'll tell them... Yes, I'd be happy to... No, not too much longer... Okay, thanks."

I hung up, and six faces were staring at me—again. "Freddy says hello. Our meal here today is on him. He already called and arranged it."

"Must be nice to have a hot-shot rich boyfriend," said Nadine.

"Put another check mark in Freddy's column," said Goodie.

"What else did he say?" asked Meredith.

I wrinkled my forehead. "That's about it."

"You told him you'd be happy to do something," said Merri. "What would you be happy to do?"

"I can think of a few things I'd be happy to do with Freddy," chirped Orpha.

"Oh, that," I replied to Merri and shook my head. "Freddy is at Jimmy's and he asked me to pick up their order to go. No big deal."

"We should have just sent him all our leftovers," said Goodie, looking at all the food left on the table.

As if on cue, Juan appeared with a stack of take-out boxes, and each of the ladies scooped up what was left of their favorite dishes to take home. Even Goodie.

I squinted my eyes at Merri. "The food has soaked up

all your earlier alcohol, right? You okay to drive home, or shall I call the taxi?"

"Of course," said Merri, "and I'll take Nadine with me."

"And I'll take care of Orpha, Goodie, and Nova," said Felicity.

Goodie elbowed Orpha and stage-whispered, "And that will give us some time to convince Felix to get on board with our next adventure."

CHAPTER 20

I would swear I could feel my blood pressure go soaring. What in the world were these little old ladies up to now? I stood, shot Felix a look, and mouthed 'call me." She nodded.

"Are you sure Freddy took care of the tip?" asked Nova, struggling to put her flannel shirt-jacket back on. I reached over and held the arm of the jacket out for her to put her arm through.

"Yes. Absolutely. I'm sure he did." I smiled. From the moment I met him, Freddy had been one of the most thoughtful and considerate men I'd ever met, and there was no indication that his inheritance was going change him in the least.

"So we're all set for our trip home," said Orpha. "And you're now free to go see your hot, rich boyfriend, Violet."

I didn't bother to protest, or scowl, or even roll my eyes. I merely said good-bye to Felix and the ladies, gave Mom a quick kiss on the cheek, and headed for the front counter to pick up the order for Freddy and Jimmy.

The enormous box filled with food was not the only thing waiting for me at the counter. Raven stood there, shifting her weight from one foot to the other.

I stopped in my tracks. How long had she been in the restaurant? How much had she heard? I looked back in the direction of the group gathering up their coats, purses, and leftovers, and felt my heart start pounding in my chest.

"Hi, Ms. Avery," said Raven.

"Hello, Raven."

For a moment I hoped she were only there to pick up an order of her own, and that our conversation was over, but that was not the case.

"I was headed for my job at the High Tide," Raven began, "and I saw all your vehicles parked out there, so I pulled in."

I said nothing, and she continued. "I owe you all a big apology," she said, looking down at her feet. "Ms. Michaels says I watch too much crime TV."

At that I smiled, as I have often been accused of the same thing myself.

"So I wanted to tell you that I'll be heading for college soon—I'm going to study to be a physical therapist—and I won't be writing any more articles for the North Beach Tribune."

Apparently, Raven had only just arrived, and I breathed a huge sigh of relief. "I'm sure you'll make a very fine physical therapist, Raven. And I wish you all the best."

She nodded, and went out through the exit door, assuming correctly that I would pass on her apology to the other women. But I decided to wait until a few more of them were sober to do so.

I nodded to Juan behind the counter, picked up the heavy carton, and headed for my car. I was pretty sure there was a lot more food there then even two very hungry men could eat, and I wondered who else might be having Chinese takeout at the Clamshell. Thankfully, it was a short trip, and my curiosity was soon satisfied.

Freddy's motorcycle was parked between the motel office and Jimmy's aging split-pea Pinto. Farther down, parked in front of Unit 6, was Kanji's Scion. Other than those three vehicles, there was no indication of more company than the usual suspects, as our dear, sweet Orpha-the-homicidal-maniac was fond of saying.

Geez, I was going to have to watch what I thought about Orpha's confession. If I didn't, then sooner or later I was bound to think out loud, and doing so could open up a whole 'nother kettle of worms for the Sheriff's Department.

But as I climbed from the car, people and vehicles started miraculously appearing from out of nowhere. First Rich wheeled into the lot in "Moby Dick," his big white beach truck. Then Kanji, trailed by the pup, came out of Unit 6 and started toward the office. Sheriff D's SUV arrived next, with Mercedes riding shotgun.

Kanji took the big box of Chinese food from me and headed indoors, while I waited by my car to speak to Mercedes before joining the others inside.

Sheriff D went around his vehicle and set a stepstool on the ground for Mercedes before he opened the passenger door and gallantly helped her out of the SUV. It was kind of sweet, really, and my heart filled with happiness for these two. They both deserved it.

Then the sheriff tipped his Stetson to me and went on inside, giving us girls a few minutes of privacy.

"How was Mateo's service?" asked Merc, hugging me tightly.

"Muy bien," I replied.

"Yes," said Mercedes, "I was wondering if the service would be bilingual."

"Wonder no more," I said. "It was very respectful, but very long, and Felicity and the Rainbow Gals and I ditched the reception to go eat at Cinco Amigos."

Mercedes nodded. "That much made it up the grapevine all the way to the top of the peninsula." She paused, then added thoughtfully, "How's Nova?"

"Nova's doing as well as can be expected," I answered. "I think she's more than a little relieved that she got solid closure on Mateo's disappearance. So many fishermen's wives are not so fortunate."

"So is it true the entire dance troupe got snockered on Chinese vodka this afternoon?"

"How, exactly, did the grapevine pick up on that little tidbit of private information?" I asked with harsh indignation. "Is nothing sacred?!"

Mercedes laughed. "Did you forget who I'm sleeping with?"

"No, I did not—you won't let me forget! But what's that got to do with..." I abruptly stopped talking.

"Uh-huh," said Mercedes. " There's a pretty tight, yet talkative, Mexican contingency here on the peninsula. Juan and José both have wives who work as hotel maids at Spartina Point, but I heard about it today from Carter, who heard it from Fernando's brother Emilio, who is an unpaid volunteer deputy. Carter says Emilio is indispensible as a court interpreter, and he wants to put him on the payroll, but he thinks the family might not be fully documented, and he doesn't want..."

I held up my hand. "Enough!" I said. "I didn't ask for the whole history of the Hispanic population on the peninsula, I just wanted to know how you knew The Veiled Rainbow got plastered this afternoon."

"Oh, right," said Merc. "It was the Mexican grapevine."

"Now was that so difficult?" I asked, laughing. "It's good to see you."

"Good to see you, too," said Mercedes, giving me another hug. "Now if we don't hurry up and get in there, I won't be getting anything to eat today!"

"Trust me," I said, putting my arm around her and walking toward the motel door, "there's enough food in there for several NFL teams, plus cheerleaders."

We entered Jimmy's living quarters and all the men had already served themselves and were camped in various chairs throughout the two rooms, busily wolfing down food. Jimmy, Kanji, Priscilla and the pup were on the living room side, using the coffee table to set their plates on, and Carter, Freddy, and Rich were seated at the dining room table.

"I guess I'm the last hog to the trough," said Mercedes, picking up the one remaining empty plate on the counter and digging in to the cartons of food.

"You didn't want us to wait, did you?" asked the sheriff.

"It's my fault," said Freddy. "I told them there was no telling how long you two would stand out there talking, and that we shouldn't let the food get cold."

Neither Mercedes nor I had a solid comeback for that, and we let it slide as she filled her plate, and sat down next to Carter. Even though I'd finished eating not an hour before, I found that the smell of crab puffs was mighty tempting, and took one to nibble on while everyone else ate.

"Like I was saying, before the women came in," said Rich, "the Mexican community came out in force for Mateo's service. The production managers at the cannery even closed it down for a couple hours." He took a swig of the beer he'd obviously brought with him.

"And all five of the Cinco Amigos were there," I contributed. "They'd just unlocked their restaurant doors when the gals and I arrived." I looked at Freddy. "By the way, how did you know I was there when you called in your order?"

"Mexican grapevine," said Freddy, shoveling in another mouthful of food.

I looked pointedly at Mercedes.

"Mars and Venus," she said with a shrug. "Men just don't know how to tell a good story."

My cell phone rang before I could reply to Merc's comment, and since the call was from Felicity, I stepped outside to answer it. "Is everyone alright?"

"Oh sure, no problem," Felix replied, "but you asked me to call when I found out what the ladies are up to, and Sylvia, you're just not going to believe this."

"Nothing would surprise me when it comes to the women of The Veiled Rainbow," I said. "Just tell me it's not going to involve bail money."

"I doubt it, but these women are determined to keep things stirred up around here," said Felix with a chuckle. "You'll probably find out soon enough, but you asked me to call and give you a head's up."

"Yes I did, and thank you for calling." I perched on the stool behind the office counter and squinched my eyes shut tight, preparing myself for the worst.

I guess I must have slammed the door too hard when I went back inside, as all conversation came to a halt, and six heads turned in my direction expectantly. Eight heads, if you count Priscilla and the pup.

"Well?" said Mercedes. "Let's hear it. What's the big news?"

"Who said there was big news?" I asked, feigning innocence.

Freddy snorted, Rich guffawed, and Carter clucked his tongue. Only Kanji and Jimmy had no editorial noises to contribute, and I'm sure that was only because Kanji doesn't know me well enough to tease me, and Jimmy knows better.

"The Veiled Rainbow have decided to try their hand at online dating," I blurted out.

Laughter erupted all around the two rooms, accompanied by much head shaking.

"Hey! It's not all that funny." I was surprised to find myself defending them. "They've decided they're still young enough to find love, if they just cast their nets a little farther afield than the guy next door, so they've decided they're going to use the World Wide Web to find the men of their dreams."

Kanji nodded in agreement. "Ladies that belly dance for fitness are certainly not beyond an arbitrary age limit for sexual companionship."

"Whoa! Who said anything about *sex?*" I could feel my eyes threatening to pop right out of my eye sockets.

"Well, what did you think they're looking for?" asked Rich. "Another old man to cook and clean for?" He laughed at his own joke, and took another swig of beer.

"I guess since Mother Merri is involved, I'd just rather not think about it."

Mercedes laughed. "Well I think it's a great idea," she said, slipping her arm through Carter's. "Every woman deserves a chance to be happy, no matter what age she is."

"Hey!" said Jimmy. "I deserve to be happy, too. I think I might sign up with them."

The rate at which this crazy idea was being approved made my head spin. "Felicity also thinks she might be persuaded to join them. Now that Walter's gone, she hasn't anyone to hang out with, and she thinks she might just give it a try."

"Are they all signing up together?" asked Rich.

"Felicity says Orpha claims she doesn't want to break in anyone new at this time of her life, but I think the others are all giving it serious consideration." I paused, then continued, "Of course, they were all talking under the influence of copious amounts of alcohol when they came up with this new idea."

"All of them are signing up?" repeated Rich. "All of them? Even Nova?"

"I knew it!" crowed Freddy. "You're sweet on her, aren't you Dad?"

Rich waggled his beer bottle like he was surprised it was empty already, and quickly got up to get himself another beer from Jimmy's fridge, turning his back to the table so we couldn't see his face. I was pretty sure Sheriff D didn't want to know if there were sparks developing between the two, especially not now when the dust was finally settling over Mateo's accident.

"Well," said Sheriff D, clearing his throat, "I suppose Meredith can put her computer skills to good use, helping them all create their online profiles."

"I am selfish to say this," said Kanji, "but I am in the hopes that, should any of these women find love again at their advanced ages, they will choose another insurance company for their future policies."

We all smiled at that. I couldn't blame Kanji for having done more than enough undercover work to last a lifetime, and I doubted he'd be too eager to investigate any future claims. But before I could voice my opinion, he tapped his coffee cup for attention.

"On another subject," he began, "I have deliberated much, and finally decided that I am going to retire—for real this time—and I'm thinking I might like to do so right here on the North Beach Peninsula."

For the most part, Kanji's pronouncement was met with positive and supportive responses. Freddy held back for just a nano-second, then extended his hand. "I hope that means you'll continue working for me at Spartina Point."

"I would very much like to do so," said Kanji, shaking Freddy's hand. Then he looked at me and smiled in a way that took my breath away.

Freddy saw the look that passed between us, and said, "You won't be signing up on any online dating sites, will you, Sylleegirl?"

Up until that moment, I hadn't given it a thought. Two extremely eligible and terribly charming, but obviously testosterone-challenged men, was more beefsteak than I could handle, and even that was at least one too many. I hadn't yet decided which one was the right one, but now was not the time or the place to discuss it.

Fortunately, Priscilla and the pup got into a minor spat over a scrap of barbecued pork that had dropped on the floor under the coffee table before I was pressured to answer. I breathed a small sigh of relief as the group was distracted by the yowling, hissing and barking in the living room. Nobody took the puppy and cat spat seriously, but Jimmy hollered at Priscilla to "knock it off" and called for her to come to him, waving another whole piece of pork to tempt her.

"Seriously?" asked the sheriff. "You really expect a cat to come when you call it?"

"She might surprise you," said Jimmy, repeating her name over and over to get her attention. "Of course, she doesn't like to show off when anybody's watching," he said, when it became clear that Priscilla was obviously not going to perform.

Kanji stood up and sharply clapped his hands twice.

"*Elvis!*" he called, and the pup instantly gave up his bickering with Priscilla, puppy-loped over to Kanji, plopped down on his haunches at his feet, and quivered with excitement.

"You finally named him!" I said, overjoyed at dodging another 'So who's it going to be?' relationship bullet.

"Yes, he did," said Freddy, eying me warily. "So at least there's one less mystery hanging in the air here this evening."

In the brief but uncomfortable silence that followed, Mercedes began chair dancing at the dining room table and singing the repetitious lyrics to Elvis Presley's "You Ain't Nothing But a Hound Dog," and Kanji's little Elvis put back his head and howled, as only a young Golden Retriever pup can howl.

"Everybody's a critic!" said Mercedes, and everyone laughed. Then Merc asked if anyone else wanted the last egg roll, and could somebody please pass her the hot mustard.

I knew I owed her big time for her intervention, but I was pretty sure she'd find a way to be repaid, in full, plus interest, before too much time had passed.

And that's exactly how it's done when you've got great friends who are always there to watch your back.

ABOUT THE AUTHOR

Long Beach, Washington, author Jan Bono has published three Sylvia Avery cozy mysteries set on the southwest Washington coast. She's written five collections of humorous personal experience stories, one self-help weight loss book, two poetry chapbooks, and one book of short romance. In addition, she's penned nine one-act plays, and a full-length dinner theater play. Jan has also written for numerous magazines ranging from Guidepost to Star to Woman's World and has had more than 40 stories included in the Chicken Soup for the Soul series.

See more of Jan's work:
    www.JanBonoBooks.com